THE DYNOSTAR MENACE

THE DYNOSTAR
MENACE

by

Kit Pedler and Gerry Davis

SOUVENIR PRESS

First published 1975 by Souvenir Press Ltd,
95 Mortimer Street, London W1N 8HP
and simultaneously in Canada by
J. M. Dent & Sons (Canada) Ltd,
Ontario, Canada

ISBN 0 285 62180 7

Printed in Great Britain by
Clarke, Doble & Brendon Ltd, Plymouth

For their extensive help in the research and preparation of *The Dynostar Menace*, the authors would like to thank:

The Astronauts and Publicity staff of the Johnson Space Centre, Houston, Texas, U.S.A.

The staff of the Culham Fusion Research Laboratories, Oxfordshire, England.

Staff members of a Psychiatric Teaching Hospital in London.

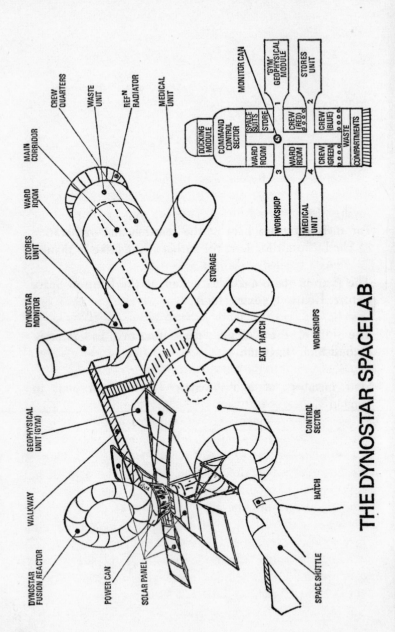

THE DYNOSTAR SPACELAB

CREW QUARTERS

WASTE UNIT

RE'N RADIATOR

MEDICAL UNIT

MAIN CORRIDOR

WARD ROOM

STORES UNIT

DYNOSTAR MONITOR

STORAGE

GEOPHYSICAL UNIT (GYM)

WALKWAY

EXIT HATCH

WORKSHOPS

CONTROL SECTOR

DYNOSTAR FUSION REACTOR

POWER CAN

SOLAR PANEL

HATCH

SPACE SHUTTLE

DOCKING MODULE

COMMAND CONTROL SECTOR

SPACE SUITS | STORE

MONITOR CAN

'GYM' GEOPHYSICAL MODULE

STORES UNIT

CREW (RED)

CREW (BLUE)

WARD ROOM 3

WARD ROOM 4

CREW (GREEN)

WASTE COMPARTMENTS

WORKSHOP

MEDICAL UNIT

The man's eyes flicked open in the dim artificial night of the sleeping compartment. Slowly, like a bat unfolding it's wings, he unzipped the sleeping bag and stretched out his arms, floating easily forward in the zero gravity air of the spaceship.

The air smelled of iodine and sweat.

He checked his two companions, hanging from the wall in their bags, studying their faces wrapped in their head cowls to assess the depth of their sleep. Then, he placed his stockinged feet against a bulkhead and launched himself out through the open square hatch of the compartment and on into the central access tunnel.

He cruised through the weightless darkness with the ease and grace of an underwater diver.

For a brief moment, his senses failed to give his brain correct information and he felt a momentary surge of nausea. His eyes began to jerk rapidly from side to side and he somersaulted in slow motion, striking the back of his head on the triangular open mesh of the deck, with a soft thump. He gripped the alloy mesh bars of the floor, and remained absolutely still in the faint deep blue light of the corridor, listening and ordering his senses.

The only sound was the low rustle of the life support conditioners and the high micky-mouse squeak of the voices of Red Team on duty watch coming through on an overhead loudspeaker. He could also hear his heart beat in his ears. It was slow.

Once sure that the noise of the impact had evoked no response, he pushed himself away from the floor, floated into the centre of the tunnel and pulled himself along by grabbing regularly spaced nylon handholds on the tunnel wall. Ahead there was a bright yellow beam of light streaming across the tunnel. The light came from the open airlock leading into the monitor can where Red Team were at work.

The three men of the team were in the last stages of exhaustion.

They were Richard Hart, English atmosphere scientist, at forty-three, the second oldest man aboard; René Lasalle, French instrument designer for "Project Dynostar" and Otto Sigmund, German systems engineer. Men already exhausted because they had spent fifty-six days in space working at a completely unplanned rate to raise "Project Dynostar" into operation.

Each was still reeling under the impact of the sudden order to close down the whole experiment.

The order to smash the results of ten years' continuous and competitive research had arrived just hours before the final fruition of their lifework. They floated in support straps cocooned in a bitter world of their own as they worked through the complex and intricately timed shutdown operation.

Four days of unrelenting concentration lay ahead of them and the other eleven men on board.

Each face showed the puffy swelling due to the effect of zero gravity and metabolic disturbance on the blood vessels of their skin.

Cautiously, the man eased himself along the tunnel towards the brightly lit airlock and then halted beside a small metal panel stencilled with the legend: "Primary M.C. circuits". The panel was about six feet away from the airlock. He silently unscrewed the four flynuts holding the panel in place, until they floated away on the end of their retaining lines. Lifting the hinged panel, he looked inside at the tight leashes of electrical cables and terminals and then unzipped a pocket in his oversuit and removed a small sheet of paper showing a circuit diagram labelled: "Main vent interlock".

In the narrow beam of a small pentorch, he compared the layout of the cables behind the panel with the diagram and selected three, pulling them slightly free of the others. Each one of them was marked in a different striped colour combination.

Inside the monitor can, the three men worked with the deft precision of a long practised string trio, each silently trying to suppress the crushing disappointment of the order to shut down the Dynostar. Hart turned to Lasalle:

"There's a positive reading on number two condenser backing pump."

Lasalle nodded and moved a sliding control. A needle on a dial fell to zero. Hart ticked off an item on a printed list.

In the tunnel, the man had removed a neatly wound coil of very thin wire from his pocket. The wire had three separate strands, each was of a different colour and ended in a sharply pointed needle probe. Carefully he inserted the three points through the insulation of the wires he had selected. Then he replaced the panel and spun the flynuts back into position, but leaving them untightened. Then he tugged at the wires until they pulled free and slid out

9

through the narrow gap between the panel and it's mounting.

In the monitor can, a red light on a panel winked briefly. None of the three men noticed.

In the tunnel the man had repeated his operation and the three needle prods were back in position, stuck through the insulation of the wires but now he pushed himself back along the corridor unravelling the coil of wire attached to the needles as he floated back down the tunnel towards the sleeping compartment. Just before entering the square hatch, he took a small test meter from a pocket and connected it to one pair of the three wires. The meter registered nine volts. He unclipped the meter.

In the monitor can the red light winked, unseen for a second time.

Back inside the sleeping compartment, the man zipped himself into the sleeping bag holding the three bare ends of the wire in one hand. He wound two of the wire ends together and then wound them onto the third. For about five seconds he held them together and then began to tug on the wires.

The needles pulled out of the cables behind the panel and moved back down the tunnel as the man reeled in the wire.

A motor whined angrily inside the monitor can. Hart looked up:

"The vent pipe!"

Behind them a pneumatic ram hissed and extended a polished metal rod.

The airlock slammed shut. There was a loud metallic bang and the air vent began to roar and shriek as the pressurised air in the now isolated monitor can exhausted away into space.

The air instantly filled with a greyish white mist of water vapour and each man's face contorted into a rigid mask of intolerable agony. Their limbs began to jerk convulsively and their bodies jack-knifed, as they fought for the last remnants of oxygen.

The German, his face swelling into a terrible suffused melon shape, made one last ineffectual attempt to dive past his two writhing companions and grab the manual control of the vent pipe.

The Frenchman, a red froth floating away from his distorted mouth, just managed to jab a finger at the alarm button. The alarm bell clamoured through the ship with a deafening shrillness jerking the exhausted, sleeping men to sudden awareness.

In the monitor can, the bodies of Hart, Lasalle and Sigmund floated in a mist of swirling dust particles.

CHAPTER TWO

It was 2.40 a.m. earthtime and the building housing the
State Department of Energy was in darkness except for
one group of brightly lit windows on the third floor.
Originally built in the early seventies to house the Apollo
Astronauts, some ten years afterwards it had been converted to accommodate the new department under it's
director, Lee Caldor.

Caldor was sitting hunched in the rear seat of the car as
it swept along the deserted bay Highway on its way to
his office. He was cold and unshaven.

The news of the accident had been given to him on
scramble-vision by a haggard mission director and he had
at once summoned his own team of assistants. What his
assistants did not know was that he was faced with a
double crisis.

Forty-eight hours before the deaths on "Spacelab Dynostar" he had received an "eyes only" document, not under
guard from a state department, but from the Council of
Twelve; the most formidable and effective environmental
action group in the Western World. It would have been
the Council's normal practise to use every organ of the
media to attack publicly someone who, in their eyes, was
offending against the environment.

The document, in full documentary detail, accused him
quite simply of suppressing vital evidence during the

year-long public enquiry into the safety of Project Dyno-star.

The Dynostar, driven into being by Caldor's relentless exploitation of power, money and charisma, had become a symbol of hope for a world almost exhausted of energy. It represented the last attempt by technical man to get cheap and abundant power.

First, man had raked the earth for coal and oil, flinging them heedlessly into the boilers of the greedy technical juggernaut. Then he had turned to the power of the atom and built great nuclear power stations. But when, soon after the lethal accident to the light water reactor at Grim Ness and its subsequent desolation of the North East of Scotland, the fast breeder reactor near Odessa in Russia had exploded, nuclear fission had reluctantly been abandoned as a cornucopia of power.

By the middle of the eighties, the landscape of Europe had become littered with vast concrete mountains sealing the radioactive remains of the fission stations: technical mausolea which gave mute testimony to the Promethean fantasies of the technicians.

The last hope was nuclear fusion, the power of the sun. The energy of the hydrogen bomb contained, controlled and made to work for man.

In the late sixties serious fusion research had begun in earnest. In England, Russia and America, complex machines began to take shape in vast hanger-like workshops, each with its own mythological name.

Stellerator, Zeeta, Beta-Levitron, Torsatron, all took their place in the history of the most difficult research ever undertaken by man. There was just one problem to solve.

This was the problem of how to contain a plasma of gas at a temperature of millions of degrees without vapourising

13

the container. The answer seemed to be a magnetic container, a bottle of magnetic fields. Gas plasmas are susceptible to magnetic fields and so research centred around the problem of generating a magnetic field so stable and intense that it would hold the incandescent plasma together while the fusion process took place.

Stable magnetic fields eluded the scientists until the late eighties, when it was finally agreed that gravity was a disturbing factor, that the hot plasma in the field sagged very slightly due to its own accelerating mass. Also the need for almost impossibly hard vacuums became apparent. Logically there was but one answer: there was neither gravity or air in space.

"Dynostar" was conceived.

The outcry was immediate. The cost of space flight was prohibitive due to increasing shortages of raw materials and energy and rapidly worsening atmospheric pollution. Eventually a public enquiry was set up jointly by the Council of Europe and the United States to examine the cost, safety and potential rewards of Dynostar. Russia was the only major non-attender, since she was already occupied with her own fusion device: the Kapitza machine.

A year of furious public argument followed and it was largely due to Lee Caldor, using his intuitive diplomatic brilliance behind the scenes of the enquiry, that the go-ahead was finally given.

The number of European countries joining with the United States was agreed, each supplying scientists, hardware or cash as the need and availabilities became evident. All were placed under the ultimate direction of the only viable organisation: the United States Space Authority.

Eventually, what the media had already named as "the Last Space Flight" was launched and a vast

14

complex called "Spacelab" assembled in space. The separate parts of the fusion reactor Dynostar were ferried up by shuttle craft and a giant copper and aluminium doughnut, over forty feet in diameter, gradually took shape.

Over the ensuing months, team after team of scientists spent fifty days at a time in space, testing, developing and preparing the vast machine for function. And now, into the euphoria of the hours before start-up, had come the first bombshell from the Council of Twelve.

They had released data showing that if Dynostar worked, its giant magnetic fields would not remain stable but would balloon outwards thrusting great lines of force down through space to disrupt the ozone layer, a mere twenty-five miles above the earth's surface.

If the delicacy of the ozone cycle layer was disrupted, lethal ultra-violet radiation from the sun would blaze through onto a wholly unprepared world. Skin would burn, crops would die, ecological systems would shrivel and collapse.

The rays which had started life on earth would bring it to a close.

There was no doubt that the figures were correct and it was finally agreed that the management of Dynostar had failed to take sufficient heed of data they already had.

After untold millions of dollars and five years of gruelling calculations and experiments, just hours before completion, project Dynostar was stopped and the order given to shut down.

Caldor had immediately taken full charge of the operation and, after consultation with Van Buren, the on-board space commander, guaranteed the President and the media that the shut-down would be complete in under seven days.

Now, with such a short time remaining, three essential crew scientists had died. A shocked and exhausted Van Buren had been unable to guarantee shut-down without both replacements from earth for the dead crew members, and spare parts. He had reported total confusion on board the Spacelab; and then made the most chilling statement of all: that part of the Dynostar operation had been under automatic control and there was now real doubt whether the divided and confused crew would be able to shut it down again.

The Dynostar was probably out of control.

Briefly Caldor's imagination saw the violet bands of radiation flashing out from the doughnut. A population running in a street screaming, their eyes covered from the flaring radiation. Flowers shrivelling, blind animals stumbling.

As the car stopped at the guardport, Caldor realised that the only possible course was to update the relief crew shot, take the only operational shuttle vehicle available and get the necessary men and spares up to Spacelab Dynostar with the minimum of delay.

The guard shone a torch on his face, compared what he saw with a photograph on a clipboard and waved the car through the tall iron gates.

Caldor visualised the state of mind of the resident crew. Three dead men floating in a partly ruined ship, gross work overload, crushing disappointment. Impossible mental stress. For a moment the possibility of sabotage or at least deliberate interference crossed his mind. Could one of the scientists—pushed to the brink by the order to shut down—have tried to complete the experiment? He dismissed the thought.

The lethal hazards of continuing the experiment had

been graphically described to the scientist crew members. No rational man could ignore them. But, at the same time, he realised that the possibility of sabotage would have to be kept in mind by the leader of the rescue team. Who to choose? Van Buren had flatly spelled it out: he no longer had effective command, so the choice narrowed down to a senior astronaut with command experience.

The rundown of the space programme in the early eighties had left many highly trained men without space work. One newspaper had referred to a "Rentanaut" situation. One by one, Caldor reviewed the potential candidates, knowing full well that he was merely confirming his first, subconscious decision. Someone he could trust implicitly as far as his own political experience would allow.

It had to be John Hayward.

CHAPTER THREE

Commander John Hayward held up a gloved hand to shield his eyes from the blinding violet glare of the sun. Seven hundred feet dead ahead lay the motionless bulk of Space-lab Dynostar, flaring white and gold against the blue-hazed background of the earth. Its colours were given a slightly purple overlay by the molecule-thick layer of metal covering the panels of the flight deck windows.

Hayward was strapped into position at the control panel of an Orbiter Space Vehicle which was inching across space towards the docking collar of the Spacelab.

His eyes were fixed on a pattern of red, green and white lights surrounding the docking collar of Spacelab and his other hand manœuvred a nine-inch joystick which he moved to retain the cruciform array of lights centred within a pair of small etched grids set on a frame between his eyes and the screen.

Each time he moved the joystick, small attitude control gas jets on the shuttle hissed loudly as they nudged the bulk of the shuttle into line with the collar.

Spacelab Dynostar was a giant corrugated cylinder over ninety feet long and twenty-five feet in diameter. From its sides and top the five smaller cylinders of the "cans" protruded at right angles from the long axis of the main ship, like bottles stuck into an oil drum. Each separate module was plugged into position by a narrow airlock.

Four of the modules were set in one plane and the fifth, the "monitor can", was set at right angles to the other four. A narrow alloy ladder with circular retaining rings stretched across space to the doughnut shape of the Dynostar fusion experiment, itself supported on a complex skeleton of girders attached to the main body of the Spacelab.

Beneath the great ring of Dynostar, lay the power assembly which stored millions of amps of sun-generated electricity, to drive the first fusion pulse start-up.

Hayward pictured in his mind the three dead men inside the monitor can. Then his attention wandered from the complex ritual of the docking procedure and, gazing momentarily down through the side panel of the screen, he could just make out the light green outline of the Western seaboard of the United States set against the blue haze of the Pacific.

For a moment his awesome responsibilities lay heavily, then remembering his training in the early years of the Apollo mission, he recalled the voice of a psychology instructor: "When you begin to feel frightened, identify the precise cause of the fear, but only in relation to your function within the mission structure." He felt his pulse rising, the weightless conditions of space, creating an audible heartbeat somewhere in the middle of his head.

Why had Caldor picked him over the heads of the many younger astronauts, with their more recent experience? At forty-five he was one of the few remaining veterans of the Apollo and Skylab flights left in the dwindling space industry. His official title, Director of Space Personnel, had for months seemed increasingly meaningless and before the sudden order to lead the emergency shot arrived, he had been giving serious consideration to an offer to become President of a bank and yet hating the idea of becoming another figurehead super-hero without real function.

Although he recognised the strength of his own record on paper, he reflected that the stamina and quicker reactions of a younger man would have been far more appropriate than his own length of experience.

He concluded that his choice must at least in part be due to his own friendship with Caldor. Unlikely in the first place, it was one of the few actual areas of warmth that the coldly ambitious Caldor permitted himself. Based upon the admiration of an intellectual for a man of more overt physical capabilities, it had grown to a point where the perennially suspicious Caldor had relaxed the mental barriers he normally kept in place. He had allowed himself to build a trust of Hayward.

But Caldor was the last person to be swayed by sentiment.

Again Hayward felt a slight chill of apprehension. Fischer's flat voice broke through his thoughts.

"M.D.A. to four four eight, extension latch—check; probe-head capture latch—check."

Automatically Hayward looked down at a panel of hexagonal lights on his right hand.

"Drogue assembly O.K. Attitude sensors O.K."

Hayward glanced briefly over at Eric Fischer, strapped into the adjacent seat. He was a German-American nuclear engineer from Berkeley, with eighteen months of training as an astronaut. He studied the pale thin face and close-cropped blond hair. A brief pulse of adrenalin spread in his stomach as he remembered his last conversation with Caldor about the possibility of either interference or sabotage.

Collecting himself, Hayward pushed a short lever and servo-motors began to whine, swinging the nose cone heat shield of the shuttle vehicle to one side and revealing the proboscis of the newly developed nose-docking module. Like a giant mosquito about to suck blood, the gold-plated tube silently extruded into space, glinting in the harsh sunlight.

In the overhead mirror, Hayward studied the dark, fleshy features of the third man on board the shuttle: Major Daniel Sicura, electronics scientist, three years of astronaut training, one tour of duty in the briefly revived Skylab programme, then a return to an earlier occupation —military intelligence. Anger rose in him as he remembered the furious argument with Caldor on earth and his initial refusal to carry what he called a "glorified cop" on the mission. Caldor had given no quarter, it was either take Sicura or get off. A mixture of pride and an overriding obsession to get back into space just once more, had forced Hayward to agree.

He had had little time to talk with the squat, heavy shouldered Sicura and had immediately registered the possibility that the man might have received an entirely different set of instructions from his own. He began to work out how to explain the presence of what amounted to a policeman to the members of the Dynostar team lying on the other side of the Spacelab docking collar, now only feet ahead. Already a wordless hostility had built up between the two men.

The collar now swung down out of vision towards the golden snout of the shuttle as the heavily sprung probe entered the conical aperture of the Spacelab collar. There was a loud clack, then a noise like slapping the side of an empty tank and the three men moved forward slightly in

21

their retaining harness, as the two great craft joined. Almost immediately, there was the loud, high-pitched hiss of pneumatic rams as remotely controlled latches jerked into position holding the two docking rings tightly together.

Somewhere beneath their feet a pump started a regular blattering pulse. The three men floated in their straps, waiting. After about a minute Fischer looked up at two pressure meters and called out:

"We have a hard seal."

Hayward's body felt awkward as he pulled himself through the docking tube. Finally the airlock seal just two feet in front of his eyes hissed briefly, then swung upwards. The green high-contrast light from the forward control sector of the Spacelab blazed in, bringing with it the stale and slightly malodorous atmosphere characteristic of a long manned space mission.

Commander Van Buren was waiting, head downwards.

Hayward pulled himself forward and swung around. After routine enquiries he began to assess Van Buren's condition.

The changes were appalling.

On earth, Van Buren had become the principal media symbol of the entire Dynostar experiment. Journalists, aware that the public were no longer interested in space hardware alone, had carefully nurtured and developed Van Buren's personality to a point where he commanded a larger audience than a pop star.

His long face, with its fine sensitive features and closely cropped silver-grey hair, looked out from practically every glossy magazine and television set.

Van Buren with his two teenage sons.

Van Buren in a canoe race.

Van Buren with the President. A man of genuinely warm and compassionate nature, he had taken easily to the publicity and had never once put a foot wrong. His own charisma had become identified with hope.

Van Buren was Dynostar.

Now Hayward saw a hunched, shrunken man. His face was yellow and waxy, and distended veins showed through on the skin of his forehead as a dark, unhealthy spiderweb. The normally friendly and slightly mocking eyes were expressionless and his whole cast of countenance was flat and completely free of emotional overlay. There were no signs of the sensitive leadership and diplomacy which had enabled the man successfully to manage a multi-national team of highly strung scientists.

Hayward introduced Fischer and Sicura who had followed him through the main control section of the Spacelab. He saw just the flicker of suspicion on Van Buren's expression as he described the purely scientific function of Sicura.

"Where do you want to start?" asked Van Buren.

"How far were you into shut-down?" Hayward asked.

There was a long pause, the speech was slow: "We had just gotten onto the automatic withdrawal routine, we were cutting out the automatic computer programmes up in the monitor can. . . ."

". . . and getting back on manual over-ride," Hayward cut in.

Van Buren nodded listlessly.

"Then what?" Hayward continued.

"The monitor can went. Just blew. No reason."

"Any ideas?"

"It was an impossible accident." Van Buren's brow furrowed.

"We've checked. All the circuits are intact, but the thing vented—there's just no reason, no reason at all."

"All right, so we'd better take a look. I'd like Dan Sicura to start going over the situation there, if you've no objection?"

Without waiting for Van Buren's reaction, he nodded to Sicura, who straight away began pulling himself clumsily towards the central access tunnel, his relative lack of space experience showing as he struck and rebounded from a bulkhead.

"And Fischer here, I want him to check the shut-down verification sequence here in main control."

Fischer looked once coolly at each man, and then turned and began to pull himself round the tightly banked arrays of controls and indicators.

"If they can get into what you guys have already done, then we can get this thing down on schedule."

Van Buren launched himself towards the access tunnel opening: "I guess you want to see the damage in the monitor can?"

Hayward shook his head: "That can wait. Sicura will do that. I want to go round and meet the crew."

CHAPTER FOUR

As Hayward floated through the corridors and sections of the ship, it was soon absolutely clear why Van Buren's ability to command had, to all intents and purposes, broken down. The atmosphere ranged between oppressive apathy to open hostility. Each man had changed completely from the confident jauntiness which had been apparent at the cocktail parties and publicity dinners back in Houston.

In place of the integrated relaxed interchanges and chipping humour, there was a gaunt, unkempt solemnity. Each man still appeared to be able to function but did so like an automaton. There was little inter-communication, except when it was vital to the task, each man acting as if he were locked into a grim private shell.

Eight men had been stopped within hours of completing an experiment which, if successful, would have put their names into the historical records of achievement. They were men who might have provided the energy-starved world with its first glimpse of free, abundant and relatively safe energy. Now they were eight men ordered to tear down the culmination of nine years of their lives.

They had been stretched beyond any ordinary limits of endurance, and were now being asked to provide one last effort, not for success, but to ensure permanent and ineradicable failure.

Hayward waited in the mess section, alone with Van Buren who was talking rapidly and bitterly:

"We've had fifty-six days here and we were already near exhausted trying to get to completion. And now the eco-freaks down there," he jerked his thumb at the blue haze of the earthlight shining through the triangular porthole, ". . . have decided that the whole thing's going to punch holes in the ozone layer. How the hell do they know that will happen?

"They haven't done any real work. They've never been up here. It's so damned easy to sit on your arse and make up phoney maths. We were only scheduled to run Dyno-star for a one-second pulse, that's not going to produce any effect at all."

Hayward remained silent.

"And now I've got three dead men back there in the freezer. . . ."

"You haven't got the message at all Eddie," Hayward intervened. "And you haven't passed it on."

He held Van Buren's stare, seeing the anger die away back into apathy.

"I'll talk to everybody—here, now."

Van Buren paused and then slowly reached up for the intercom speaker 'phone in its conical holder and fumbled. The instrument floated out on the end of its line and a small spray of sweat droplets detached themselves from his face and floated free, glinting in the earthlight from the window, like rain. As he tried to recover the mike, Hayward reached out, took hold of it and spoke urgently:

"This is John Hayward. I want everyone here in the mess section, right away."

Above the squawked chorus of protest on the return

speakers, he repeated the instruction, clicked off the mike and poised himself in the straps, waiting.

It was nearly twelve minutes before the assembly was complete. The last to appear were the three men who were off duty and had been sleeping. They seemed almost deliberately, to Hayward, to be lying in attitudes which made it impossible to judge their facial reaction.

The French electronics scientist, Jean Lucas, hung in toe retainers, his small body sideways on to Hayward's position. Will Patterson, the Australian nuclear engineer, had parked his large muscular frame bent up between two control panels, and the English doctor, Philip Lyall, sat in the tethered astronaut manœuvring chair, his hand toying with the control joystick.

On two of the four T-shaped jockey bars protruding from the central mess table sat Mel Freeman, medical biochemist and assistant to Lyall and Russ Walters, American physicist. Over their heads, floating horizontally, was the English nuclear scientist, Bob Townsend, and beside him, the German Theodore Neumann.

Hayward sat watching the crew, his fingers hooked under the water injector assembly, trying to appear at ease and at the same time trying to force down a sensation of nausea. He had not been in space for seven years and the balance canals in his inner ear had been made permanently unstable from previous flights. Beside him, Eric Fischer was leafing through a wrist clipboard of data sheets apparently unconcerned about the multitude of tensions so clearly visible in the faces around him. Sicura was holding onto a flexible ventilation shaft. His eyes were cold as they flicked from face to face, measuring.

"I'm Hayward, John Hayward," he began.

"You're kidding!" Patterson drawled, adjusting his

attitude so that he was right way up to Hayward. His accent was made to seem more strident by the frequency changes of the weightless atmosphere. There was a short laugh.

"We've a tight schedule, Commander," Patterson continued, "so let's have it."

Hayward glanced at the faces, the wall of hostility was almost touchable. He fought down the nausea. "I'll be brief." His voice rang off the metal walls. "The air of self-pity aboard this craft is thick enough to choke on." There was a complete silence, Lucas began to pick his teeth.

"There's no-one to cry to, no-one to blame, it's over, finish. The evidence is a hundred percent."

"Who the hell says?" Patterson grated.

"The figures are obvious," Hayward replied calmly. "And someone in the design set-up has either got some data wrong, or suppressed it. The neutron field strength from Dynostar was under-estimated by at least a factor of six!"

There was a murmur of protest. Hayward gestured for silence: "Hear me out. If the ozone layer is hit by that flux, all ultra-violet absorption there will be completely disrupted and short-wave lethal wavebands will get through from the sun to the surface and shrivel everything living. Skin cancer—ruined ecologies—dead animals, you name it."

Hayward paused and looked for reaction. The resentment was still present, but he had their attention. Lyall, the English doctor, nodded slightly. Walters, the American physicist, stared back thoughtfully as if his imagination had been caught. Mel Freeman, the biochemist, seemed attentive, but otherwise unaffected.

Neumann shifted position, his voice had a slight European inflection:

"Those figures are entirely open to misinterpretation. It would take a good radiation physicist to make the necessary analysis."

"They *had* the best." Hayward went on. "We're not back in the seventies, the environmentalists didn't know what the hell they were talking about then, they guesstimated.

"This Council of Twelve, they're nothing like the old Club of Rome, they've got money, laboratories and as much computer time as N.A.S.A.

"They're also very well informed politically and diplomatically. When they release a report, they know damn well that they're as right as any large organisation."

"We're going to need a week minimum to examine this Council of whatever's figures!" Bob Townsend retorted angrily. "A computer analysis is only as good as the data fed into it. Their premises could be complete crap!"

"And so could yours," Hayward replied evenly. "Anyhow, forget the debate. The order is to shut it down."

"Of course," Jean Lucas moved forward in his retaining straps. Hayward saw a short, wiry frame, cropped black hair, and a sad, lugubrious expression. "So what shall we do? We leave the Dynostar here for a year until we prove that it is safe? Then we come back and make it work, eh?"

Hayward nodded, wrongly sensing an ally.

"Then that would be most stupid!" Lucas continued. "Because as you know perfectly, after a year up here, the whole torus of the Dynostar will be ruined. One year of ion bombardment, one year of micro meteorites, heat, cold and short wave radiation. It would be wrecked. Just a pile of space junk at two thousand million dollars."

"And where the hell's the money going to come from for the next shot?" Patterson demanded angrily. "The people down there aren't going to allow another flop. Any way you look at it, Europe can't afford it alone."

"Then the way is open for the Aussies to spend some of their out-back oil profits, isn't it?" Dr. Phillip Lyall's voice was well modulated. Patterson swung round. Hayward summed up the two faces and then glanced down at his wrist chronometer:

"Any other comments?"

Russ Walters and Mel Freeman shook their heads. Townsend looked across at Lyall and shrugged. Hayward gingerly eased himself into a vertical stance and noted that the crew had all oriented correctly to his own vertical position. A minor victory, he thought, making an analogy in his mind with the attitudes of submission of apes.

"One thing more. There's no talk of failure either at Space Centre, Congress, the European parliaments, the media—anywhere. They all say you've done an almost impossible job and if we can shut down the Dynostar without damage," he nodded towards Lucas, "then we could still get a little ticker-tape when we get down."

He looked around the room and watched for a reaction to his speech. It was almost non-existent.

Apart from a slightly supercilious expression on Lyall's face and a raise of the eyebrows from Russ Walters, there was still no real sign of response. All looked away or down, sunk firmly within the prevailing mood. Hayward felt a slight breeze of fear as he recalled his briefly held idea that the death of the three crew members might have been deliberate.

Freeman stared back at him, his lips pursing. There was something unusual about the man's face, just a faint form within the expression, nothing to define. He dismissed the thought, angry with himself for giving way to even a momentary paranoid reaction.

Each man was poised to react violently towards Hayward, the interloper.

He remembered the arrogant management term that Caldor had used in their last talk before take-off: "What was needed was low-profile leadership." Low-profile, my ass, he reflected. There's nothing in management technology to deal with eight super-intelligent and furiously hostile men in zero gravity conditions with disordered senses and in the last stages of psychological exhaustion. The tone of his voice, in spite of the squeak of the spaceship conditions, was confident, entirely belying his thoughts. He had already abandoned dignity as an approach since no one could be dignified with a voice sounding like a eunuch!

"One advantage of having Sicura, Fischer and myself on board is that we can spell you all a bit." He looked down at his wristpad. "So I've re-allocated the duty turns." He gestured to Sicura. "Blue team will have Dan Sicura here, Bob Townsend and Theo Neumann." He anxiously hoped not to make a mistake with the names.

"Green team, you Eddie." He nodded at Van Buren, "Russ Walters and Jean Lucas. Red team will comprise myself, Eric Fischer here and Will Patterson." He looked over at the big Australian. Keep trouble on a short lead, he thought.

"As before," Hayward continued, "Phillip Lyall and

31

Mel Freeman will monitor the life-support systems in addition to their medical duties. And that's all. Any questions?" He paused, looking around slowly. "Right, blue team pick up on the shut-down sequence now and continue as before. Red team stay here with me."

Like a shoal of fish moving away from food, the crew slowly cast themselves loose and floated away down through the square aperture of the crew quarters into the central access tunnel. Van Buren, Fischer, Patterson and, he noted, Sicura, stayed behind.

He looked enquiringly across at Sicura. "You're due with blue team in control."

Sicura's heavy Italian face remained expressionless: "I'll stay in on this one." There was a pause. "With your permission, Commander?"

Or without, thought Hayward. An angry retort started to form. He turned to Van Buren:

"What's the current status in the monitor can Eddie?"

"After it happened," Van Buren began, "we realised that some of the manual systems up in the can were damaged. We don't know why yet, so we started to connect them up by emergency lines running up through the airlock and we're trying to patch them into main control up front. It's not complete—another few hours maybe." He loked down. "There's nothing in the book about this, not a goddam thing!"

"Who's been inside the monitor can since the accident?" Hayward persisted.

"Only Dr. Lyall and myself. To take out the three . . . bodies. They're sealed in bags in the waste freezer aft. There'll have to be an autopsy when we're down."

"How far did you get with the control check inside?" Fischer queried.

32

"No so far," Van Buren continued. "The start-up procedure is on total automatic and proceeding. The main computer programmes are running and we're trying to shut them off."

"What's the problem?" asked Hayward.

"The problem is a necessary peak magnetic field of twenty-four kilogauss." Fischer's voice was precise and monotone. "And to sustain that, there is a total of stored electrical energy in the power can of about one hundred twenty-four kiloamps, this is linked by feedback cables to sensors examining the magnetic field stability in the torus. If you just shut it off, there is a probability of about fifty-four percent, that the condensers in the power assembly would break down and explode and this would almost certainly blow the ship in half."

Fischer gazed into the air as he talked. He seemed to relish the figures and the totally unemotional description of their deaths.

"So why in hell haven't you got men back in there now?" Hayward demanded.

"Because of the M.H.D. reactor." Van Buren replied. "It's driven by a small plutonium pile, a development of the design fitted to the Apollo series. It's linked to a small magneto-hydrodynamic electrical power generator. There's a high gamma count near its casing and we decided to wait for Fischer here, since he had a hand in its design."

"Have you got the radiation readings?" Fischer asked.

"They're up there, in the monitor can," Van Buren replied. "On the data log."

Hayward turned to Fischer: "What about shielding? Can't we seal off the radiation?"

Fischer stroked the front of his nose: "No, not enough material, too heavy. We'll have to go and take a reading."

"And worry about your balls later?" Hayward asked.

"No, no, not necessary. I'll measure as we go." Fischer smiled slightly. "They can transplant anything these days! Hey, could I have a time with four!"

There was a slight ripple of laughter and the tension eased momentarily.

Hayward turned to Van Buren: "Eddie, you're not going to be needed right now. Why not hit the sack for a while?"

Van Buren started to protest.

"Eddie, I want you functional," Hayward insisted.

CHAPTER FIVE

Inside one of the vast concrete monoliths that made up the Johnson Space Centre at Houston, a complete mock-up of Spacelab Dynostar had been built. Unlike the previous replicas of Apollo and Skylab craft, which had been mechanically and electronically complete in every detail, the strained economies of the nineties had necessitated the construction of the mock-up in plywood and plastic. There had been few operational parts for the trainee astronauts.

It had been sufficient, however, to give Hayward a complete working knowledge of the interior so he was able to lead Sicura and Fischer towards the narrow airlock of the damaged Monitor can.

He inspected the partially closed circular door over his head; a matt grey saucepan lid, three-quarters of a metre in diameter. It should have been closed, not because there was any pressure difference in the air on either side, but because of a ship rule isolating each component unit of the Spacelab complex in the event of fire or explosion. In fact, it lay open about fifteen degrees to allow the passage of a leash of multi-coloured cables forming the connections the crew had already set up between the automatic systems in the monitor can controlling the start-up of Dynostar, and the new jury rig being assembled for crew operation in the forward control sector.

As Hayward swung the circular door downwards and

aside, Sicura floated up and began to enter the locking collar, edging Hayward aside.

"Get back," Hayward shouted. Sicura, his two hands on the second door, looked back over his shoulder. "Come back. We don't know the radiation level."

Sicura remained poised, staring at Hayward. His expression gave no hint of acknowledgement. Hayward already disliked the coldly glabrous expression of the other man. He controlled his tone: "Get back down out of there —now!"

With studied insolence, Sicura pushed himself off with one hand and launched his feet in a direction which meant that Hayward had to move to avoid being struck. As he pulled himself back, he beckoned Fischer to replace him in the locking collar.

At the entrance to the monitor can, Fischer uncoiled a small metal cylinder resembling a microphone which was attached by a lead to an oblong metal meter strapped onto his wrist. As he advanced, the cylinder towards the door, a grille on the box began a staccato clicking, and, as he thrust the cylinder forwards, the rate of clicking rose. Fischer fixed his eyes on the dial needle as it swung upwards.

"Ten point six Fermis. It's O.K." He swung the airlock door to one side and floated upwards into the monitor can. Hayward and Sicura made to follow, but the radiation counter on Fischer's wrist began to click at a steadily increasing rate.

"Stay where you are," Fischer called out. "It's over fourteen here."

Hayward peered upwards through the hatch: "Come back out of it Eric," he called.

"Not necessary—the reading gives me fifteen minutes,"

came the reply. Fischer swung the inner hatch closed until it just touched on the leash of cables passing through the circular aperture.

The interior of the monitor can or "Control Module" as it was listed in the inventory of Spacelab, was a cylinder approximately ten feet in diameter and twenty-eight feet long. It stood vertically above the main larger cylinder of the Spacelab, like the conning tower of a submarine, at right angles to the other four cans.

At the end farthest from the double airlocks, was the main control desk, nicknamed Gemini by the crew. Over the desk were two triangular windows looking directly out onto the massive gleaming doughnut shape of the Dynostar device, fifty feet away. There were two jockey seats in front of the desk resembling two heavily padded bicycle saddles. Steel rings on the seat mounting tubes held brackets from which hung retaining straps.

On perforated alloy beams underneath the control desk, were the complex block of the automatic control computers controlling Dynostar. A rectangular array of coloured lights was flickering and pulsing like multiple reflections in a crystal.

There was a slight overall humming sound, punctuated at irregular intervals by the discordant groan and click of programme tapes starting and stopping on the computer.

Beneath the computer blocks and nearest to the airlock was the M.H.D. reactor and generator. The reactor itself, the size and shape of a large melon, was attached to the plasma generator and charge extraction tube of the magneto-hydrodynamic generator, a machine which extracted electrical energy directly from a high velocity stream of charged gas atoms. It emitted a soft, low-pitched roar like a muffled blowtorch.

Beside it, on a bulkhead, was a fluorescent orange clover-leaf radiation hazard signal.

Fischer drifted upwards and strapped himself onto one of the two jockey seats and began to check the myriad of black toggle switches and indicator lights. Directly in front of him was a ten-inch-square read-out screen on which figures came and went in continuous profusion. He looked down at his wrist chronometer, recorded both minutes and seconds on a wrist pad, and then began to work over the shut-down check list, ticking each item as he verified readings on the controls. After about three minutes, he eased himself back in the retaining straps and gazed out through the triangular port at the Dynostar device.

A sensation of sheer physical pleasure at the appearance of the great machine completely overcame his concentration. Dynostar was in the shape of a forty-foot-diameter doughnut made up by parallel circles of gleaming copper field coils.

Set at regular intervals around the copper circles, like giant wedding rings on the continuous ring of copper, were a set of highly polished alloy hoops, each one machined to a design tolerance which would have caused an average metal worker to give up in sheer disbelief.

Between the inner circular rings of copper and the outer hoops were complex spirals of black tubes winding round and round the doughnut or "torus" as the scientists preferred to label it.

The whole assembly was attached to the main Spacelab hull by a shining filigree network of precisely machined magnesium alloy girders.

Had Dynostar been designed to work in an atmosphere, it would have been necessary to create an airtight inner ring or tube in the general shape of a tyre so that the air could be pumped out of its interior to create the necessary vacuum for the fusion process to be confined. But, in space, nature had provided a near perfect vacuum and so, through the elegantly woven assembly of red and silver metals, Fischer could see the light blue haze of the atmosphere against the distant night horizon of the earth.

He came to with a jerk, his eyes briefly checking along the twisted leash of cables leading across from the Dynostar, down to the side of the monitor can out of his field of vision.

His eyes wandered over the giant windmill shapes of the solar power cells spread out from their attachment to the power assembly underneath the Dynostar ring. Each blade contained tens of thousands of minute Lead-Caesium crystals. These were connected together to collect the energy in the rays of the sun and turn it directly into electrical energy, to be fed to the giant condenser banks in the power assembly, and stored ready for the giant pulse of electrical current which would blast for one brief second through the giant electro-magnets of Dynostar.

He reflected sadly that all the years of theoretical research and experiment, all the magnificently skilled fabrication, were already a matter for history.

The delicate and finely balanced operation of shut-down had to be controlled to within rigidly defined standards. Any departure from the tautly interwoven pattern of the operation would not only destroy the ship and every man on board, but also release bands of highly charged radiation which would sweep downwards through the ionosphere in interlocked lines of force, unbalancing and destroying the diaphanous protective ozone layer twenty-five miles above the earth.

But if all went according to plan, in four short days,

the human crew would file into the converted spaceshuttle docked onto the control sector of the Spacelab and would leave the most sophisticated machine ever made by man, to be eroded and pitted by the fierce particle bombardments of space.

Would they ever return? Fischer looked down at the controls and ran his long sensitive fingers over the protruding dials, like a mother feeling the contours of her baby's face. An impoverished world would be unlikely to finance another shot. . . .

There was a muffled clang from the airlock hatch and an overhead speaker squawked. With a start Fischer glanced at his watch, six minutes. Hayward's voice came through:

"Eric, you O.K. in there?"

He leaned forward and pressed the answer button, his voice sounded strained even to himself:

"Yes, I will start the removal of the first programmes. Someone'll need to come back in for another eight minutes approximately. I shall have had my maximum permitted dose by then. There are fifteen items, I've done six and should be able to complete another three—there's no real problem, everything's functional."

"O.K." Hayward's voice came back on distort. "We're timing you and give you around seven minutes to be on the safe side."

The speaker clicked off, Fischer turned back to the written schedule and looked up at the bank of indicators labelled: "Prime Reactor Parameters." He frowned and compared the reading on a dial showing "core temperature", then turned to a sliding lever with the legend, "moderator position". He slid it forwards, the needle on the "core temperature" dial remained stationary, then crept upwards.

Fischer began to look agitatedly from one bank of controls to another, then he pulled the lever backwards, the core temperature needle still went on rising. From beneath him there was a dull thump, followed by a muted whine. The whine grew louder, he looked over his shoulder, but the computer banks and reactor casing showed no abnormality.

The geiger-counter probe was floating beside him, undulating like a dancing snake in the zero-gravity air. He grabbed it and pointed it down towards the reactor casing beneath him; its rate of clicking rose abruptly. He glanced back at the "core temperature" needle, it was hard over on the maximum reading.

His brown T-shirt stuck to his back with sweat.

Looking at the reading on the wrist geiger dial, he began to do quick, frightened calculations.

"Hello, hello, Eric, can you hear me? We're coming in."

Fischer jabbed the return button and shouted hoarsely: "No, for God's sake! Stay out! The reactor core—I can't control the temperature, it's rising. I can't control it!"

"We're coming in to get you out now."

"No, stay away," Fischer yelled. "Keep this line open and when I shout, pull me out as quick as you can."

He unstrapped himself and launched the geiger probe on its lead down the can towards the reactor, until it stretched out, whipping from side to side. The needle on his wrist was hard over and the clicking had changed to a continuous note.

Suddenly, to his horror, he saw the matt green paint on the reactor casing discolour and begin to blister and char. The air in the can was now becoming intolerably hot and sprays of sweat were breaking away from his face and

41

hanging in glinting clouds reflecting like jewels off the surrounding fluorescent tubes.

He pulled himself quickly down towards the airlock, trying to fight down panic and to think out the nature of the fault. Moderator rods out of position—they'll over-heat and distort—they must be gotten back in to stop runaway fission. How to do it? If the temperature goes up too far the core geometry will distort and they won't go back in. There are two sets of rod controls—one auto-matic linked by a feedback to core temperature—that must be the primary fault. . . .

Without warning, bright violet flashes appeared in the air in front of him, then brilliant crimson snakes seemed to dance and wriggle their way across his field of vision. He screamed and covered his eyes. The flashes and snakes continued.

They were inside his head!

Suddenly he remembered—radiation phosphenes. Direct stimulation of the retina of the eye and the seeing part of the brain by radiation. Slowly he collected himself and moved on down the can. He remembered—the last fail-safe mechanism for the reactor, which had already been fitted with double vote-catcher electronics, electronics which ex-amined each one of its own pieces of equipment and then voted to itself on which one was functioning most efficiently. . . .

The manual controls!

He tried desperately to remember where they were sited. He looked around trying to peer through the exploding brilliance of the phosphene flashes in his head. He tried to reason clearly. They must be sufficiently far away from the reactor to be operated safely—they must be near the exit for safe removal of the crew.

With a shout of relief, he recognised the manual override wheel on the section of the hull leading down to the airlock. It was behind a glass seal in a metal box.

He raised his hand to smash the glass, but there was a sharp, ugly cracking sound from behind him. He swung round. The reactor casing and generator had split and were burning; black particulate clouds of smoke were floating away from a jagged tear in the metal.

Beneath his feet, there was a second explosion which flung him across the width of the can, to rebound back off the wall. Tongues of orange flames were licking around the glass-sealed box with the manual rod control wheel inside. The paint on the box was bubbling. The air was now intolerably hot and Fischer could hardly see at all through the flashing violet fire of the phosphenes and the gathering clouds of black oily smoke, pouring from the reactor.

Coughing and retching, he pulled off his T-shirt and wrapping it round his left hand and arm, thrust his covered fist through the flames at the glass over the wheel. Again and again he struck the glass, his strength waning, the flames charring the shirt around his arm. Finally, with one last surge of strength, he smashed the glass and grabbed for the wheel. On the rim of the wheel there was a cast-in arrow pointing clockwise. He began turning it, his eyes tight shut against the flames billowing up around his arm.

Automatic powder fire extinguishers began to flood the can with choking white clouds.

The communicator squawked: "Stay where you are. We're coming in.

His shirt sleeve had now charred and crumbled away from his blistered arm and his face and hair were singed and blackened. From behind him, the smoke pouring from the reactor had diminished and the flashes in his eyes from the radiation phosphenes were dimming.

The hatch beneath him swung open, Sicura and Hayward quickly reached in and, each grabbing a leg, pulled the almost unconscious Fischer down through into the locking collar, then shut the hatch as far as it would go against the leash of cables passing through the aperture.

Together, the two men bundled Fischer down through the neck of the locking collar and into the central access tunnel.

"Eric," Hayward shook the injured man. "Did you shut it off?"

Fischer nodded, then his face contorted in a spasm of pain and he vomited a stream of thin watery fluid which hung in the air of the tunnel, undulating like a giant yellow amoeba.

Sicura jerked his head back to avoid the breaking globules.

"Get him down to the medical unit, fast." Hayward began to manœuvre the writhing scientist down towards the rear of the tunnel. Sicura stopped for a moment, and looked back up the access way to the monitor can:

"We'll have to take a look back in there."

Hayward looked down at Fischer's singed and blackened features: "Leave it. Nobody goes in there. Come on."

At the aft exit from the tunnel, the two men bent and manœuvred the now motionless body of Fischer around the access way to the medical unit.

The medical unit was of the same size and shape as the other cans attached to the main Spacelab. Suspended be-

44

tween the circular bulkheads there were two stretcher beds with retaining straps, each supported by single bearing rods at each end to enable the whole to the rotated in its long axis.

On the opposite half of the cylindrical module were racks of squeeze bottles, a small laboratory bench with sintered glass electric heaters and a light alloy binocular microscope mounted on a gymbal joint.

One cabinet contained clipped rows of shining surgical instruments, alongside, a second row of spring clips holding capped test tubes. Above the tubes, there was a small refrigerator and a single triangular port admitted turquoise earthlight.

The air smelt of medicinal alcohol.

Van Buren, Dr. Lyall and Mel Freeman were inside. Lyall launched himself forwards, gesturing to one of the stretchers: "Get him up there."

Van Buren's face puckered at the sight of the burns on Fischer's arms and face, but between them, they manœuvred Fischer, his face working now with pain, into the stretcher bed and buckled down the shoulder and leg harness.

Lyall turned to Freeman: "Start getting that charred cloth off his arm."

Freeman floated over to the cabinet and took out a large pair of forceps and blunt-ended scissors.

Patterson's head appeared at the airlock opening.

Hayward saw him and unstrapped the wrist geiger counter from Fischer's arm and handed it, with its trailing probe, down to the waiting Australian. He spoke deliberately and quickly:

"Get back down to the airlock collar of the monitor can, put the probe into the space between the door and the cables, then go back into the access tunnel and start getting readings . . ."

Patterson started to protest, then glanced up at Fischer.

". . . take them every ten minutes. I want to see a baseline and I want to know whether the count is going up or down."

Patterson hesitated for a moment, then took the geiger counter and eased himself backwards into the airlock.

For nearly an hour, Lyall and Freeman worked on Fischer. The right arm was carefully débrided of charred tissue and covered with oiled gauze. He was given intravenous Methionine sulphoxide to help protect his tissues against the ionising ravages of the radiation.

Finally, Lyall set up an intravenous drip, connected by a needle to a vein in Fischer's forearm. The drip bottle was connected to a small air pump which pressurised the interior to push the contained solution of electrolytes into the vein.

On earth, the bottle would have been on a high stand and gravity would have forced the fluid in, but in the zero gravity conditions of the Spacelab, it had to be pumped. Hayward sat, watching. Finally, he spoke:

"I want to talk to him, as soon as he's round."

Lyall was hostile: "The man's three quarters dead! When we've done the white-cell count I'll be more exact. He's got to be left alone."

"I must have the information. I need it now." Hayward's voice was firm.

Lyall paused, then shrugged: "Only a few minutes then I'll have to sedate him."

Hayward floated over to the stretcher bed and shook Fischer's shoulder gently: "Eric, it's Hayward. Can you hear me?"

Fischer's eyes opened with a start. At first they stared straight into the room, then focused back on Hayward's face. His voice was weakened to a painful whisper:

"The reactor—the moderator control—it just can't do what it did! It can't—it is not possible—the radiation. I will tell you what I did—so you can follow the sequence. . . ."

Hayward listened, carefully making notes as Fischer painfully described his battle with the runaway reactor. He was interrupted by Patterson's voice from the airlock. The Australian's face was ashen as he entered:

"The level in the monitor airlock is twenty-eight—it's not safe to go anywhere near it."

He caught his hand on a bulkhead and released his hold on the geiger probe. It snaked forward on its cable and touched Fischer's body. The clicking of the speaker soared to a screech, then went down again as the probe rebounded away from Fischer.

"Jesus Christ!" Patterson backed away, mouth open.

"What?" Hayward was startled by the vehemence of the other.

"Can't you see?" Patterson's voice was hoarse with fright. "When you get a dose of radiation—you *don't* turn radioactive, unless you've got some hot material on you! The reactor casing must have blown. It's released some plutonium.

"The poor bastard's covered in it!"

47

Forty-five minutes later, Hayward was giving his final instructions to the hastily assembled crew members in the mess section:

". . . we can't seal off the monitor can because of the cables running through both airlocks, and there is insoluble plutonium dust in the air, so unless we seal off the gap in the airlocks, we'll all get it—and I don't need to remind you that one microgramme is a hundred percent carcinogenic, quite apart from its radioactivity.

"Townsend, Walters, make up a temporary seal of—use anything, wet clothing, towels and jam it into the gap, seal off any airflow between the can and the main hull of the ship.

"Lyall, you and Freeman take Fischer to the shower tube, wash him down, vacuum all the water off him and put the water and his clothes in a bag in the waste freezer. I'll contact Mission Control."

* * *

Caldor leaned back in his chair surveying the ten men seated round the table in front of him. Each represented the best available expertise. There were two designers from the Spacelab team, a radiation physicist, a psychiatrist, two physicists, a systems analyst and an expert in computer design logic, backed up by a medical doctor and a pathologist specialised in space physiology and disease.

They had been in session for three hours and the air was heavy with the tang of coffee and old cigar smoke. Faces showed lines of fatigue. On the table in front of each man was a small computer data terminal which let him share simultaneous time with the vast blocks of the Mandrake computer system set in the basement tunnels honeycombing the earth underneath Mission Control.

The principle of the operation was itself based upon computer design logic. It enabled each man to debate his own subject with all the data of his own speciality instantly available to him on recall, through the small read-out screen over the data terminal in front of him.

The ten-man human computer had the official name of "Multiplex Heuristic Decision System" and was the most accurate way known to decide upon the future of a complex operation with a number of dependent and independent variable quantities.

It was known among its participants as "Hydra".

Probabilities of failures and operations were estimated and votes taken every ten minutes. Each man contributed a proportional vote varying between nought and one, measured in tenths.

They had exhaustively debated the status of the stricken Spacelab Dynostar and made a series of decisions involving the life and death of the crew with as much overt emotion as if they were comparing the prices of meat on a butcher's slab.

They all eyed Caldor, waiting for his decision. They already knew there was only one.

Their own anxieties were small, since they had each contributed proportionately.

Caldor's were massive since it was his final overall decision. He gave no external sign of anxiety, his small well-formed mouth appearing to be entirely at rest. He was gazing fixedly at a computer-generated perspective line liagram of the Spacelab interior flicking on a large, coloured read-out screen on a nearby wall.

As he pressed a button repeatedly on his own data console, the perspective position of the diagram flickered into a new position. He seemed to be playing with the control.

Suddenly, he flicked the switch off with a quick backhanded movement and leant forward, elbows on the table:

"I think we all agree, therefore, that . . ."—he ticked off the points with his hand—". . . estimates of stress factors in the crew members are one of the main pivot points in this operation. Three men are dead, and one vital replacement will probably die within hours.

"The Dynostar is still running to start up on automatic computer control and is probably unreachable because of lethal radiation in the monitor can.

"Now the crew have run temporary lines from the computers in the monitor can to the main control sector in the hope of building a safe manual over-ride, so that this will achieve shut-down and avoid explosion in the power can. But there is no absolute certainty that this will work.

"In fact I would give it no more than point six, first, because they'll have to make a jury rig and secondly, because the men doing it are already close to the point of breakdown.

"Now most of you on the technical side have argued strongly that the crew continue the attempt to shut-down Dynostar from the main control area; and the remainder of you have attempted to justify an extra vehicular operation to cut the cables leading from the monitor can to the Dynostar. I myself have serious doubts about this on two grounds. First, it will probably do irreparable harm to the Dynostar and so hinder any future continuation of the experiment. Second, fatigued men in an E.V.A. situation are considerably more likely to make a mistake and so there is a real danger of accidental discharge of the condensers in the power can.

"On the credit side of this suggestion. . . ."

He punched a button on his data terminal and columns of figures appeared on the read-out screen.

". . . and you may wish to recap on your voting, is that division of the cables will be completed more rapidly.

"So the first operation is less hazardous, will take longer and is more uncertain. The second, quicker and considerably more hazardous."

He rose to his feet and his chief aide, Colonel Joseph Robertson, began to gather papers off the table into a large briefcase.

"My decision is that we give them a further eight hours to achieve manual shut-down and then, if that fails, they will have to go E.V.A. and cut the cables directly." He nodded curtly. "Thank you for your time gentlemen. I will tell the President directly."

Once out of the room, he turned to Robertson. "Joe, two things: there are about three hundred journalists waiting up in the P.R. block, give them a written release —no talking. Keep off the crew fatigue part of it, otherwise tell them exactly what's happening, but keep Fischer's accident out of it." Robertson nodded.

"Then make sure I have a secure private line to Hayward. We already have a scrambler line, so transit a pad tear-off code to Hayward now, then we can alter the scramble sequence every hour. There's a slight risk there that someone may pick up the initial transmission of the tear-off sequence, but that's one we're going to have to take.

"I'm not sure yet what's going on up there, but one thing I've got to have is a totally private line to Hayward."

CHAPTER SEVEN

Hayward saw that Caldor's decision had improved the morale of the crew. The possibility that Dynostar might still be saved for the future had led directly to several practical suggestions as to how the construction of the manual control could be speeded-up.

Hayward terminated the meeting in the crew quarters by suspending all watch and team arrangements, giving the order that food and rest periods were to be taken as and when the operation allowed.

Patterson and Sicura were given the task of preparing the spacewalk operation should the first plan fail. They immediately began to study the circuit diagrams of the great leashes of cables stretching across space between the Dynostar and the crippled monitor can. Both were aware that any mistake they made would in an instant turn the whole Spacelab Dynostar into a thousand incandescent fragments.

Although each man appeared totally concerned with the task, Hayward noted an uneasy mutual suspicion only just hidden beneath their apparent concentration. He made his way as quickly as possible to the medical unit.

Inside, the English doctor and the medical biochemist, Freeman, with his brushed forward silver hair and protuberant blue eyes, were setting up a system of clear plastic tubes connected to a peristaltic pump fixed to a bulkhead over Fischer's head.

Lyall looked up: "He needs blood."

Hayward looked at Fischer's face, horrified. It was ashen white, the dry lips were showing purple against the deathly pallor of the skin. The eyes were closed and there were penny-sized dark red blotches scattered over the skin of his cheeks. He moved towards him, but Lyall called out tersely:

"Don't go near him, he's still radioactive, even though we showered him."

Hayward moved back. "What blood group is he?"

"I've only had time to do a tile test," Lyall replied. "O, Rh. positive will do. It'll have to anyway!"

"That's mine," Hayward replied. "When do you want to start?"

"You need yours," Lyall replied quickly. "There are two more on board who'll do, I've their med. cards here. It'll leave you too weak. It's not like being a donor back on earth, one's blood volume is already smaller than it should be."

Hayward began to roll up his sleeve.

"And I can absolutely do without heroics," Lyall replied turning away.

"Phillip, take a look at this will you?" Freeman was holding out a small square of film negative divided into a number of parallel stripes of varying greyness. "It's Fischer's lapel radiation badge. I've just developed it, careful it's still wet!"

Lyall took the negative and held it up against a fluorescent tube, studying the lines intently. Finally he pushed the negative into a spring clip and turned to Hayward:

"You can keep your blood Commander. Fischer's had a minimum dose of two thousand R. Six hundred R. is the minimum lethal dose, 1,000 R. is irretrievably fatal in between four and seven days. Two thousand R. is now destroying his central nervous system, he will probably live for a few hours." Lyall spoke as if he were quoting lecture notes.

Hayward hung his head. In his short aquaintance with Fischer, he had grown to admire his tenacity and integrity. He felt a sickening disgust at his next words:

"Wake him."

"What?"

"I said, wake him. I need to know what he found in the monitor can."

"I can't, he's dying! He's full of analgesic, the pain would be intolerable."

"I have to know what he found. The survival of all of us may depend on what he knows. Use anything you've got and get him round, now!"

For several moments, Lyall stared back at Hayward, his lips drawn in disgust, then he relaxed suddenly and turned to Fischer and touched the pale forehead lightly with his fingers. He spoke in a low, flat voice:

"I can give him Durufan, it's the most powerful analeptic there is. I don't know what it'll do to him." He shook his head slowly from side to side. "There's no point in your waiting. I'll call you on the intercom if anything happens."

Outside, in the access tunnel, Hayward felt a surge of nausea, his sense of balance deserted him and he cannoned into the wall.

"You all right, Commander?" Freeman's questioning blue eyes were wide. "Hey, why don't you take a couple of these?" He unzipped a thigh pocket and took out a small glass phial containing white tablets.

"What are they?" Hayward asked, trying to bring his discorded senses into line.

"Like Hyoscine," Freeman replied. "They soon settle your semicircular canals."

Hayward took two of the pills out of the special ejector and put the tablets in his mouth. Freeman floated through out of sight into the mess access. Hayward immediately spat out the two pills and palmed them.

Freeman returned a moment later with a plastic sachet of fruit juice. Hayward put the drinking tube in his mouth and squeezed the flexible container until it was empty. Freeman moved aft along the access tunnel.

The speaker overhead gave a single tone, followed by Lyall's voice: "Commander, will you come at once?"

Back in the medical unit, Hayward noted that Freeman had already rejoined Lyall. There was something about the man that repulsed Hayward. It was hard to identify. He was too calm, and the tone of his voice unctuous. There was also a quality of over-familiarity and when he spoke he tended to put his face too close, to hold on to an arm too tightly. The characteristics might have made him a successful television front man. Too solicitous, too sympathetic, too intense.

Some of the livid blotches on Fischer's face were already confluent. In spite of the drip pump, he was obviously dehydrated, his hands showing the washerwoman's appearance of wrinkled finger pads. His breathing alternated between deep slow chest movements and rapid shallow jerks.

Lyall turned: "He's breathing, that's about it."

Hayward turned to the stretcher bed: "Eric, can you hear me? It's John Hayward. Eric!"

Slowly, the eyelids opened. The eyeballs were jerking slowly to one side and then flicking back. Gradually, they steadied, the voice was a whisper, saliva rattled at the back of the throat:

"The moderator controls. I designed them, every circuit has a possibility of—failure. . . ." His face twisted in pain, a thin yellow bile floated away from the dry lips.

Haywards voice was gentle: "What happened?"

"There was a modification! The vote-catcher back up system had—been connected so that it selected—elements with the lowest success record. It was bound to produce destructive feed-back. Once someone changed the position of the moderators—they would come fully out and stay out?"

"What modification?"

Fischer's expression was incredulous. "Someone had *worked* on the circuit, the seals were broken—someone had *worked* on it. Why?" Fischer's face was working, his knees moving up in agony.

Lyall pushed Hayward aside with one hand, a full syringe in the other. He pushed the needle home into Fischer's arm muscle. Bubbles of foam were breaking away from Fischer's mouth and hanging still in the air, like frog spawn.

Hayward felt an intolerable wave of nausea and turned away from the dying man. He eased himself out of the medical unit.

* * *

Hayward pulled himself sideways through the hatch of the empty mess section, his mind racing. Fischer's remarks were repeating again and again in his head. "Some-one had been working on the circuits!"

Working on them! What for? Fischer was dying of acute radiation poisoning—he was suffering—what was the description Lyall had used—Central Nervous System Death—his brain was dissolving? So was his opinion to be taken seriously? Two accidents, three dead men, their corpses stacked in plastic bags like so many sides of beef in the waste freezer, and one man dying.

All four "accidents" in the same section of the ship. If someone had worked on the reactor moderators first of all, they were unlikely not to have received authorisation from Van Buren, and secondly, if the work done on the circuits was the cause of the accident, it could only have been deliberate. A booby trap!

The idea seemed completely outlandish to Hayward. He went over to the coffee dispenser and squeezed a sachet full of black coffee into his mouth. He felt his self-control slipping. Fischer's putty white face reared in his mind's eye like a ghoul.

Why had they picked him? He was unfit, his inner-ear disturbance of balance, Menière's syndrone the doctors had called it, was still producing attacks of nausea and he could also feel the involuntary flick of his eyeballs which was associated with the condition.

Why him? Answer: middle-aged and expendable!

Self-pity gained a hold. A younger man would have been far more resilient in this sort of situation, he wouldn't have the deep sense of empathy for another's pain that an older man would have. He had been through enough in his forty-five years to be able to understand anybody's situation when it was centred on pain, fear or confusion.

He squeezed out another plastic sachet of coffee. As the

liquid began to warm his stomach, he realised he was hungry. He'd had nothing to eat for six hours. He turned to look at the long row of food cupboards, which resembled a diner automat with perspex windows. He selected a frozen steak meal and slipped the package into a small microwave oven.

The food quickly relieved the inevitable feeling of head congestion experienced by everyone in a weightless environment for a period of more than a day. The digestive processes of the stomach and intestine pulled blood down from the head, so relieving the constant feeling which was similar to an uninterrupted head cold.

He remembered his first duty tour in "Spacelab Two" when the crew had learned to break up their meals, eating as many as five or six meals in a single duty period to keep the congestion at its minimum.

After a few minutes, he called up Van Buren on the intercom and asked him to come to the crew section. On his arrival he repeated Fischer's claim that someone had worked on the reactor moderator circuits.

Van Buren shook his head emphatically: "No way. The entire moderator system was in the "no need to touch" category. We were shown their layout in training, but they were so safe with this vote-catcher control thing, that we didn't spend more than a two-hour period on them. René Lasalle did have a quick look a couple of periods back before he died, but it was more like reassuring himself there was nothing wrong. Fischer must have dreamed it up."

Hayward nodded slowly in agreement but, after Van Buren had left, he realised that his words had only served to intensify his doubts. What Van Buren didn't know was Fischer's character, his obsessional dedication to tech-

59

nology. If Fischer said a circuit was in a particular condition, it was in that condition and no other. Even under the stress of the reactor accident, it would have been entirely uncharacteristic for him to make mistakes.

If Van Buren did not know of any repairs or modifications to the moderator circuits, and surely Van Buren would have known if any were contemplated, then what Fischer had seen took on a much more serious, sinister interpretation.

"Can I get you anything Commander?" Mel Freeman's head had appeared at the hatchway.

Hayward, startled out of his thoughts, reacted almost guiltily. Freeman floated in: "If you want something I can easily fix it. I'm sort of unofficial chef around here."

Hayward collected himself, keeping his voice carefully neutral: "No, I've eaten, thanks."

"You know where to find me if you want anything. With everyone working flat out, we've no time for all the routine blood tests and I'm kinda under-employed." He smiled and left.

Hayward swore briefly to himself, searching around for privacy. On one curved wall of the mess deck was a built-in Hi-Fi system, a pair of stereo speakers and a cassette unit with a rack of cassettes dating from the earlier Skylab experiments of the seventies. It had been found then that the private world of stereo headphones and music had been one of the most effective relaxation procedures for the first generation astronauts.

He selected Beethoven's Eroica symphony, put on the earphones and hooked his tethering line onto a nearby clip. As the great opening bars of the symphony filled his head, he closed his eyes and pursued his thoughts once again.

Three key crew members dead. Three replacement men sent up, a further accident, one replacement dying and the automatic controls continuing, the Dynostar start-up permanently out of reach because of a lethal radiation barrier. He completely rejected the idea that one man could sacrifice his life by going back into the monitor can to complete the shut-down procedure.

If there was someone on board ruthless enough to kill to prevent shut-down, what was the motivation?

There was not a man aboard who had not developed an acutely personal stake in the success of Dynostar.

They had already mortgaged their futures in this one last great technological experiment. They had given up academic futures, families. The sacrifice had been voluntary and enormous. But if so, which one? Who among the eight men would cold-bloodedly kill to achieve success? He shook his head and then realised with a shock that, because of the music, he had been speaking out aloud. He glanced round the mess section to ensure that it was still empty.

The symphony had now reached the long golden horn passages, like shafts of sunlight falling on a winter's land-scape. Today he was totally oblivious of the music.

Personal motives maybe? Political? Financial? He reflected on the list of hundreds of firms who had each been responsible for some small element of the Dynostar complex.

At least one multi-national corporation was involved. But not deliberate murder! No stake could be high enough. Besides, the man would have no certain chance of success.

Then he recalled the deadly interior of the monitor can and the Dynostar inexorably clicking away to start-up, to receive the giant pulse of electrical energy which might bring life on earth to a virtual halt. He thought back over the technology of the accidents. Could one man be responsible?

He realised, anxiously, it could have been a conspiracy involving as many as three men. He found himself unable to believe that so many could be involved. Van Buren—not a chance. Walters—thoroughly pleasant, the archetypal regular guy. Townsend—mean, but capable, a political innocent. Lucas—a typical European technocrat, but not murderous. Neumann—no, introverted, too fastidious to kill. Patterson—physically one of the strongest, awkward, rude, but open. No guile. Freeman—he battled with an irrational dislike—a weak personality, quite impossible to believe him a premeditated killer. He wondered whether to tell Sicura.

Why had Caldor put Sicura up against his wishes? Skilled space experience—yes, but there were many men with similar training in the Rentanaut situation back on earth. Only one reason for Sicura, he thought grimly. Caldor knew something he, Hayward, did not. What had Caldor told Sicura? The man was an astronaut, but he was also a cop. Either way, he reflected, he had to tell Sicura about Fischer's allegation. It could be a vital piece of information and Sicura at least would make a relatively unbiassed assessment and then pursue it.

Did he want it pursued? The effect of Sicura being revealed as a trained investigator, might turn out to be the last straw for an already overstretched crew. The overriding priority was to achieve shut-down, and secondly, to get the crew back safely.

Hayward suppressed his own resentment of Sicura. He imagined the effect of a security operation on the delicately balanced shut-down operation and then, almost without effort, his decision was made.

If there were any further "accidents", then obviously Caldor would hold him accountable for not passing Fischer's statement on to Sicura. But Fischer was dying and his statement might not be reliable. In spite of his actual belief in the accuracy of Fischer's statement, the other reason took priority.

Successful shut-down had absolute priority.

He took off the headphones and switched off the cassette player.

His decision was not to tell Sicura.

He moved out through the hatch and pulled himself forward along the central tunnel to the workshop can.

* * *

The workshop can was the only one of the five modular units to possess its own exterior airlock hatch.

Bolted onto the bulkheads of the module were a pedestal drill, a small turret lathe and a grinding jig, all shrouded by light alloy hoods connected by flexible trunking to a fan-driven dust and swarf extraction unit.

On another part of the hull was a small hand-bench with a series of magnetic jig clamps for holding pieces of metalwork in positions relative to each other for assembly.

A small Argon arc welding unit was connected by red and blue tubing to high-pressure cylinders in a wall frame. A series of hand-tools clung to rows of magnetic racks.

Sicura and Patterson were working through diagrams of the cable leashes connecting the Dynostar power assembly to the monitor can. They were preparing for an E.V.A. or Extra-Vehicular-Activity.

For the previous forty-five minutes they had been going through the complex ritual of "suiting-up". First they had donned a long cotton skin-fitting overall, then struggled with the liquid cooling garment composed of a network of water-carrying tubes to provide body cooling, and finally, added to their bulk still further by shrugging into the pressure garment assembly. Then they had each strapped the pressure control unit around their waist. With its dial upwards, the unit looked exactly like a more compact version of the instrument panel from a sports car.

It had been decided that, since Patterson had the greater experience of Spacelab, he would remain at the E.V.A. control panel in the airlock of the workshop can, where the life support systems from Sicura's suit was connected and controlled. Patterson was completing the last of the five connections. First had come the multipin electrical systems plug, then the oxygen connectors, the water inlet and then the water outlet. He had just hooked the bayonet fitting of the nylon tether to its bracket.

Sicura meanwhile had strapped the S.O.P., or secondary oxygen pack, to his right thigh and sealed off the clumsy E.V.A. gloves. His face was free of any reaction as he placed the helmet and visor in place over the neck collar.

Patterson was similarly dressed and connected, except for the gloves and helmet. He floated towards Sicura from the E.V.A. control and completed the sealing down of Sicura's headpiece, going immediately back to the E.V.A. panel to check his own umbilical connection.

When he was satisfied, he unplugged the connections of his Life-Support Umbilical and floated back out of the air-lock into the interior of the workshop can. Picking up a microphone, he spoke to Sicura:

"You getting this?"

An arm of the bulky figure raised and Sicura's voice came back on distort from a nearby speaker:

"Yes, I hear you."

Patterson continued: "Now remember, there's the braided cable containing the main field sensor lines, that's the one. Pick it up at the insert into the torus. Unpick the braiding and you will see two cables, one blue, the other yellow stripe on green. Cut yellow stripe on green and, for Christ's sake, leave the blue one alone."

He referred to a circuit diagram clipped up in front of him: "And listen sport, once you've done that, don't forget to pull the ends well back. Come to think of it, cut a few inches out altogether, so that they can't touch again, all right?"

Sicura's voice on the speaker sounded thin and nasal: "Yellow on green, right."

Patterson closed the inner airlock door and twirled the wheels controlling the locking bolts. After checking the seal on nearby controls, he turned a wheel labelled "lock vent" and spun it. From behind the door there was a sudden loud hiss, which gradually diminished in pitch to a softer roar. Finally, there was silence.

At the single triangular port Patterson watched Sicura's bulky figure shining in the harsh sunlight, the canvas-covered umbilical cord uncurling behind him as he launched his body awkwardly across the black star drop towards the power assembly. Hayward had entered and was floating beside Patterson, watching.

Patterson picked up the hand mike: "Sicura—you getting me?"

There was a slight crackle overlaying the reply: "Yes, you're a bit faint, give me more gain."

Sicura had reached the handholds on the tracery of girder work supporting Dynostar and was pulling himself up towards the power assembly. Patterson was checking the E.V.A. control meters showing the condition inside Sicura's suit. Each dial showed a different parameter: skin temperature, atmosphere humidity, air temperature.

Sicura's voice still crackled. "I am at the walkway. Do you read me?"

"Yes, loud and clear," Patterson replied.

"I can't get much further, the umbilical's almost fully out."

"You've got ten feet to spare minimum," Patterson replied evenly.

"Hey! What are you doing?" The voice held acute alarm.

"Doing to what?"

"The oxygen, what do you read?"

Patterson glanced at the metering dial.

Sicura's voice was rising in pitch: "Oxygen . . . I can't. . . ."

Suddenly Patterson yelled: "Sicura, your pressure. . . ."

Simultaneously, there was a thin, high-pitched scream from the overhead speaker. Hayward and Patterson gazed out of the port, horror-struck.

Sicura's suited figure had broken away from its umbilical cord and was cartwheeling away beyond the Dynostar assembly, diminishing steadily in size.

There was just static from the speaker.

CHAPTER EIGHT

Eighteen minutes later, the inner airlock door swung to one side as Patterson floated back into the workshop carrying the broken end of Sicura's life-support umbilical. Hayward snatched it out of his hand and, without waiting for Patterson to take off his head visor, moved quickly over to an inspection lamp and started to examine the connectors. After a few moments Patterson joined him.

"What in hell happened?" the Australian queried anxiously.

Hayward was subjecting each of the five connectors to a minute scrutiny and had already cut away the rough canvas tubing which acted as an external protection. Silently he picked out the nylon tether. It had been cleanly cut about nine inches from the end. There was a piece of adhesive tape wrapped around the end. Looking at the canvas tube and putting it back into position, Hayward pointed silently to a small transverse slit in the cloth opposite to the cut end of the tether. Both water tubes and the oxygen line had similarly been cut cleanly through at the same point and rejoined over short lengths of alloy tubing using high tensile polyester tape.

"They're all low pressure lines." Patterson was almost whispering. "When Sicura jerked at the end of the umbilical, the tether would have protected the water and air lines from tension, but with the tether cut, the jerk broke

the seals on the tubes and look—yeah—the electrical plug
—the two little brass retaining pins look, they just
sheared!"

Hayward was staring fixedly at Patterson's pressure
control unit still strapped to his suit, the life support umbilical was still in place. Without a word he unclipped a
hand knife from the tool rack and ripped open the canvas
cover and pulled out the tubes.

There was no damage; they were all intact.

"Right," Patterson said, "I'll get straight out and look
for Sicura. There's not much chance, but he may've caught
up somewhere on the outside." He picked up his head
visor.

"Get out of that suit." Hayward's tone was peremptory.

"Why?"

"Get out of it, now. We've got a saboteur aboard and
you're not going anywhere until we've tested that suit."

"I've already been out man, nothing happened."

"You were in the lock for what? Around thirty seconds,
yes?"

"Yeah, about that."

"Right! Out of it!"

Two minutes later, the two men had refixed the head
visor on the empty suit hanging in the air of the workshop
like a giant rag doll. They had fixed the life-support umbilical to the E.V.A. control in the airlock. Hayward was
looking at the sweep second hand on his wrist chronometer. He called out:

"One minute."

Patterson was studying the instruments on the E.V.A.
control panel:

"It's O.K. It's all holding."

The distended empty space suit bumped against a bulk-

68

head and then rebounded, twisting its attitude, so that it was upside down to the attitude of the two men.

"Two minutes," Hayward called.

"That's long enough," Patterson said. "Sicura's got to be on his secondary oxygen pack. Let's get weaving." He moved towards the suit. Hayward motioned him back.

"Jesus Christ man!" Patterson shouted. "Sicura's only got a few minutes left. . . ."

There was a muffled explosion from inside the pressure control unit of the empty space suit, black fumes shot up inside the empty headpiece, then bright orange flames burst out of the suit. There was a second heavier explosion, sending the two men reeling. Smoke began to billow out into the oxygen-rich atmosphere of the workshop.

Recovering his balance, Hayward pulled down a fire extinguisher, pulled out the lock pin and fired it at the burning suit. Immediately a hissing flood of greyish-brown foam ballooned out from the extinguisher and clung to the front of the suit, like a monstrous amoeba. The flames snapped out abruptly.

Patterson had reached the E.V.A. control board and rapidly disconnected the umbilical leading to the smouldering suit. The foam had already begun to set in a solid cake and only a few bubbles in it were still moving and expanding.

The sound of the explosion had brought some of the crew to the workshop airlock. Walters and Neumann peered in, trying to see through the fumes.

Hayward turned to them: "Everybody out!"

He turned back to Patterson who had already torn away some of the solidified extinguisher foam and was undoing a panel the the blackened suit pressure control unit, his face wincing at the heat from the distorted metal.

69

Finally, he levered part of the panel away with a screwdriver and unlocked an oxygen connection pipe and withdrew it. He stuck the end of the screwdriver down into the open end and then pulled it out. Something brown and glistening was adhering to the top. Patterson smeared it onto a finger, smelt it and held his fingers out to Hayward.

"What is it?"

"Grease! First bloody law of oxygen technology—no grease. All joints have got to be dry, otherwise you can get a spontaneous fire when you turn on the oxygen."

He smelt his fingers again. "Something else with it too, peroxide maybe, something to stoke it up a little. Whoever your man is Commander, he's a clever bastard. He knew it would have taken a few minutes for that fire—long enough to get away out in space on the end of the line, right?"

"Get up to the suit-drying chamber," Hayward said. "Check all the other suits. Sicura's gone, there's no hope there. He'd be two miles away at the end of his S.O.P. supply by now. That leaves mine, Fischer's and the four already on board."

After Patterson had gone, Hayward pulled himself over to the port. Once, against the hard, brilliant stars, he imagined he could see a small bright moving spot of light. He looked again, but it had gone. Sicura's body would eventually be calcined in the burning centre of the sun.

Unless the other suits were in working order, he was inescapably trapped on board an uncontrollable fusion bomb with a coldly ingenious murderer!

CHAPTER NINE

Caldor heard the news of Sicura's death at two a.m.

He had been lying in bed for an hour, trying to integrate the details of his defence to the accusation from the Council of Twelve. Major Douglas Phillips and Joseph Robertson, his chief aide, were already waiting for his car at the entrance to the Mission Control building.

Phillips, in his fifty-third year, was the Public Relations Officer to the State Department of Energy. He was a Texan who had been recruited by Caldor over the heads of several more highly qualified men, a simple political act of fealty to the state which housed the Space Administration. His face, with its close-set eyes and leathery red-veined skin, and his manner of consistent throw-away banter, were already known to millions of television viewers. He spoke slowly as they rushed upwards through the darkened building in the main lift:

"Hayward's already got the line open. The **tear-off** code's checked, but he won't say much till you've identified your pad tear-off sequence."

They entered a communication room lined by complex arrays of electronic equipment. Four technicians were busily at work.

In one corner, there was a closed-off glass booth. Phillips unlocked the door and ushered in Robertson and Caldor.

A technician stood up and made to follow them in but Robertson gestured him away and closed the door behind them.

Inside there was a single console. Caldor seated himself in front of it and pressed the open line button. Then from his coat pocket he took a small notepad. On the top sheet were ten numerals in a sequence. Caldor looked down at the tear-off code pad.

It had been one of the most ingenious inventions of the cold war in the fifties. It had been found that all codes, even transmitted through scramblers, were eventually breakable by a computer technique called Iterative Loop Recession Analysis. To retain privacy any two people who wished to communicate alone were each given a series of ten digits chosen from stocks of random number tables. The digits were not used as part of the code but as an instruction for the programming of the scramblers.

As each time period for transmission approached, a new series of numbers was exposed by tearing off the top sheet of the pad, so that by the time an enemy had begun interative analysis on the last message, the operational mode of the paired scramblers would have changed. The best any enemy installation could ever hope to do would be to decipher about one transmission in fifteen, a ratio which would be likely to give such unimportant and out of date information as to make it not worthwhile.

In the early days of the code, an English security office had spent fourteen hours of computer time and thousands of pounds of Foreign Office money in deciphering the tear-off code message from a Russian nuclear submarine to its base.

He had found that the message read that the cook on board had run out of yeast for the blinys!

He dialled the numbers in sequence on what looked to be an ordinary telephone dial, then waited.

A red light winked on a panel and Hayward's voice came through a speaker as clearly as if he were in the next room, although his voice had first been converted into a random series of meaningless tones and then reassembled once more after passing half way round the world and on down through the atmosphere.

First of all he checked and acknowledged the tear-off sequence from Caldor then went on to give a short, precise account of Fischer's allegation and Sicura's death. He concluded:

". . . and we now have overwhelming evidence of sabotage directed at keeping Dynostar operative till start-up. And it is being carried out by one or more people who are prepared to kill. . . ."

Caldor stared at Robertson's face as he listened to Hayward. Robertson, a tall man in his early forties, looked in fact many years older. An angular mid-westerner from North Dakota, he had a long neck, slightly receding jaw-line and a protuberant Adam's apple. He looked type-cast for a film about Oklahoma dirt farmers. He had a naturally awkward manner and always sat in a chair as if it was causing him acute pain.

In fact he was a brilliant administrator whose total loyalty to Caldor was already a departmental by-word.

Hayward wound up: ". . . it will depend entirely on the condition of the remaining E.V.A. suits as to whether we can get out to the cables or not."

"John, listen," Caldor spoke calmly as if he were a doctor discussing symptoms with a patient. "We're already looking at the time to shut-down again. We're going to have to recalculate it. Let me know directly you've checked the E.V.A. suits. We can't mount a shot for at least eleven days, so we can't get more suits up to you."

He clicked off the voice switch suddenly and turned to Robertson: "You getting this all on tape?"

Robertson nodded silently and pointed to a needle on a dial which fluctuated as Caldor spoke. He switched the voice switch again.

Hayward's voice queried: "What happened? I lost you for a minute!"

Caldor ignored the question and, looking straight at Robertson, replied: "John, we will proceed here with a complete background check on your crew. . . ." As he spoke he held his hand out to Robertson.

It was one of the features of their partnership that Robertson always carried a bulging leather case full of papers and statistics instantly available for inspection and it was Robertson's boast that he was rarely at a loss for a factual or analytical answer. The case was known to his colleagues as the "Caldor brain pump" and odds were frequently exchanged as to when it would actually burst.

Robertson burrowed in the depths and came out with a typed list of crew members. The names of the three scientists—Hart, Lasalle and Sigmund—killed in the first vacuum accident, had already been scored through in red. Alongside the eight remaining names, there were brief notes in pencil.

Caldor continued: "When we've completed the check, I'll get straight back on to you." He flicked off the voice switch.

It was not until they were seated in the car and driving away across the campus-like grounds of N.A.S.A. to Caldor's private office in a nearby building, that Caldor began to unburden himself to his assistant. He stopped the car

74

and looked out of the window. It had just begun to rain. Warm gulf-coast rain. The sky to the east was growing lighter and he could just make out the giant shapes of the N.A.S.A. buildings across the clipped, well-cared-for lawns.

He turned to Robertson: "Better get this down, Joe."

Robertson, without a word, pulled out a small tape recorder and clipped the mike onto the underside of the driving mirror.

"First," Caldor began, "we've got to decide whether Johnny Hayward is telling the truth. Well—no logic there —I know Johnny real well and he's just the last guy to flip, so we're going to have to take that as basic, all right?"

Robertson adjusted the volume control on the recorder and nodded without looking up. Caldor continued:

"So, at least one of eight men is a saboteur and almost certainly a murderer. He knows space technology well, and he wants Dynostar to start-up. O.K. so all of them up there want that, I know, but our man is actively working towards it.

"Assuming it wasn't a simple vacuum accident, then apart from the atmosphere scientist Hart, our man disposed of instrument engineer Lasalle as well as the systems engineer Sigmund. We send up Hayward with Fischer and Sicura, now Fischer's probably dying and Sicura's on his way into the sun!

"Hayward's job is to get shut-down. Ours is to get the man." He paused. "Or men! And that's exactly what we can do. We're going to have to sift every available detail of their past. I'll take personal charge."

Caldor glanced quickly down at his watch. "I'll get up to Clear Lake. If I drive to Robert's Field now, you get them to lay on a jump-jet. I should arrive between seven and eight a.m. I want you to get me a land-secure line here in the communication room and check that out with security, now!"

Robertson nodded.

"One last thing, I'll need a call to the White House from Clear Lake when I get there. Time it for the first Oval Office session around 9 a.m. He'll have to decide how much we tell the Europeans.

"When you've done that, get up to Clear Lake yourself, tell Federal Intelligence the bare bones. Krentzer will arrange the details of that, all right? I'll drop you off."

Caldor turned the starter key.

The rain on the windscreen was heavier.

CHAPTER TEN

Clear Lake camp had been chosen as a base for the personnel and families of the Dynostar Project largely because of its proximity to the Redcliffe Nuclear Research Station.

The contrast was extreme. The Research Station with its low, squat laboratory complexes, massive cooling towers and reactor spheres stood out in harsh contrast against the jagged snow-capped background of the Rocky Mountains. It had been built alongside the massive Redcliffe Dam so that it could draw power directly from the generators of the newly completed hydro-electric station.

Clear Lake was nearly two thousand feet below the station, along a winding mountain road in one of the most beautiful valleys in Colorado.

The camp itself had started life on a much smaller scale as a Y.M.C.A. summer camp and had then been enlarged to serve as a major international conference centre. Finally, it had been bought by the Space Administration and fitted out as a village of permanent residences.

The lake itself was about three miles in length and one-and-a-half wide and, at several points, a long army of pine trees advanced right down to the waters edge, partly concealing the varnished wood cabins which lay scattered around its shore.

The central administration building had once been a

large pine bordered Assembly Hall and its exterior appearance still suggested its old function.

There was a white painted verandah and two dilapidated elk heads remained fixed to its front wall. Inside, the technological era had completely taken over.

Each air-conditioned office contained every conceivable business machine and each room clustered around the central operations and communications centre where permanent and land-secure lines stretched to every important centre in the political administration of the country, also to the Research Centre and Space Administration.

Any man working within its complex could guarantee to talk within seconds to one or twenty men—it made no difference, scattered anywhere throughout the United States or Europe. Every aspect of its abundant equipment showed the urgency and importance with which Project Dynostar had been regarded by those who had funded it.

Alongside, the American flag drooped in deference to the three dead men, at half mast in the cold early morning air.

The atmosphere of the Camp was clear, unpolluted and beautiful, and many an obdurate senator or visitor from a European government had found himself seduced into agreeing with a point he had argued firmly against after a few days in the heady atmosphere of good food, boating and scenery.

The landing engines of the jump-jet swivelled downwards and blasted clouds of dust into the air from the surface of the helipad. The lashing roar of the engines echoed back from the foothills on the far side of the Lake.

Finally, the ungainly machine wobbled slightly in the billowing dust cloud and touched down, its suddenly increased weight bending the hydraulic knee joints of the insect-like undercarriage.

Moments later, Caldor ran up the steps to the verandah of the wooden administration building. He stopped for a moment and surveyed the scene, his breath misting in the air. He reflected wryly that in a few years time the Clear Lake camp might revert to one of its previous roles as an holiday camp.

* * *

By 10.30 a.m. Caldor had almost completed his re-organization of the administration building.

Operating on a strict "need-to-know" system and speaking only of an unspecified emergency concerning the Spacelab Dynostar, he had brusquely told the team of project engineers and draughtsmen to clear out of their officers and to make for Caldor's hastily gathered team of investigators.

The main security probe was to be headed by Krentzer and Wallace, two men who were highly skilled in the discovery of political and criminal activities. They had cut their first teeth during the last years of the Watergate investigation. They were both already in the air, on board a military jet from Washington.

His aide, Robertson, had just arrived and was already installing himself in an adjacent office, together with two secretaries. One male, one female.

Before starting his reorganisation, Caldor had spent some time in the office of the Chief Administrator, Dexter. Hanging on the walls and adorning desk tops and tables were various gifts to Dexter from the members of the Spacelab crew.

There was an unopened bottle of Alsation brandy from

Jean Lucas on the side desk, a beautifully machined model of an old stationary engine in a glass case from physicist Russ Walters, and a reproduction copper hunting horn from the English doctor, Phillip Lyall. Around the walls were framed, signed photographs of the crew, each carefully posed, showing the unstressed and jaunty confidence of highly trained men in the peak of condition.

Caldor had installed Sue Annenberg in the next room. She was Dexter's personal secretary, tall with long flowing chestnut hair and an attractive jolie-laide face. In fact, there was no single good feature on her face, but it was universally agreed among the male personnel that she simply gave off ordinary pure and simple sex. During the summer months, the timing of her daily bikini-clad appearances at the lake shore were plotted by the men with all the precision and logistics expertise of a space shot.

She had acquired the nickname of "Earth-Mother" from the Dynostar crew and more than one man had shown signs of depression after the arrival at the camp of his wife and family.

Caldor had chosen her for one reason.

If anyone knew and understood the eight Dynostar crew members, it was Sue Annenberg. She had nursed them through gruelling ballistic trajectory flights, helped them cope with the horrifying nausea caused by the human centrifuge and gymbal cabins.

She had looked after their bank accounts and helped the Europeans with their language problems.

Her salary was one of the highest ever paid to a secretary in the space administration and Dexter had neither grudged her a cent nor committed the full amount to any official report.

Caldor had already spent time in the jump-jet deciding how much she needed to know. He had told her to assemble the files on the eight astronaut scientists and she had already pinned their photographs on a green soft-board opposite to Caldor's desk.

Eight faces. A potential rogue's gallery.

He had reasoned that she already knew about the vacuum accident from the media, but did not know either about Fischer's accident or Sicura's death, even given the camp grapevine.

Caldor put his feet up on the desk, leaning back in the leather padded swivel chair. He was finishing the account he had decided to give her:

". . . and so we just might have one of them—well—pushed over the edge. They have a completely abnormal stress pattern up there and what we've got to do very quickly is to look through their character structures and try and work out which one would be most likely—or the other way round if you like—which of them are the most unlikely to have any sort of breakdown."

"Are you really suggesting one of them is crazy?" She sat down on the edge of the desk, crossing her brown legs slowly. Caldor ignored the only partly conscious provocation.

It was his second night without sleep, but fatigue had not begun to show on his smooth, youthful face. He returned her gaze with slightly hooded grey eyes.

"Not at all. But a month and a half of weightlessness, sensory disorientation, stress, and disappointment are more than enough. I'm suggesting no more than an inability to cope. Probably well covered by a semblance of normality."

He paused, waiting for her reaction, but she continued

81

to sit on the edge of the desk. Her pose was now openly challenging.

"How do you feel about it?" He felt the weakness of the question. As he spoke he also knew that Krentzer and Wallace would already have instigated a search into her own file. The data computers would be rattling out all the dissected fragments of her character and background.

She glanced out of the window where the waters of the lake were already reflecting the clear blue promise of a perfect day. She sighed:

"If it's as dangerous as the Council of Twelve say, well, I guess we're going to have to leave all this—either way. If it shuts down, the whole project's kaput, and if it works— we'll all live underground. The survivors that is!" She turned back to him: "That answer your question?"

Caldor nodded: "I want every scrap of information we can get. Political affiliations, stock holdings, directorates, friends, everything. Attitudes to technology, versus the environment, kinks, hobbies, sex, blackmail potential. . . ."

"To find a man with a potential nervous breakdown?" Sue's eyebrows were up, her expression disbelieving. "They've been through all that before." She pointed to the files. "It's all in there."

"That was two years ago," Caldor countered, too late to rectify the slip. "We'll need it updated."

"And what's all this sex life bit?" Her eyes smiled. "It isn't a bordello they're running up there!"

Caldor leaned back, realising the name "Earth-Mother" had probably been well earned. For a moment he let his concentration slip and enjoy her intense, frank sensuality.

Nothing showed on his face: "In the next two hours, I'm expecting two more people, Paul Krentzer and David Wallace. They're both from Federal Intelligence, look after them please and arrange quarters for them. I think that's all. Thank you."

He nodded briefly and looked down at the papers in front of him. She slid off the desk and went out.

He studied Van Buren's photograph on the soft-board. Van Buren had been his own choice as chief astronaut scientist for the Dynostar project, not only because of his scientific and technical abilities, but also because of his position as a figurehead for the project.

His face and persona had contributed significantly to the sale of the project. Now he had to look again at the face. To examine the bland friendly smile, to look instead for signs of weakness and treachery.

Try as he would, he could find none.

CHAPTER ELEVEN

The internal access corridors of the Spacelab Dynostar complex were in uproar. A confused traffic of men and equipment passed awkwardly along its length as the new controls for the manual shut-down operation were assembled in the forward control section. Shouted commands echoed in the claustrophobic atmosphere.

For Hayward there was no place to hide. Unlike the navy ships in which he had served prior to his training as an astronaut, there was no executive office, and no door to close off behind him.

Life in the Spacelab was a true egalitarian community and each man got to know his fellow crew members in every small detail and habit. Continuous proximity led even to the recognition of particular body odour and a repetitive coughing pattern was often sufficient to send tempers soaring.

Hayward decided that he would occupy the least frequented part of the ship: the Geophysical Module. It had been included in the Spacelab complex since it was essential to establish regular data and parameters about the upper atmosphere and solar wind before the start-up of Dynostar.

Since the deaths of Hart, Lasalle and Sigmund, it had been almost unused.

The module also contained the exercise equipment whereby the crew kept their muscles in a healthy state of tone, but these too had lain largely unused since the emergency, except for the vascular suction apparatus which was used in brief duty periods to draw blood temporarily from the head into the legs and so relieve the head congestion caused by weightlessness.

The module was known to the crew as the "gym".

Hayward closed the airlock door behind him.

In many previous missions he had gradually worked out a routine for weightlessness that gave a sense of relaxation similar to that which came from pacing the deck of a ship.

First he launched himself from one side of the module, then, somersaulting neatly in mid-air, landed with his feet touching the opposite side. Then he propelled himself backwards and forwards repeatedly in a rhythmic routine. After a few minutes, he found that his thoughts began to run more calmly and freely.

He went back to the vacuum accident. Fischer's allegation and Sicura's death. The vacuum accident could still be a technical malfunction, in spite of Van Buren's denial. Fischer's judgement was certainly affected, but the damage to Sicura's suit was premeditated, ingenious and murderous. Did whoever was responsible want Sicura's death? Or the death of anyone who went into space?

Patterson's suit had also been sabotaged. Nobody with the training the crew had received would put grease anywhere near an oxygen line. It was a first principle they must have had drummed into them time and time again in ground training. But if Patterson's suit was also damaged, that did not necessarily exonerate the Australian. He could have done it to provide himself with a cover.

The hatch door swung open.

Patterson's voice was quiet, all the aggressive quality of his speech had gone. For the first time his face showed actual fear:

"Better come with me Commander."

He immediately backed down through the hatch and turned into the central access tunnel. Hayward followed; apprehension rising.

Patterson silently led him to the closed off space-suit drying chamber, lying between the mess section and the forward control section.

In the early years of manned space flight, it had been found that perspiration absorbed into the cloth of the space-suit linings was a potentially serious problem leading to bacterial and fungal growth, and also to the misting of face visors. Consequently the suits were stored in an electrically heated cubicle maintained at minimum humidity by recirculating the air across mesh trays of silica-gel to absorb water vapour.

Patterson slid the door of the drying chamber to one side. Seven space suits floated on Velcro retaining straps like huge robots waiting for activation. He silently turned one suit towards Hayward:

"This one's had all the L.S.U. connectors removed." He selected a second and pointed to the pressure garment connector sockets. "The connecting rings are gone from this one."

Together they went from suit to suit. Each had been destroyed beyond any reasonable repair.

Three had been crudely ripped open, as though the saboteur had had insufficient time to complete his work.

"How soon could we repair one?" Hayward asked.

"Can't say. We could maybe stick up some of those

rips, but there's no guarantee they'd hold up in space. I wouldn't go out in one. As for those connectors, we could just make one up on the workshop lathe, but there isn't time and we've got no drawings to work from."

Patterson stared at Hayward: "Anyway round you look at it Commander, we're stuck inside!"

To a space veteran like Hayward, the discovery was the worst possible psychological stress. He reacted as any naval officer would have done to the loss of lifeboats from a ship in distress.

To astronauts, space-suits were the most important security symbol of their control over their environment, the one vital element of their surroundings that gave some release from the ever present tension of claustrophobia.

They were imprisoned with a murderer. He felt the nystagmoid twitch of his eyeballs, nausea ballooned in his throat.

His face was grey and aged.

Patterson spoke softly: "Well, we may be able to patch one up. We might as well get used to the idea that we can't go E.V.A. in time, so we'll have to get the control unit put together double quick."

He turned to go. "I'll get back forward."

Hayward remained at the entrance to the drying cabinet, fighting down waves of anxiety and nausea.

Which one? Van Buren, Walters, Townsend, Lucas, Neumann, Patterson, Lyall, Freeman?

Which one?

Soon, each man must know that one of his fellows was a deliberate killer. His mind raced over the complete destruction of relationships, the complete abrogation of trust that that would mean. They were all working continuously on the equipment to stop the runaway Dynostar and one

87

of them was determined that the machine would start on schedule.

Or was it one man?

The conspiracy idea recurred uneasily. His mind spun.

Caldor! He might have got something by now. Fear started again. Even if they could expose the man, there were no arms aboard.

How do you restrain a murderer in space?

As he pulled himself along the central access tunnel towards the command sector, he eased past three men.

Their eyes followed him silently.

Finally, he reached the forward airlock and pulled himself into the shuttle, sensing their eyes in his back.

Once inside, his level of anxiety diminished. Like an animal recognising its own territory, he climbed up into the cramped living quarters directly beneath the flight deck, squeezed in between the waste disposal unit and the food dispensers. He looked up through the cabin window.

Outside, there was a blinding white reflection of sunlight from the front of the main Spacelab body. Above him, the great windmill-like sails of the solar panels partly obscured the huge doughnut shape of the Dynostar and its power assembly. The shapes seemed unreal, like something implanted on the Spacelab by the Gods themselves.

For several moments he gazed at the meshwork of girders glistening brilliantly in the perfect clarity of space, then he moved back to the communicator panel, taking the tear-off code pad from a zipped pocket.

*   *   *

Caldor compared the tear-off digits on a screen with his own code pad, dialled his figures back to Hayward, waited for the red light to indicate acceptance by Hayward.

Caldor noticed that Hayward's voice had become more nasal, free of overtone. He gave no preamble as he told Caldor about the sabotage to the space-suits. He finished by asking whether Caldor had found anything in his character search to indicate which man was responsible.

"Nothing John, nothing at all," Caldor replied. "They've all had a complete vetting, a total re-examination. We've had London, Paris, Berlin check out the Europeans. There isn't anything. Politics, money, multi-nationals. There are no clear motivations as yet."

There was a long pause before Hayward replied: "For God's sake keep trying. I've got to know who that bastard is!"

Caldor paused: "John, there's something you don't know."

The speaker in front of him crackled. There was no reply.

"You still there?"

"Yes?"

"Sicura was armed."

"Who authorised that?"

"I did."

"Why the hell didn't you tell me?"

"I figured you had enough on your plate."

"Why? What reason?"

"John, for the first time, after the accident, we obviously had to think about sabotage. I needed someone who could deal with a criminal, if it turned out that way."

The speaker in front of Caldor remained silent for about fifteen seconds. Hayward's voice was cold, angry:

"What I need now is more space-suits. Then I need to know who that character is and why he's doing it. So far you've got me nothing. And now you are telling me you armed one of my crew! After putting me in command of the operation! What is this?"

"Keep to basics, John," Caldor said. "What else do you need to know?"

"I've got to know who I'm dealing with. If there's no ordinary motive, then I've got a psycho aboard."

"It's possible." There was a pause, then, "What do you make of Dr. Lyall?" Caldor asked.

"Lyall? I don't know much about him."

"We've had the transcript on him from London, England. He checks out. I think you'll need to trust him."

"Let's get one thing straight. I trust nobody!"

"Look, the killer knows you, you don't know him, you need a second pair of eyes."

There was a pause: "I'll talk to him and let you know."

Hayward's voice clicked off.

CHAPTER TWELVE

Hayward leant back in the retaining harness and gazed out
through the cabin window at the Dynostar. With increasing difficulty, he tried to force his thoughts into some sort
of order, but gradually, he was overcome by an irresistible
lassitude and he slept.

In the dream, he was back on earth standing outside the
low fence of the ranch-style bungalow he had built; it lay
at the end of the garish urban sprawl that had grown up
along the Gulf since the inauguration of the Johnson Space
Centre in the early sixties.

He basked in the warm sun, enjoying the flowering
shrubs with their attendant bees and humming birds.
Through the open kitchen window he could see his wife,
Nancy, preparing lunch, her long dark hair pinned up
over her head as she moved about the room.

Along past the white painted timber frame of the house
were his two sons. John junior was hanging down by his
legs from a tree branch trying to catch a rope that Peter
was throwing up to him.

Nancy came to the window smiling and beckoned him
in. As he tried to move through the gate, an enormous
and irresistible force held him back. A crawling inertia
swept down his limbs as he struggled to move forward. A
grey turbulent cloud swept over the sun and, as the air
grew dark, the scene drained of colour down to a frighten-

ing monotone mixture of greys. Nancy had stopped smiling and was looking increasingly anxious. The darkening air thickened as though he was surrounded by huge wet balloons.

The boys had stopped their game and were watching him. He forced himself wearily forward, and, as he moved, his wife and sons began to look relieved but it was no use. A force, like a metal bar, pressed against his chest. . . .

He awoke with a shout; the hard edge of the control panel pressing against his chest. The harsh sunlight which had blazed in through the screen panels had given way to an impenetrable blackness as Spacelab Dynostar swept around the earth and into the earth's shadow.

For a moment, there was a crushing sense of deprivation as the image of his family receded into the poised and terrifying reality of his surroundings. Automatically, he reached out and switched on the panel lights. He consciously relived the dream. Why? Nancy had died so many years ago, the house long since sold.

Every year the boys seemed to grow further away from him. It was a penalty of his public life that his eminence became an insurmountable ego problem for them. The tears broke away from his eyes and hung as crystal globes in the light from a fluorescent tube. He yearned for Nancy and her sweet embrace, trying to shut out the succession of faces he remembered on the pillow beside him in the mornings.

A fruitless search for the warm years.

As he stretched his limbs into action, he saw that there was no real fear even deep inside his imagination. Apart from a brief tightening of the stomach at the thought of the pain there might be before death itself, he discovered a complete disinterest in the idea of extinction.

There was little to return for.

He looked around at the triangular shaped cabin, then at his watch. He had been asleep for roughly forty minutes. An ideal target for a killer! He had even placed himself in the one part of the complex where there would be the least likelihood of interruption. Caldor was right, he needed an ally.

As he pulled himself back through the airlock, across forward control and on down the access tunnel, he found himself almost unconsciously entering the medical unit.

Lyall was sitting at the bench examining some slides. He turned and, as Hayward came up to him, the astronaut marvelled again at Lyall's unwearied face. He must have been on his feet as long as anybody in the Spacelab and yet looked as if he'd just walked out of a Harley Street consulting room.

There were many times when Hayward would have found the other man's slightly supercilious attitude and phlegmatic air of detachment highly irritating. Right now it was worth more than the entire U.S. marine corps. He doubted if, after the last few hours, anything could occur which could knock this quietly spoken man out of his cool.

Hayward suddenly remembered Fischer and turned to look at his bunk. But the bunk was empty and, as Hayward's face framed the question, Lyall replied:

"He died fifty minutes ago."

"Why the hell didn't you tell me?"

"I thought you realised it was inevitable. I haven't told anyone else," Lyall continued. "I didn't see any advantage."

Hayward's anger slowly spent. "What did you do with him?"

"In the freezer, with the others."

"I didn't authorise that."

"There was no need. The body was still radio-active and the waste freezer is farthest from any crew members. Have you any other suggestions? As to disposal that is!" The eyes hooded, there was no mistaking the challenge.

Hayward remembered Caldor's words—"if there was a man to trust, Lyall was the most likely." He began to talk.

First, he gave Lyall a complete account of his discussion with Caldor and ended by describing the absence of conventional motive and the possibility that one man had cracked psychologically and was hiding it. He concluded by asking Lyall whether he, as a doctor, had noted any abnormality, new or old, in any of the crew members.

Lyall considered the question for several moments before replying:

"Difficult. They're all about nine-tenths, I'd say. Any one could flip, but no, there's nothing really hard-nosed, nothing I'd put any money on. Freeman's got some problems. . . ."

"What are they?"

"They're just medical."

"Tell me."

"They're not relevant."

"Goddamit, I need to know!" Hayward exploded.

"Commander, if I thought they were relevant, I'd tell you, but they're not. They're private to him and, of course, to me. I'm sorry but there it is."

Hayward paused: "I want you to think about the men in a completely different way. We've got a killer aboard and he may be mentally disturbed."

Lyall's eyelids drooped: "I've not much experience. I only spent a short time in psychiatry, at the Maudsley, in London." He paused. "Maybe I could do something. I do regular blood and electrolyte tests, urine that sort of thing.

Freeman does the benchwork. What I could do is to fire off a few questions when they come in for test."

"What do you expect to get from that?" Hayward was doubtful.

"There's a form of questioning. I'd have to disguise it of course. Some people call it the psychiatric interview. It can give you leads if you do it carefully. I haven't time to do it properly, but I'll have a go if you like?"

"One more thing," Hayward began. "With two men killed, probably murdered, I need somebody to keep an eye on my back and . . ." Hayward looked embarrassed for the first time, ". . . someone to assess my own performance."

"O.K. I'll keep an eye open, but one thing—you're dead beat. You need sleep."

"No way!"

"Commander, if you're going to go on functioning, you'll have to have proper R.E.M. sleep just like anyone else. I can guarantee you three to four hours and no hangover. The pharmacopeia's quite sophisticated these days."

Hayward paused: "I'll check round the ship first."

Lyall shook his head: "What is there you can do? Why not delegate for three hours?"

For a moment Hayward seemed to want to go on arguing, then wearily shook his head and pulled himself up towards Fischer's bunk. Lyall deflected him down to the second:

"That one's a bit hot at close quarters!"

Lyall started to fill a long, thin, blue syringe.

"I don't need that," Hayward protested. "I thought you meant pills."

"I can get the dose more accurately this way," Lyall replied as he put the syringe into a clip and adjusted the straps around Hayward's body. He unclipped the syringe and swabbed Hayward's upper arm. Hayward turned his head away grimacing briefly at the wasp-sting of the needle.

After some minutes, he felt the buzz of the drug as it took hold. The lassitude and euphoria were irresistible. He tried to focus on Lyall's face through the fog, but night roared through his head.

CHAPTER THIRTEEN

By the time Hayward was two hours into his drug-induced sleep, Caldor had already made contact with, and assembled, a group of five specially trained experts to investigate the possibility of mental breakdown in one of the crew members.

The group comprised two civilian psychiatrists, who had been largely responsible for the personality testing of the Dynostar crew, two military psychiatrists from a nearby airforce base, and a female psychiatrist with a special interest in behavioural patterns caused by extreme stress.

Caldor's first task had been to smooth ruffled feathers. With the full authority of a Secretary of State, he had whisked them from breakfast table, clinic and barracks into cold helicopters for a totally unplanned journey with a quite unreasonable amount of time to rearrange their lives.

They had arrived angry, hungry and shaken.

In the Seminar Room at Clear Lake, he had rapidly outlined the critical position on board Spacelab Dynostar and given an account of the individual crew members and the details of what they had already managed to assemble about characters and backgrounds. At the end of his address, he had asked for comments and advice as to which of the men might be responsible.

The reactions had caused him total dismay.

The two civilian psychiatrists had immediately taken

up an aggressively defensive position, since they clearly felt that they were responsible for having vetted and approved the characters of each of the crew members.

Finally, they had moved onto the attack and one had commented, without bothering to conceal his anger, that had the crew members of Spacelab Dynostar been subjected to the year-long character vetting of the Apollo and Skylab programmes, there would have been no possibility of any failure to spot any signs of incipient mental instability.

They concluded by pointing out that, since the Sortie-Can European experiment early in 1977, there had been no long-term psychological appraisal of potential candidates and that moreover some of the crew were not even American!

Caldor had attempted to press them into more practical suggestions without success and had then passed to the two airforce psychiatrists.

Their response was more positive. They had both delivered long and technical assessments of the crew members and seemed entirely at ease whilst dissecting characters with as much emotion as if they were playing a game of chequers.

Their language had been replete with "exogenous and endogenous reactions", loaded with "depressive aetiologies" and topped with "functional—organic—defect—pathologies".

Caldor had listened with an outward appearance of patience, realising that although the two were more able to discuss the problem, they were no more likely to make any useful decision. He glanced at his watch anxiously, visualising the rapidly deteriorating situation in the Spacelab. He chose his words carefully:

"Thank you for your comments gentlemen, but I'm afraid you have entirely missed the point. We are not engaged on a theoretical discussion of an A.M.A. paper, we have to get to the man in a matter of hours or we may all die."

Quelling the immediate and angry chorus of protests with his hand, he turned to the psychologist, Irene Andler. Throughout the meeting she had sat almost completely silent; a half-smile playing on her face.

She was small, dark, neat and of Jewish appearance, and she sat with her upright back clear of the chair, her hands folded in her lap. Her attraction lay in the calmness of her features.

"I'd value your opinion Dr. Andler." Caldor sat back and braced himself for another onslaught of jargon, but the woman, who could have been any age between thirty-five and forty-five, merely looked back at him with heavy-lidded black eyes. Her failure to answer disconcerted the other men.

"Well?" Caldor asked sharply.

Her voice was quiet, the expression reserved: "It appears to me that we should never be able to agree about any practical modus vivendi." She looked from one man to another, the same half-smile playing. "There are too many —vested interests." One of the civilian psychiatrists flushed angrily.

"But I have another suggestion. We already have some more highly qualified experts here. . . ."

"Where? The civilian psychiatrist interrupted brusquely.

"Here—on the base," she continued. "Wives, families, friends, relations. They have a lifetime of knowledge and experience. They have done all our testing for us."

The men relaxed, smiling among themselves. One of them lit a cigarette.

Unexpectedly, Caldor rose to his feet and turned to them:

"Thank you gentlemen. You have been most helpful. Mr. Dexter, our Chief Administrator, will show you to your quarters. I shall keep you fully informed of any development."

Before the startled psychiatrists could answer, they found themselves ushered firmly out of the room. Irene Andler made to follow, but Caldor restrained her gently.

"You'd better stay."

She paused for a moment, then turned and sat down without replying.

Caldor took his seat behind the desk, pressing down an intercom switch: "Sue, coffee, two of us. O.K.?" He flicked the switch off without waiting for a reply. "Now, can you enlarge on what you've just said Dr. Andler?"

There was the same irritating pause: "You tell me that most of the wives and relations are here?"

Caldor nodded.

"Well then, you have a most interesting community. They presumably all meet one another socially?"

Again Caldor nodded.

"They get to know gossip, Pillow talk is, I think, often more valuable than clinical testing." She smiled thinly. "You don't need so many statistics. Somewhere there will be a wife, a mistress, even a mother who can tell us.

"I'm not talking about real madness," she continued, "I mean that there are tendencies, categories of behaviour in the man we're looking for, which they might not recognise."

She paused, looking down at her fingers. "On the other

hand, somebody might already know his state of mind and be doing everything they can to conceal it."

The tall sentinel firs at the shore of Clear Lake were outlined against the vermilion sunset, giving the scene an unearthly loneliness. Across the lake, lights were beginning to appear in the buildings surrounding the control centre.

Caldor stood for a moment, gazing out through the immense picture window at the violet and gold reflections on the surface of the water, remembering Sue Annenberg's description of the Van Burens' home where he stood. She had said: "You'll find it all a bit like a motion picture set."

The décor was carefully contrived early American. The fireplace wall with its long, rough stone hearth was dominated by an enormous bearskin stretched out on a pine frame.

The head had been set in an expression of unimaginable ferocity. On the inner wall there was a display of antique guns: an early Winchester rifle, a black-iron colt revolver and a muzzle-loading pin-fire musket. The floor was highly polished redwood and several American-Indian rugs were scattered over its surface. An over-large dark brown leather suite of chairs surrounded the stone hearth, each one too pneumatically upholstered for comfort.

Sarah Van Buren, casually immaculate in Park Avenue jeans and matching shirt, was mixing drinks at a small corner bar. She handed Caldor a scotch on the rocks and then gave a tomato juice to Irene Andler, who was trying to maintain her normal stiff posture in one of the chairs which was doing all it could to make her collapse backwards.

Caldor took a small sip of whisky and began to lie.

First of all he outlined the incident which killed Hart, Lasalle and Sigmund, then described how it was probably an accident.

He omitted any mention of the deaths of Sicura and Fischer and failed to describe the deliberate and murderous sabotage to the space-suits. Instead, with Irene Andler's gaze fully on him, he drew a picture of the stress the crew members had been under since the accident and suggested that the situation had led to dangerous mistakes on the part of one man.

He ended by saying that the man who had begun to crack under stress was probably covering up his failures and that this meant that one of them might have some background of instability which had failed to surface in the routine psychological testing.

Therefore, the reason why he and Dr. Andler wanted to talk to all the families on the base, was to try and identify the man, not, he added quickly, for any punitive reason, but so that whoever it was could receive help and not be left in a work situation where his behaviour could put the crew in further jeopardy.

He performed well and caught a hint of amused approval in Irene Andler's expression. To his surprise Sarah Van Buren was staring over his shoulder at the doorway behind him. He turned and made out the shadow of a woman. Her voice was low, the accent middle south:

"I didn't mean to eavesdrop."

As the shadow moved forward into the room, Caldor quickly scanned his visual memory of the photographs he had studied and recognised Eunice Walters, wife of Russ Walters, physicist.

After the introductions, Eunice sat down beside Sarah,

drink in hand. Caldor remembered Sue Annenberg's description, "Sarah and Eunice are as thick as thieves, sort of queen bee social leaders around the place."

He reflected on a difficult-to-define similarity between the two women. It was not in build, since Eunice was taller than Sarah and was ash blonde to Sarah's cropped, brown hair.

It was a question of style.

Both had a hard brightness about them, a poised way of holding their bodies as if they were modelling their clothes. There was an unmistakable air of confident authority. These were the wives of astronauts: the magazine companions of super-heroes. Although both were, by conventional standards, beautiful and exquisitely dressed, each failed to generate any real sexuality. It was as if they were role-playing as women rather than having any genuine femininity.

Caldor decided quite irrationally that they would both probably be very dull in bed.

He thought quickly how to use the unexpected appearance of Eunice Walters.

"It seems to me," she was saying quietly, "that you've got your suspicions already. I think you're just wanting to confirm what you already know!"

Caldor reflected that her voice was either very tightly controlled or she had lost any deep attachment to a husband already in a highly dangerous situation.

There was a faint suggestion that she was enjoying the situation.

"Don't waste our time," Caldor intervened shortly. "We need your help. We have a major problem building up in space. We need to know anything you can tell us about the background of the Dynostar crew.

"Not just your own husbands, but anything you may know about the other men."

"It would help," said Sarah, "if Dr. Andler here could tell us more. What kind of things you're looking for."

Irene Andler toyed with her empty glass: "We're looking for patterns of reaction to stress. In a way the seeds of breakdown."

"Surely you've got all that on record!" said Sarah.

Caldor shook his head: "We're not talking about a major event. Small upsets, perhaps inability to cope with some situations, evasion of responsibility, even." He smiled thinly. "Leaving too many decisions to their wives!"

"They all do that," Sarah smiled. "But we don't run the thought police here, yet. We all get on, we have to. There's a lot of stress for us here. We don't ask too many questions. I mean O.K., Eddie gets mad when the kids swim into his fishing line, but that's all I guess." She turned to the woman beside her. "Can you think of anything?"

Eunice Walters remained silent and put an empty glass back on the table. When she spoke, the drawl had almost completely gone. The face she turned towards her friend was hard:

"You're kidding!"

Sarah's eyes widened.

"You know what I mean, honey. They're not talking about someone who kicks the spokes out of junior's bike when he's high. They mean someone who's different, just a little different."

Sarah's face coloured: "Leave the dirt out of it Eunice."

The voice of the other woman had an edge: "Sarah baby, aren't you doing the camp mother a bit hard! Well, sorry if it hurts your delicate feelings, but Russ is in danger just the same as Eddie." She turned back to Caldor:

"Supposing one of your big he-men up there was—ah—homo-sex-ual?" She emphasized each syllable. "Would that represent the sort of defect you're looking for?"

Sarah's eyes blazed.

"Go on," said Caldor. He glanced quickly at Irene Andler, who shook her head almost imperceptibly.

"Well now," Eunice Walters leaned forward. "You see I've got a family problem. A little gay brother, a fag. We had a party before Spacelab went off and you know how it is, like recognises like?"

"Someone on the present team?" Caldor asked.

"Sure, up there right now. My little brother really dug him, I'll tell you. . . ."

"Who is it?" Caldor broke in harshly.

"Why Mel Freeman, that's who—your medical bio-chemist." Her manner became more confidential. "And little brother told me he was being bled white for money. Someone here at Denver." She sat back, waiting.

Sarah walked over to the bar: "After that I need a drink. Anyone else?"

Caldor shook his head and turned back to Eunice: "I'll check that out."

"Please do," she replied sweetly.

"Who was doing the blackmailing?" Caldor asked.

"I don't know." She thought for a moment. "I didn't get that, but little brother did tell me the name Mel uses in Denver. Like the old time movie star—Holden. That's it!"

"We'll check that out with criminal records," Caldor said.

"So that's the sort of dirt you're looking for?" Sarah protested angrily.

Caldor got up and walked to the door. He turned:

"Mrs. Van Buren, I'm not in the least interested in what people do with their genitals, just what pressures they have to put up with in the process."

CHAPTER FOURTEEN

By the end of Hayward's drug-induced sleep period, the entire atmosphere in the echoing bulk of Spacelab had changed. Almost as if he had previously been acting as some sort of inhibitor of progress, the work of building a completely new control system to bring about a safe shutdown to the Dynostar was well under way in the forward control sector.

Jean Lucas had taken effective control of the operation since it was he, as chief electronics officer, who knew most about the control systems and how to knit together quickly redesigned circuits.

Their combined problem was immense and dangerous. The final stages of the start-up operation were under automatic control of computers in the wrecked and lethally radioactive monitor can.

No one could enter and bring about a successful manual over-ride operation without dying in the process. Neither could they merely switch off the computers and so stop the operation, because there were feedback links between the computers and the power assembly rigged underneath the Dynostar.

The links were to sense and control the stability of the stabbing pulse of electro-magnetic energy to be released around the doughnut coils of the giant machine.

If the computers were merely switched off, it was almost a certainty that the loaded power assembly would discharge millions of watts of energy prematurely and then explode and destroy the ship and its crew.

If the Dynostar did actually pulse into its designed one-second burst of fusion, it would send looping fields of magnetic energy sweeping down through the ozone layer destroying its delicately held balance and admitting lethal ultra-violet rays to the earth's surface.

Each separate programme in the computers in the monitor can had first to be tapped, read out in the forward control unit, then rewritten from data transmitted from computer complexes in mission control and, finally, retransmitted by the jury-rigged line back into the computers.

Finally, the crew hoped to be able to perform what they referred to as an inching operation. To bring about the shut-down of the computers and the slow discharge of the power assembly, stage by minute stage, without either causing explosion or start-up.

The forward control sector had completely lost its previous tidiness. Wall panels had been removed and hastily assembled complexes of multi-coloured wires were already bound to stationary projections by black tape. The wires connected a number of bare printed circuit boards which had also been taped to a crude framework of alloy tubing, bound together by knotted plastic tubing and fixed to a work-top by twists of electrical cable.

The scene resembled a child's first attempt at electronics rather than the product of highly trained scientists.

Lucas was copying electronically generated circuits as they flickered onto a green read-out screen from Mission

Control. Neumann and Van Buren were totally absorbed in noting the complex wave patterns rushing over the coloured face of an oscilloscope screen.

Patterson and Townsend were in the workshop can, binding together another support frame, and Walters was checking cable connections at the junction between the central access tunnel and the airlock leading to the hastily sealed hatch of the monitor can.

Dr. Lyall was quietly and unobtrusively passing from man to man taking blood samples from earlobes and at the same time talking earnestly and quietly, observing reactions.

Freeman was strapped into a support frame in the medical unit processing urine and blood samples and testing them against banks of colour indicator charts. His was the first face Hayward saw on waking.

Freeman was shaking his shoulder, his face peering close:

"Phil Lyall told me to wake you."

He moved back as Hayward fought the dwindling remnants of sleep. Again, he felt a stab of irritation at the other's inquisitive stare.

"Where's Lyall?" Hayward asked shortly.

"Taking samples in the control sector, Commander," Freeman replied evenly, gesturing at the rows of capped tubes on the bench.

"So far we're all O.K. No leucopenia—so the radiation can't be all that bad. Electrolytes too, they're all within normal limits."

Hayward nodded, trying to control a surge of nausea from his damaged balance canals. He moved towards the exit lock and pulled himself down into the access tunnel and along to Walters, who was wiring a small repeater unit into the leash of cables leading into the monitor can. Walters looked up, grinned broadly, waving a small tool and immediately went back to work. Hayward watched.

Walters' thin, almost birdlike face with its easy mobility was entirely reassuring. The endless stream of college-boy humour, normally a little irritating, again was a source of confidence to Hayward. A snatch from a long-ago musical comedy came to Hayward's mind: "I'm as corny as Kansas in August, I'm as normal as blueberry pie." The lyric fitted Walters.

He spoke rapidly and jerkily: "Jesus, when I get back—correction," he grinned broadly. "If I get back, I'm going to get me a job in computers." He gestured towards the control sector. "By the time Jean Lucas' finished with us, we'll all have a master's degree!"

"How is it?" Hayward asked.

"Better since you've been asleep." Again the quick crinkled grin. "Nothing personal, Commander."

"When did you last sleep?" Hayward asked.

"Hell, I don't know. Not doing any harm, leastways, not yet!"

Hayward touched his shoulder briefly and floated on towards the forward control section.

As he moved out from the dim lighting of the tunnel into the glare of the conical chamber, he was immediately surprised by the atmosphere. He had expected to have to deal with the tensions and animosity following the knowledge that at least one man among them was prepared to kill them to make what they were doing impossible. But, on the surface, there was no sign.

Just as war forges unlikely comrades, the final threat to their personal safety seemed to have temporarily suppressed suspicion so that the task in hand became totally dominant.

Each man was in fact treating his colleagues with an exaggerated politeness as if to reinforce the belief that he was to be trusted. He approached Van Buren, who seemed almost entirely to have recovered his self-assurance. He asked about progress.

Van Buren looked up: "We're doing O.K. If we don't hit any more snags—eight, ten hours." He gestured at Lucas. "Jean there says twelve, but I always give his predictions a twenty percent cut." He grinned. "You always look on the bright side, don't you Jean?"

The Frenchman looked up for a moment, the set of his drooping, lugubrious face showing only a brief reaction. He jerked his spectacles up his nose and turned back to his task. Beside him, Neumann was bending an aluminium bar into shape with a composite space tool called a plench. A combination of pliers and wrench.

At the entrance to the workshop module, Hayward paused for a moment. Inside, Patterson and Townsend were testing the lashed-together alloy frame for stiffness. Hunched over the bench, there was a superficial resemblance between the two men. Both were above average in size and of a similar hair colour. There was also a common expression. Both had a firm, almost cruel, set to their features. They worked in silence and communicated in short effective gestures.

The Australian also communicated a sense of recklessness and his hand movements often anticipated those of the slower Englishman as he concentrated on the task of pop-riveting an alloy corner plate to a frame. Hayward realised that he understood Townsend least of all, partly because of his Northern English origin and partly because of his naturally taciturn manner. Often, in argument, he would relapse into the accent of the Tyneside as a kind of non-verbal joke.

The conspiracy theory again flickered into his consciousness as he watched the two at work. He moved closer and steadied the frame as Townsend fired the pneumatic rivet gun. The sound cracked and echoed unpleasantly in the confined space of the workshop can.

"Van Buren gives the operation eight to ten hours," Hayward said.

"If we're not away by then, I'll want to know the reason why," Townsend replied.

"What's the hurry?" Patterson drawled. "Mr. Nobel hasn't anything for us this trip!"

As the three men worked on, Hayward heard another voice. He turned. Lyall's face had appeared at the airlock:

"If you can spare a minute, Commander, I'd like to do your blood samples."

It was not a request.

Hayward followed Lyall down to the stores module.

"What're you going to tell me?" Hayward asked.

Phillip Lyall looked back at him thoughtfully. The compact, youthful features were showing anxiety and strain:

"I'm not quite ready yet."

"Have you got something?" Hayward asked shortly.

"More than something!"

"Then who? How many are there?"

Lyall shook his head: "You can rule that out completely. There's no conspiracy. There's just one man."

"Just tell me who it is," Hayward said quietly.

"I want to have just one more talk with him—if I can set it up, just to be sure. If I tell you now and I'm wrong it could be the last straw in the whole bloody shambles. A wrong accusation at this stage and God knows what would happen, except that we certainly wouldn't be able to shut the thing down in time."

"O.K. What about the others?"

There was a moment's pause and then Lyall nodded, unzipped a pocket and brought out a notepad. He press-studded it to his wristband:

"I've made quite a few notes. I know these men, we trained together. It's just a question of elimination. . . ."

Suddenly Hayward became aware of the shadow of a figure in the access tunnel below him. He whirled to see Freeman.

How long had he been there?

"What is it?" Hayward snapped.

"Clear Lake is starting transmission, Commander. Mr. Caldor's on the shuttle com set."

Hayward turned back to Lyall, but the doctor merely nodded, smiling slightly:

"I'll be in the medical unit."

He moved up the access tunnel.

CHAPTER FIFTEEN

Hayward gave Caldor a tersely condensed report on the shut-down operation, emphasising the likelihood that it would be achieved in time.

"Fine, but what have you done to prevent any further sabotage?" Caldor demanded sharply.

"The work load itself is probably enough," Hayward replied. "They're all completely dependent on each other for actual manual help now. I don't think the man can do anything serious by himself. He wouldn't have the time."

"What about more than one? A group? We're still not sure about that, are we?"

"I don't want to discuss the reasons now, but it's very probably just one man."

"How do you know?"

"I don't for certain, but I'm assuming it for the moment."

"Is Lyall helping?"

Hayward briefly described his talk with Lyall and its implications.

"Which brings me to Mel Freeman," Caldor said. "It's the only lead we've got and it may not amount to anything. . . ."

"Go on." Hayward tensed, reflecting on his own personal dislike of the man. Caldor was still talking and he forced his attention back.

". . . and so we ran checks with Denver police. They've recently hooked a fairly big-time blackmailing group. They ran a whole network apparently. Anyway they've got all their books in the round-up. Freeman was on the list. He's a homosexual and the syndicate threatened exposure just after Freeman was chosen for Spacelab. There's also some suggestion of narcotics, but we're checking on this."

"And that would have killed his chances?" Hayward said.

"Right. No way could he have got up. The selection board would have reasoned—wrongly in my view—that he would be considerably more likely to be subject to blackmail . . . depression and general instability, quite apart from the effect of any public exposure. The syndicate had photographs—an agent provocateur—you know the set-up. They settled for a small monthly payment. It was actually to a phoney insurance front company, to keep his bank manager happy.

"And another thing. He's made at least one attempt at suicide. Apparently under an assumed name at a hotel at Salt Lake City—barbiturates. They only got that through the blackmailer's records, which were pretty damned comprehensive.

"They even had a computer, for God's sake!"

"I can't act on that," Hayward said.

"I agree, but it just means he might go first under stress."

"He's the only guy I can spare right now," Hayward said. "The others are going very well and we'll probably come in on time. But they're all on the brink. I don't want to take any further action right now. The situation is too unstable."

"John," Caldor interrupted. "We've done checks on the details of how the space-suits were wrecked. The man who did it had really studied their design."

"To rip them open with a knife?"

"O.K. But on the others—the operation was more sophisticated. One of them was missing a two inch stainless steel junction pipe.

"Just two inches, something you could put in your pocket.

"But he must have known, nobody could replace it or make it. He's devious and clever, so take care."

"What about Mission Control?" Hayward queried. "Lucas is in constant touch over the circuitry, how the hell can we keep this quiet? There must be at least one hundred and fifty men on the operation back there. One of them's bound to leak it. You've got to be swarming with media."

"Don't worry about it," Caldor replied. "We've had White House approval to close the whole station off. Off duty men are confined, they're all hopping mad about it. Threatened a walk-out! But they won't. The Governor has put out the National Guard complete with Federal approval. Nobody gets in or out of the place."

"But one 'phone call. . . ."

"Total monitoring. Let me worry about that, John. You just get that thing turned off. One last thing. The European Committee's getting very agitated. I'll have to tell them that all's going as planned. The President as well, he's holding off a siege of journalists in the White House."

Hayward clicked the transceiver off and gazed at his own reflection in the metallised windshield. He decided that the broad brow, the strong thatch of greying hair and the deep-set, almost saturnine expression, belied the insecurities he felt. He fingered an incipient double chin.

Suddenly for the first time since he had been on board, he laughed out loud. Super-hero Hayward's main concern is about a double chin. The laughter evaporated in a sudden chilling doubt. Nobody had checked the shuttle control systems. Suppose the man had decided to prevent their return altogether. Some sort of crazy logic, burning boats. A suicide!

He paused, anxiously looking around at the banks of controls in the cockpit. He realised with a new surge of fear that beyond the near certainty that the killer meant to achieve the start-up of Dynostar at any cost, neither he nor Lyall, nor even Caldor, knew anything about any other motives the man might have.

Was he hoping to return to earth—the energy hero, the provider of endless cheap power? Or did he merely want to report a successful experiment and then die?

Pulse racing, Hayward unclipped the flight briefing and sat down at the check-out patch board. Sweat broke away from his face, hanging in scintillating clusters.

The board consisted of a shiny nine-inch square of plastic with a rectangular array of four hundred small holes regularly set out over the square. With a small prod terminal connected to a wire, he started down the list of checkpoints in the book. For each one, he inserted the prod into a hole and kept it there until a labelled green indicator light lit up on an array in front of him. He worked methodically for an hour. His hand often shook and he frequently missed a hole with the prod.

Eventually, with a deep sigh of relief, he pushed himself back in the straps and closed his eyes. He hadn't allowed any thought time to deal with the possibility that the shuttle had also been sabotaged, or what the reaction of the crew would have been had it happened.

He glanced at his wrist chronometer and realised, with a sudden prickling along the spine, that he had been in the shuttle for ninety minutes. Lyall! Perhaps he had got something more.

Perhaps he had already questioned Freeman!

Logically, it would be the least harmful to the shutdown operation if it was Freeman who was expendable. If it was one of the others, he would have no alternative but to let the man work. Each man was essential.

As he pulled himself through into the forward control beyond the glare of an inspection lamp, he was just able to confirm that the three men were still totally immersed in their task. The floating cables had been more neatly strapped together and a bank of indicator lights were glowing steadily on the lashed-up frame holding the printed circuitry.

He nodded to each one in turn, then pulled himself on down the central access tunnel in search of Lyall, looking briefly into each section of the ship as he went.

Townsend had finished the alloy framework in the workshop and was mounting three small electronic units already connected by cables. Patterson had gone.

In the medical unit, there was no sign of Lyall, but Freeman was staining blood smears on slides by immersing them in sealed plastic envelopes containing the stain. He looked in, nodded a greeting.

Hayward found himself out of his depth. His experience of homosexuals was almost non-existent. The screening processes which had consistently followed him throughout his career as an astronaut had eradicated all but the most covert of sexual deviations, so that in that respect at least, his life had been sheltered. But such is the power of suggestion that it now seemed obvious. He wondered why he had not recognised the signs before. Sparse silver-blond hair combed forward, a slightly puffy face with an indecisive expression, large heavy lidded eyes, quick deft hands.

He realised he was staring and spoke curtly: "Where's Lyall?"

"Hasn't been here for over an hour. I wondered myself."

He gestured at the slides hanging in their bags on clips: "I'm almost through with this batch."

Hayward turned and floated out of the unit, across the central access tunnel to the airlock of the stores module. He entered and peered around the circular arrays of cabinets and bags. At the far end, Russ Walters was struggling to unravel a coil of wire, the strands looping out uncontrollably in the weightless air. Hayward moved forward to hold the reel while Walters wound the wire loosely in coils around his wrist. He smiled: "Thanks—nearly got me a bird's nest there!"

"Seen Lyall?" Hayward asked.

Walters clipped the wire free: "Hasn't been here."

Hayward nodded and left. At the rear of the ship, he approached the crew's quarters, which were divided into two main compartments, each broken up into four separate cubicles shaped like the pieces of a cut cake. Each cubicle was entered by the narrow end. On one wall were regularly arranged rows of lockers and on another, a series of small cabinets containing personal effects.

A privacy curtain could be drawn over the entrance and a brown quilted sleeping bag, like a large papoose, was suspended from special hooks bolted to the wall. The bags were zipped up the front in a Y-shaped pattern around the neck to prevent the occupant from floating free while asleep, and to give a more psychologically secure sense of enclosure.

A huge circular bulkhead terminated the quarters and separated them from the most rearward section of the ship: the waste disposal and storage area. Access to this unmanned and refrigerated section was by a single central hatch.

Hayward rapidly searched each cubicle, finding nothing. He moved on to the shower area, or "personal hygiene module" in the jargon of its designer.

The shower consisted of a cylindrical tube of plastic stiffened by circular rings. In normal operation, the crew member would position himself under the tube and then pull it down around him, sealing the end of the tube to a circular fitting around his feet wedged into toe retainers.

He would then be effectively sealed into a flexible tube while he washed himself down with a hand shower unit. There were no towels, only a combined hot-hair drier and hand-held vacuum device to suck away the weightless water droplets which would have hung like glistening marbles in the air inside the plastic tube.

Washing is a difficult and expensive operation in space and a single shower normally occupies an hour-and-a-half and is taken approximately once a week. Since the emergency, no-one had used the cumbersome apparatus. Hayward remembered a brief flare of temper in the mess section when Neumann had accused Freeman of taking an extra shower.

There was no sign of Lyall.

He moved to the mess section and looked in. Patterson

was straddling a jockey seat at a table, eating with such total absorption that he failed to see Hayward. The Australian had long been the butt of the other crew members for his apparently insatiable appetite and had been in constant trouble with Lyall for breaking the strict rules of the dietary input-output charts which the doctor kept on each man.

No Lyall.

Hayward swung open the airlock door leading to the geophysical module or "gym". A man was strapped into the devasculariser suction apparatus; his back was towards Hayward.

"Lyall!" Hayward moved forward eagerly, but as the man turned, he saw that it was Jean Lucas, who reached out and switched off the whining pump motor. In the silence Hayward felt a completely unreasonable anger. He had finished his search.

"What the hell are you doing in here?"

The Frenchman's lugubrious hang-dog expression lengthened. He shrugged: "It is necessary—my head, it is bursting. I cannot think, so I put the blood into my feet."

Hayward's anger evaporated. Lucas was the most vital member of the crew, essential to the whole operation. Success depended on his special skills.

"I want Lyall. Has he been here?"

The sad brown eyes stared back. "No, he has not been here." Lucas fingered an earlobe. "Not since he took his last sample."

Hayward nodded and, as he turned to go, Lucas switched on the electric pump motor which started its whine and repetitive throbbing pulse.

In the forward control sector, Van Buren was strapped

in front of the read-out screen. He seemed to be dozing, the clipboard he had been holding was rotating slowly on a tethering line in front of him. There was no sign of Neumann.

Back in the central access tunnel, Hayward felt a sudden nauseating surge of giddiness, acid bile rising in his throat. He remembered the training instructions he had received after the doctors had told him he was suffering from Menière's syndrome. Gradually he reorientated the position of his head until the almost uncontrollable nausea diminished. He floated for several minutes until the anxiety which always followed an attack had diminished to a tolerable level. He refused to believe what he feared.

Doctor Lyall was not on board the Spacelab and there were no intact space-suits!

Then, in a flash of optimism, he realised that Lyall might have been following him and could easily have reached the shuttle while he had been in one of the modules.

As quickly as he could, he pulled himself along the hand holds in the central access tunnel through the forward control sector and into the shuttle airlock. As he reached the matt black circular hatch, his vision blurred and a second wave of nausea swept through him. He held on to the rim of the lock until the attack had weakened.

Then, as his vision cleared, he saw that the seal he had placed on the airlock was still intact. On his previous return from the shuttle, he had wound some green tape between a bolt on the lock door and a handle on the surround. He had scribbled his name across the tape to make sure that if anyone had entered the shuttle, the tape would tear. Someone could replace the tape, but not his signature.

He pushed himself back. His head thudding. The nausea

was recurring in regular waves, he swallowed desperately and forced himself to logical essentials—no man disappears from a space craft unless he gets out of it.

Lyall could not get out.

He must still be on board!

CHAPTER SIXTEEN

Van Buren tacked the clipboard into a magnetic bar, his voice flat: "It'll take longer."

"How much?" Hayward replied.

Van Buren nodded at the glowing read-out screen: a computer logic flow diagram was picked out in red and green lines.

"We're trying to rewrite the final sequence of sensor withdrawal programmes. They're having trouble at Mission Control."

"That's all we need!"

"It'll maybe take only thirty minutes, an hour perhaps."

Hayward examined Van Buren's lined, sallow features. Although his demeanour had improved since Hayward had taken over command, there was still a nagging doubt about his efficiency in Hayward's mind as he spoke.

"I can't find Lyall. He's disappeared."

He saw a sudden alarm in the other's eyes. He gave Van Buren a quick account of his search.

"What about the space-suit drying chamber?" Van Buren asked.

Hayward cursed inwardly as he realised his simple omission. Van Buren continued:

"Lyall was using it to talk to some of the guys. I went up there with him myself a couple of hours back. He was asking a lot of questions."

Hayward pulled himself through the access panel. Van Buren followed. The space-suits were floating in their retaining harness just as they had been. The chamber was otherwise empty.

The two men quickly repeated a general search of the ship with a growing fear. Behind them, previously confident expressions once again turned to anxiety, doubt and fear.

In the crew quarters, the two men quickly unzipped each sleeping bag in turn, until, with a sickening sense of realisation, they both saw that only two places remained unsearched: the lethally radio-active monitor can and the waste disposal area at the rear of the ship.

Hayward looked silently at the central hatch leading to the refrigerated waste section and remembered the bodies of Hart, Lasalle, Sigmund and Fischer beyond it. The hatch was closed and the dial temperature indicator registering minus twenty-five degrees centigrade. Hayward shivered involuntarily:

"We'll take the monitor can first," he said.

Again a flash of alarm crossed Van Buren's tense features.

At the entrance to the monitor can, Hayward looked up following the leash of cables along through the slightly open airlock hatch. On each side of the cables, the mass of wet tissues and clothes which had been put there by Patterson and Townsend had dried and hardened in the overheated atmosphere of the airlock tunnel. Van Buren looked over Hayward's shoulder. The two men exchanged a glance.

"Found him?"

They looked back down the narrow airlock tube and saw Patterson and, behind him, Townsend and Walters peering upwards. Even Patterson's face was strung into tight lines of anxiety.

Hayward and Van Buren backed down, feet first, into the tunnel.

"He's got to be somewhere aboard," Van Buren said quickly. "We haven't checked aft in the crew's quarters. He could be asleep or showering."

The lie had a mollifying effect on the others and they began to disperse, only Patterson remained for a moment. Then he spoke:

"Commander, what's really going on here?"

Hayward smiled: "I'll worry about that."

Patterson paused for a moment, then hunched his knees up to his chest, somersaulted and started to pull himself into the tunnel.

Hayward reached the waste compartment access hatch first. He spun the retaining clamps and swung the hatch to one side. An icy damp flood of air poured out of the pitch black interior, swirling around his head. He switched on the interior lights and pulled his way in through the aperture. Van Buren followed.

The compartment was in the shape of a drum, twenty-eight feet in diameter and nine deep. Around half the periphery were closely packed racks of trays, each partly full of sealed black plastic containers labelled with the names of individual crew members. They contained frozen urine and faeces for final analysis on return to earth. There were also rows of large trash disposal bags sealed off with Velcro tape containing used tissues and wrappings. Each was clipped into its position by press-stud restraining tabs, labelled and dated. The surfaces glittered with a light coating of frost rime.

Hayward scanned the racks then, steeling himself, turned to follow Van Buren's gaze.

Behind them, an alloy mesh frame was divided into small rectangular areas. Just visible in the dimness of the freezing mist were the lumpy outlines of three large, clear, plastic pags partly covered in frost. Each was bound to the alloy mesh by nylon straps.

Hayward moved closer until he could make out the faces of the three dead crew members inside the plastic. The corpses looked as if they were giant embryos still enclosed in the membranes of the womb. The faces were irregularly stained with the indigo patches of post-mortem lividity.

The fourth body, farthest from the two men, gleamed metallically in the mist. It was less securely tied and entirely covered in aluminium foil, a vain attempt by Dr. Lyall to contain Fischer's residual radio-activity.

Hayward's teeth began to chatter and he saw Van Buren's breath was labouring in the intense cold. He was exhaling long trailing clouds of vapour.

"That's it, let's get the hell out of here," Hayward gasped. The cold had started to bite and the deathly atmosphere was eroding his control.

In the freezing mist of their chromium and aluminium mausoleum, the pathetic faces of the dead in their plastic shrouds seemed to appeal mutely for help. He turned to leave and the loosely tied body of Fischer was disturbed by an eddy of air from the movement.

It moved away from the alloy mesh on it's retaining line. Hayward caught a brief glimpse of another crinkled plastic surface, then Fischer's body reached the limit of it's tethering cord and rebounded slowly back into its previous position.

Van Buren had already reached the exit. Hayward reached up and grabbed his ankle, pulling him back in again. The older man gave a gasp of fright. Hayward pointed and together, in slow motion, they moved over to Fischer's body. Van Buren tried to restrain Hayward as they approached.

Hayward pulled his arm free and pushed Fischer's body aside. In a corner of the alloy mesh was another large plastic bag tied to the bars of the mesh. Even in the dim light and through the freezing mist, they could see very clearly what it contained.

Phillip Lyall's long white face was fixed in an attitude of incredulous horror. The dulled eyes were staring open and his lips were jammed apart, the mouth full of white tissue.

CHAPTER SEVENTEEN

Hayward turned quickly to Van Buren, who had dragged himself awkwardly backwards towards the exit. His mouth was open, his head shaking from side to side:

"Get back in here," he snapped. "Help me get him out!"

Van Buren hesitated.

"Eddie! He could be alive still!"

As he spoke, his own voice seemed to come from a distance. Part of his mind had switched off as though protecting him against the implications of this fresh horror. He fought for release in action. Grabbing hold of Van Buren's ankle, he pulled him savagely back down towards Lyall's body.

"Eddie!"

Slowly, Van Buren seemed to force himself back into reality and, after a few moments, helped to untie the retaining straps and manœuvre the stiffly frozen body out through the entry port and into the crew quarters. His movements were automatic.

Hayward stabbed a finger at a control, turning up the cabin heating to maximum. Immediately a flood of warm air poured down from the overhead grille. Van Buren was floating in the centre of the room, waiting.

Then Hayward wedged the body down between a food dispenser table and the hull and started to tear away the plastic sheeting still stiffened by the cold. He exposed a pallid head, glistening with frost crystals.

"Quick!" He bent his ear down to the open mouth, then held a food tray in front of the nostrils. There was no misting of the polished surface. He ripped away the covering plastic and put his fingers on the frozen wrist, but his movements became less and less urgent, until finally, he stopped and turned to Van Buren, shaking his head:

"Nothing." He turned back to the body: "Have to find out how he died, before the others do."

"You're too late."

Hayward whirled as Patterson's flat tones echoed behind them.

Patterson and Townsend had both entered and were floating just beyond the opening of the central access tunnel.

Hayward shouted: "Get up to the Medical Unit. I need blankets and oxygen, fast!"

The ring of command in his voice quelled further reaction and the two men somersaulted and pulled themselves out through the tunnel.

Hayward continued to tear away the softening plastic. The frost crystals on the face were melting and looked like globules of sweat on the putty-white skin. The dead eyes had moistened and appeared to be full of tears. On one cheek there was the beginnings of purple staining.

His hands shaking, Hayward started to extract the bundle of tissues stuffed in the wide open mouth. It was still partly frozen and eventually came away as a single piece, it's inner surface stained dark red.

"Holy mother of God!" Hayward heard the sharp intake of breath beside him. Van Buren was holding on to the perforated floor mesh with one hand pointing a shaking finger at Lyall's face, he was gibbering, stumbling over the words of a latin prayer. He followed Van Buren's gaze.

The mouth had been propped open by a short gold propelling pencil. But the cavity was larger than it should be.

There was no tongue. It had been hacked off at the roots.

Van Buren suddenly retched and then vomited. Hayward turned away. Beside him was a pair of brown trousered legs, and another, and another.

He looked up.

Neumann, Lucas and Walters were all floating in a silent half-circle, their feet anchored into the floor mesh. They were staring fixedly at the body with its dreadful silent scream.

The atmosphere in the confined cabin took on the terrifying immobility of a nightmare where the participant is completely unable to move or get away. No one spoke.

Patterson pulled himself back into the compartment, elbowing his way between the men. He was dragging a small oxygen cylinder behind him, a flexible tube and bright yellow facemask trailing. Behind him, Townsend was unfolding an Alumesh thermal blanket.

Caught by the atmosphere, he stopped and looked down at Lyall's body. He showed no outward sign of reaction at the sight of the missing tongue.

A small globule of blood emerged from the dead mouth, broke loose, and floated towards the staring men. They shrank back to avoid it as if it were the germ of a terrible plague. It hit a bulkhead and broke into a shower of smaller droplets which rebounded back into the air of the cabin. One struck Neumann on the forehead and it appeared for a moment as if he had been shot.

Patterson put the oxygen cylinder aside.

Hayward had freed the body of its plastic shroud. Towards the left-hand side of the chest there was a ragged hole in the brown cotton T-shirt. The hole was uneven in shape and approximately five inches in diameter. It was heavily stained with blood which had emerged from a small circular puncture wound in the skin underneath.

Lucas drew his breath sharply: "Dieu!"

Patterson swore softly, then put a hand out and gingerly touched the blood-encrusted hole: "A bullet wound! Who in God's name's got a gun?"

The discovery of the wound and its implication removed the last vestiges of ordinary behaviour from the men. One by one they drew away from each other like animals withdrawing from a predator. Each one shifted position so that some part of the ship protected his body.

Hayward looked around the circle of faces. His mind still refusing to accept the situation.

"Freeman," he called. "Where the hell's Freeman?"

No one replied. Hayward suddenly saw the printed name on a locker in front of him. He jerked it open.

"This is his, isn't it?"

Townsend moved to restrain him: "That's personal!"

Ignoring the comment, Hayward reached inside. Some loose papers floated out and started to move upwards towards the air filter grilles. Inside, were four clear plastic compartments, like small domestic ovens. The lower two held clothing and spare foot covers, the upper pair, personal effects and more papers.

"You've no right!" Van Buren had moved alongside. Hayward swung round:

"If Lyall was shot, there was a gun."

He pulled the compartments open and more papers

floated into the air. Some of the others began to collect them, their training still subconsciously working to prevent blockage of the air filters.

Hayward suddenly noticed a diagram in among some papers folded into a small manual. It was a flow diagram of the Life Support System of the space-suits. One tube connector fitting was ringed in red ball-point ink. He glanced at Van Buren to make sure he had not seen, then folded the diagram and thrust it into his tunic. He turned to face the others.

Townsend's expression was feral, just under control.

"Where's Freeman?" Hayward grated.

Lucas was wedged into a corner of the cabin, his fists clenched and his hands crossed on his chest, like a life-size Netsuki:

"He went onto the devascular iser after me. He will still be there in the gym."

Without replying, Hayward somersaulted and dragged himself into the central access tunnel.

The airlock to the geophysical can was shut. He quickly spun the lock wheels and swung it open. Freeman was lying in a retaining harness, the lower half of his body encased in the negative pressure overgarment that drew blood away from the head. He looked back over his shoulder, raising his voice above the pulsing whine of the machine:

"Hi Commander."

Hayward immediately noticed a difference in his voice, a lack of precision with consonants as if he had been drinking. In spite of the devascular iser, his face was still flushed, his mood euphoric.

Hayward controlled his voice carefully: "Why aren't you with Lyall?"

133

Freeman shrugged and clicked off the pump motor: "I get migraines, can't see straight. This thing works for me." He stared directly back at Hayward: "We're not all men of iron, Commander."

For a moment, Hayward's anger flared and he started to reach forward for the other man's throat, then, getting himself back under control, he took the diagram of the Life Support System from his tunic and held it over Freeman's head so that he could not avoid seeing it.

"Recognise this?"

Freeman shook his head as if in a daze: "No, what is it? You tell me!"

"You know goddam well what it is!" Hayward faced Freeman. "I found it in your locker."

Sweat glistened on Freeman's face. The pointed ends of his silver-blond hair stuck to the forehead. He avoided Hayward's gaze.

"How did it get there?" Hayward said.

"I was, well, trying to work out a way of making the missing connection. I thought, maybe I could copy its shape." His voice was slurring.

Hayward gripped him by the front of his tunic. "What the hell are you on? What have you been taking? You're tripping!"

"No, I swear to God I'm not. . . ."

"Don't lie. I've seen enough to know. You're on drugs."

Freeman looked away without replying.

"Lyall is dead," Hayward said quietly. "He's been killed."

Freeman shook his head, his mouth flopped open.

"Do you understand what I'm saying?" Hayward continued. "Phil Lyall's been murdered." He paused. "And you killed him."

Freeman's gaze was fixed now, like a frightened rabbit hypnotised by a snake. "No! I was trying to work out the space-suit. I got the diagram. . . ." His voice was hoarse. "He can't be dead!"

"You're lying," Hayward said, "and as far as I'm concerned you've killed five men."

There was abject fear in Freeman's eyes as he struggled ineffectually to escape from the negative pressure garment which still enclosed the lower half of his body.

"What do you mean? I haven't killed anybody. Oh my God!" He was trembling. "I couldn't kill anyone."

"Right now," Hayward interrupted, "you don't know where the hell you are, or what you've done. But I tell you what's going to happen. You're going to stay right here. You're not leaving this module. If you try, I shall have you physically restrained. Got it?"

Freeman gave a frightened nod.

"I'll be back to ask you some questions, and by God, you'd better have the answers."

Hayward turned and launched himself back through the airlock and took the small roll of green tape and sealed the door in the same way as the airlock door of the shuttle.

As he swung his way back down the access tunnel, he heard a confused hubbub of voices echoing down through the airlock leading into the Medical Unit.

He entered. Lyall's body, now stripped to the waist like a grotesque doll, was being propped into position by Townsend and Walters in front of a small X-ray machine. In place of the large rectangular plateholder in normal use in hospitals on earth, there was a small scanning video-camera on a swivelling gymbal linked to a dry printing machine. The camera was swinging from side to side across the chest of the body and jerking down a little more after each traverse.

Patterson was waiting by the print-out machine. The others floated expectantly in various attitudes in the air of the cabin.

The camera finally reached the end of its scanning, whirred once loudly and returned to its starting position. Townsend switched off the X-ray tube behind the body, Patterson clicked a switch on the printer. There was a pause of several seconds, then a print began to curl out from a long narrow slit. Impatiently, Patterson tugged at it's edge. Finally, he tore it off. The others crowded round.

The print showed a positive X-ray of the dead man's chest. Slowly, one by one, the assembled men drew back. Patterson silently handed the print to Hayward:

"There's a bullet wound and no bloody bullet! See for yourself!"

"Well maybe it came out the back of him," Walters suggested.

"No," Townsend said. "There's no exit wound. I've looked."

"A bullet can sometimes bounce off a bone inside," Lucas intervened. "Perhaps it is somewhere else. Maybe in his stomach?"

Patterson was tugging the remains of the torn plastic sheeting back of the glistening white skin of the body. Hayward moved forward quickly to stop him and felt inside a breast pocket of the dead man's tunic. He had remembered the notepad containing the names of the crew that Lyall had shown him. It was a companion to the pencil which had been used to prop open the mouth.

It had gone. He became aware of the others staring at him suspiciously and drew back.

A few minutes later, Hayward waited, floating to one side of the open hatch to the waste refrigerator, avoiding the billowing mist of freezing air flowing out into the crew quarters. Walters and Patterson re-appeared at the opening, their breath puffing out in clouds.

Hayward assessed their condition.

Patterson was still moving confidently and Walters also seemed relatively unaffected as he fastened the circular door, shutting off the flood of icy air. There was no sense of threat in their movements, each seemed to be dealing with the macabre and claustrophobic situation on a level which did not apparently involve their feelings. Of all the crew, Hayward reflected, the two seemed to have the greatest reserve of control.

"What about Freeman?" Walters asked.

"I've confined him in the gym. The evidence is very strong."

"Mel Freeman! You really think he's been doing all this?" Walters said incredulously.

Hayward nodded. "I found something in his locker. I'll make a statement about it in forward control in thirty minutes. We'll assemble there at. . . ." He looked at his digital chronometer, "thirteen thirty-five, right? Now I have to talk to Caldor."

He pulled himself round and floated into the access tunnel.

CHAPTER EIGHTEEN

Caldor sat hunched in a chair in the glass walled Communications Room. Hayward had given a complete account of Lyall's death, Freeman's arrest and the state of the Dynostar crew. Although he had desperately tried to offer Hayward some crumb of comfort, he knew there was none.

For some minutes the weight of responsibility seemed impossible. Lyall's death was the final symbol of failure.

He visualised the delicately balanced cycle of atoms of the ozone layer flying apart. Flaring bands of deadly ultra violet radiation pouring through. Crowds screaming in the streets, running for cover; blind and burning. Outside his house a mob chanting for his blood. "Kill Caldor!" The chief scientist of the Council of Twelve intoning the accusations of suppressing information. He trembled involuntary, then felt a hand kneading one shoulder, and then the other. He turned. Sue Annenberg smiled at him:

"Relax, let go."

A defensive retort sprang to his lips, but there was something totally insistent in her voice and movements. He put his head forward and relaxed, feeling the tension in his muscles die away.

Five minutes later, in his office, he sent for Irene Andler. After she had settled into a chair, he sensed an over-riding need to drive the conversation as he spoke:

"It's two steps back, one forward. We've lost one of our

best men, the effect on the others in incalculable, but we do seem to have the killer."

There was a pause, she shook her head: "We can't be sure of that."

Caldor's tone hardened: "You consulted with your colleagues?"

She nodded. "We cannot agree."

"That doesn't surprise me. But you can't dismiss the evidence against Freeman? A known homosexual with a police history of drug taking. Lyall would have been the first to notice. The Denver police record showed he'd taken both acid and psilocybin, they're both hallucinators. What more do you want?"

He rose and began to pace.

"He goes on a trip, Lyall starts in on a psychiatric interview, Freeman sees the doctor as some sort of gargoyle or monster, and kills him. Hayward's found the missing space-suit diagram in his locker. It's enough for any jury."

"But," she said quietly, "we're not the jury, are we? And Commander Hayward may be prejudiced because of the history of homosexuality."

"So what! That doesn't dispose of the evidence."

She shook her head: "The pattern is not conclusive. There's nothing in Freeman's history to suggest a massive delusional state of the sort which would lead to a murder like that."

"But they were all subjected to intense psychological scrutiny. Surely a disturbance of that magnitude would have been picked up?"

Irene Andler leant back. "Why do you cut out a tongue? To stop a person talking. But if you cut the tongue out of a dead person, that is completely irrational because he cannot talk. It's not the pattern of a man like Freeman, even under drugs. Your other evidence, the diagram — even if Hayward did find it in Freeman's locker, there is nothing to suggest he used it to sabotage the space-suits. He might have been doing exactly the reverse as he maintains. He might have been trying to work out how to fix the suits."

Caldor looked around the office. Personal mementoes from the Dynostar crew were jumbled together on a shelf facing his desk.

"All right, who the hell is it, if it's not Freeman? They were all checked."

"They were not checked in the way that the men of Apollo and Skylab were. You know that. Even by the middle of the seventies in the first European Sortie can experiment, everyone agreed there wouldn't be time to put civilian astronauts through the same sort of grill that the military had to undergo."

She picked up a sheet of typescript.

"You yourself were one of the main defenders of this change. I quote you." She read from the typescript: ". . . It is far more important to get the right skills into space, than to produce stereotype astronauts. We no longer require men of extraordinary physical abilities now that the technology of the operation has become sufficiently reliable. . . ."

Caldor's face tautened. There was a long silence; when he spoke his words were measured and slow:

"Dr. Andler. We only have a few hours. What I need from you and your colleagues is constructive assistance. So just define accurately what sort of character you expect the murderer to have. Assuming that we're wrong about Freeman."

She got up, walked to the wall board and picked up a chalk. "I can give you the more likely characteristics of this type of psychosis."

Caldor nodded: "Go ahead. I guess we're looking for some past event, a cause?" His tone was slightly derisive. "His father used to beat him. His mother was a tramp."

She smiled: "No, that's strictly Hollywood psychiatry. There is no cause and effect. It doesn't happen like that with real cases. All we shall find, even if we are lucky, is that one of them has more of these characteristics than the others."

"Like what?"

"Like categories of behaviour which alone might be negligible but together would lead to a pattern. There's no cause, as you put it. One of those men, previously acceptably normal, has developed an acute psychosis. The man could now be in a totally abnormal state. He is completely out of touch with reality.

"It's most probably an acute schizophreniform psychosis. It could be a simple schizophrenia or a paranoid psychosis. . . ."

Caldor stopped her: "Jesus! I don't give a damn what you call it Dr. Andler, nor does Hayward. Just how do you recognise it?"

Irene Andler wrote on the board, ignoring his outburst: "The man has a severe thought disorder. But he can easily hide that. It's quite common. The way they think embarrasses them at first, so they often develop a front to hide it. A style of real wit—wisecracks. Although the humour may be completely inappropriate."

She paused. "They are often without the ordinary response to emotional situations; a flatness of response. They can have flights of ideas. They start on a concept, start to develop it, and then it trails off." She wrote on the board for a few moments. "They often have hallucinations—the most common are auditory."

"Noises?"

"No, more often voices instructing them or threatening. Sometimes they will have visions."

"For Christ's sake! No one can hide all that!"

"Mr. Caldor, each one of your crew members is completely brilliant at his own subject. They are all highly individualistic. Trained to be entirely logical and to solve difficult problems successfully. If the man is in the early stages of a psychosis, he won't have any personality deterioration. He will be thinking well, although his thoughts may have nothing whatever to do with what you and I regard as reality."

Caldor surveyed the board. She had itemised each characteristic in small, neat print.

"O.K. What do we do?"

"If I could talk to each of them over the radiophone, I might find something. Patterns of speech, an occasional neologism—a new word."

"No way." Caldor interrupted quickly. "They are all under the most extreme stress already. Each one is vital to the shut-down operation. Time is almost gone and if I take them away, even for a second, to talk to a complete stranger, that could easily be the last straw for any one of them, let alone the guy were looking for." He shook his head. "No, anything we do has got to happen right here."

As he spoke, she had completed the list of categories on the board. Caldor watched silently. He spoke softly:

"You know, that could apply to half the population, including me!"

She turned. "There is one crucial difference. The man

is absolutely in an unreal state. He's not mad in the theatrical sense, he doesn't gibber. He's cunning, brilliant, resourceful and is probably being advised by hallucinatory voices."

She looked at the list on the board: "The Dynostar machine could even be a religious symbol for him. He may see himself as a saviour of mankind. Perhaps he even fantasises a hero's return to earth. He may have got a messianic sense of purpose. Remember he is not a murderer in any normal sense. The people he has killed, including Lyall, simply interfered with the sense of mission. Therefore it was entirely reasonable to dispose of them and to hide his action at the same time. To stop Lyall talking. It made him feel less surrounded, less threatened."

Caldor stirred impatiently: "I'll buy that." He glanced down at his watch. "Right now I've got to fend off the world's media. They want a statement and I've got to write it. What do you need?"

"Eight people here in the centre, with the set-up to contact as many of the relatives as possible. Those who aren't living on the base. Then I need to interview all the families of the men here, at the base, with full authority from you."

Her expression hardened: "What we have to do is to make an objective study of each character, step by step, and then try to see the Spacelab through the psychotic's eyes." She paused. "Do I have your permission?"

Caldor nodded quickly and rose to his feet. "We are going to have to be a hundred percent sure about Freeman. Do you accept responsibility for taking him off the hook?"

"Not at all. I can only deal in probabilities. I'm never going to be categoric about this man or that one. I can only point the way to slight shades of behaviour."

143

Caldor had reached the door. He wheeled: "Jesus Christ!" He pointed to the board, his finger shaking. "All that crap about messianic schizophrenics. I have got to stop one man wrecking our planet in just a few hours and you talk about shades of behaviour!"

Her voice grew even softer, more modulated: "I'm merely trying to prevent you and, even more important, Commander Hayward, from taking a glib, facile way out of the situation."

Caldor glared at her speechless for a moment, then the door closed behind him.

CHAPTER NINETEEN

Hayward resealed the shuttle airlock behind him and pulled himself along through the docking collar into forward control.

The tension in the atmosphere was palpable. He was immediately aware of a circle of blank, hostile faces as he floated over to Lucas, who was studying a series of regularly flashing lights on the jury rig.

"Are the programmes complete?" Hayward asked.

Lucas shrugged: "Almost. We have to reinject a long sequence now, to disconnect the secondary field sensors. They are unstable at the present."

Hayward turned. The others had not moved from the positions they had taken as he entered. Van Buren was strapped into a man-manœuvring cradle, toying with the joystick control on one arm. He avoided Hayward's eye.

Patterson had both arms around a leash of taped cables like a boxer on the ropes. Townsend had his knees hunched up to his chest, his arms above his head, gripping a perforated floor mesh. Neumann stood, the reverse way up, his face gargoyle-like in the upside-down attitude.

Only Walters, braced against the rim of the shuttle docking collar, met his gaze with any sign of recognition. The others offered no response at all. Patterson broke the silence:

"We've had a talk, Commander."

Hayward waited.

"Those figures showing the higher field release from the Dynostar. Well, we don't buy them at all. Jean Lucas there, reckons at a first approximation they could be out by a factor of two.

"So, to cut it short," Patterson continued. "We don't accept the need for shut-down. We think it's safe. The one-second pulse isn't likely to do any damage. Which means we leave it and get off in the shuttle now."

"We can't make that decision ourselves," Hayward replied. "It's not up to us."

"Now it is," Patterson continued. One by one, some of the others nodded slowly in agreement. "There's no real certainty that all this jury rig will get the thing inched down safely. We've had to take God-almighty risks with some of the rewritten programmes. If there's any iterative error, the power assembly is likely to go up and that's it for all of us. So it's time to go."

"And there are five dead men in the freezer!" It was Townsend who spoke. He jabbed a finger at Hayward. The normally taciturn Englishman's face was pale with anger: "There's a killer aboard . . . a maniac. . . ."

"Drop it!" Hayward said. "Get a hold of yourself! Freeman is in the gym. I'm keeping him there until we've got shut-down and are ready to evacuate. As far as I'm concerned, he is the man responsible. . . ."

"Mel Freeman!" Townsend's voice was openly sneering. "Look, you may've got a scapegoat, but that's all you've got. Freeman hasn't guts enough to kill a fly!" There was a general murmur of assent.

"If any one of you have got doubts about Freeman," Hayward said, "go into the geophysical module and see for yourselves. He's under the influence of a hard drug. A hallucinogen—he's as high as a kite. And what you don't know is that he had a history of drug taking."

"Drugs!" It was Neumann who spoke. "Then how did he get through the system? How did he manage to get selected for this mission?"

"He used an assumed name which didn't show until they asked for a police record search back on earth. He's also a homosexual, and was being blackmailed."

There was a murmur at this and Hayward felt the mood changing. Nobody seemed ready to contradict him.

"But I cannot believe it," said Jean Lucas. "Why would he do these terrible things? For what reason?"

Hayward turned: "I'm not a psychiatrist, but he may have some crazy idea of stopping shut-down and getting back to earth a hero." He looked around. "Like you all did. Perhaps it meant more to him because of his background."

"Bullshit!" Townsend spat out.

Hayward wheeled round. "Fifty-six days in space, stress, weightlessness, sensory disorientation and then acid! That's enough to smash up anybody's stability!"

"You're not certain it's acid," Patterson said.

"No, I'm not," Hayward replied. "But I'm almost certain he was in some sort of hallucinatory state. I've seen it many times before—in one of my own sons as a matter of fact. The effect of acid is unpredictable. Some people think they can fly and jump out of windows. They see everything completely haywire."

"How come the doc didn't get on to it?" Walters queried. "They were working pretty damn close."

"Maybe he did," Hayward replied. "But there's something else you don't know yet. Before his death I had

147

asked Dr. Lyall to question each one of you from a medical-psychiatric angle."

Hayward expected a reaction and got it. There was an angry protest.

"You bastard!" exclaimed Townsend.

"It was necessary," Hayward replied. "I told him to find out as much as possible about each one of you. And in the last talk we had," he looked at each man in turn, assessing their expressions, "he told me that he had probably found the murderer."

In the silence that followed, Hayward continued:

"He refused to tell me who, until he'd had another talk with the man. Now that man knew that Lyall was onto him, so he killed him. And that man was Freeman."

"You'll have to prove that," Patterson protested.

"Look at yourselves," Hayward replied. "Just look around. You know each other, you work together, you trained together. Which one of you is crazy enough to kill and cut out somebody's tongue?

"Can you really believe that of yourselves?"

He waited. The men were grey-faced, strained beyond endurance; their nerves shot. They exchanged weary glances. The image of the doctor's mutilated body was burnt into the memory of each one. It was impossible for any one of them to accept that one of the others was a sadistic murderer. Gradually the mood of resentment began to recede. Hayward turned to Patterson, continuing to use the advantage of the moment:

"If you've still any doubts about the hazards of the Dynostar start-up, that's your privilege, that's a scientific decision and I respect that. You could even be right."

He looked slowly at each man in turn and spoke very deliberately: "But is any one of you prepared to maintain

148

your disbelief to the point of putting every living thing on earth in danger?"

He waited, each man remained absolutely still.

"Are you going to take that risk? To go back to a starved, decimated earth which you alone are responsible for? You know damn well you can't do that on the basis of one discussion.

"You're all dead beat. Can you honestly say that your own assessment is going to be as accurate as theirs? That a group of tired, frightened scientists, after fifty-six days in space, were able to challenge an extended study using thirty scientists and six weeks of computer time? That's not something I could do."

He waited.

Patterson looked at the others and raised his eyebrows in query. For several moments there was no reaction.

"Lucas, have you got real doubts? Can we get this thing shut off?" Hayward said.

Lucas paused: "If all goes to schedule, yes."

"All right," Hayward continued. "Then let's get back to it."

The lights in the cabin dimmed abruptly and then came back up to normal again.

"What the hell . . ." Van Buren began.

A red light was flashing on the indicator board. Lucas peered: "The gym, there's a direct short on an E.H.T. circuit there!"

Hayward started on his way towards the central access tunnel. Patterson and Townsend followed.

The seal Hayward had placed on the airlock was still intact. He ripped it off, spun the locking bolts, swung the door upwards and pulled himself in. Townsend and Patterson followed.

149

For a moment there was no sign of Freeman, then Townsend pointed silently towards the terrestrial telescope mounted at the far end of the module.

Surrounded by a flexible dust collar the eyepiece and camera end of the telescope protruded into the module through an array of instruments and controls. In front of it was a black plastic skeleton chair and, just visible above the back of the chair, the men could see the silver-blond hair of Freeman. Hayward started forward, Patterson followed.

Hayward reached the chair and was just about to touch Freeman's shoulder when Patterson yelled out: "Don't touch him!" He was pointing at a unit labelled: "E.H.T. Video-pack", a small square panel had been removed revealing two large copper flynut terminals. Two wires had been roughly attached to the terminals and led to the chair.

Townsend swung the chair around. Freeman's head lolled, his eyes wide open, teeth bared as if in some final jest. Around his head one wire had been bound around wet pieces of tissue, the second wire was gripped in his left hand, the fingers taped into a fist. To the three men, the effect had a horrific resemblance to an electric chair.

Townsend spun round to Hayward, his face drawn into furious hostility: "What in God's name did you say to him?"

Patterson had moved to the open panel and, with a single tug, pulled both wires off the terminals. Hayward put his hand over Freeman's chest and felt for a pulse. He spoke quickly:

"Patterson. The Medical Unit, there's a hand respirator there."

Patterson turned to go, Townsend pulled Freeman's head

backwards: "Mouth-to-mouth respiration! He only collected a few seconds ago. Go on!"

Hayward's whole being revolted at the idea of putting his lips down onto Freeman's. He hesitated. Townsend spoke angrily:

"For God's sake!" He pulled Freeman's lips forward, away from the face and put his own mouth down to them, making a seal. Then removed his lips, took a deep breath and exhaled into the stricken Freeman, whose chest swelled as he exhaled. He went on repeating the movement until he had established a rhythm. After about a minute, he paused and looked up, Hayward was still feeling for a wrist pulse. "Anything?"

Hayward shook his head and Townsend resumed the rhythmic inflation of Freeman's lungs.

He continued for another minute until Patterson returned carrying a small rubber bellows, like a concertina, fitted with a hand strap at one end and a flexible mouthpiece at the other. Townsend took it, fitted the mouthpiece into Freeman's lips, held the lips around the mouthpiece with one hand to make a seal and started to move the bellows up and down with the other. He worked in silence, the valve of the bellows respirator giving a regular hiss and a click on each cycle.

After more than five minutes, Hayward let go of Freeman's wrist: "There's nothing at all. He's gone."

Patterson glanced up at the opened panel and shrugged: "He must have had two and a half K.V. Twenty amps minimum."

Townsend was glaring fixedly at Hayward: "You bastard! You're responsible for that." He lunged forward, his face contorted. Patterson launched himself off a bulkhead and cannoned into Townsend in mid flight. Both men struck the black chair together, dislodging Freeman's body, which tore away from its Velcro retaining straps and floated upwards, trailing the two wires behind it. Patterson grabbed both of Townsend's arms, restraining him:

"Bob. Cool it! He wouldn't have done that unless he was guilty."

Townsend hacked away against the hull, his fury slowly subsiding. Finally, he wiped his mouth with the back of his hand:

"What the hell are you talking about. He was a sensitive bastard. If anyone made that sort of accusation, it would just crack him up completely." He wheeled on Hayward. "When we get back you're going on record as hounding him to death!"

Hayward turned to Townsend: "You've work to do, get back to it." He beckoned to Patterson and reached up and pulled the body down towards the mesh floor, Patterson assisted him.

A few minutes later, as the two men manœuvred the corpse back aft along the central access tunnel, Hayward tried to assess the effect of Freeman's death on the crew. Perhaps it might lessen the tension since they would probably get some relief from the mind's eye picture of a demented man locked away in one section of the ship. He had to tell Caldor.

CHAPTER TWENTY

The press conference had proved to be an ordeal, but Caldor had given the performance of his life. Sue Annenberg had been beside him throughout, ready with appropriate data. For the first time, he had felt the warmth of her support.

Mustering all the instinct and training of a man who had spent years of his life facing the savage skills of the Washington press corps, he had realised before entering the tightly packed hubbub of the seminar room where the conference had been called, that none of the journalists would settle for a "no details", or "no comment" approach.

They had needed a water-tight story without mention of the deaths of Sicura, Fischer and Lyall and without reference to a man whose mind was disturbed.

He had given a concise and dramatic account of the operation being mounted to shut down the runaway fusion device, and described the state of the monitor can after the vacuum accident with its deadly plutonium content. Then, with the aid of a hastily prepared line diagram, he gave a carefully fabricated account of how unsafe it was for the crew to go out into space and how, therefore, they had had to build an entirely new control system out of spare electronic apparatus.

He had based his approach on an incident in the early history of manned space flight when a returning moon-flight, Apollo 13, had almost ended in disaster. During the whole press coverage, the world's attention had been focussed on the technical details of how the crew had managed to alter the mechanics of the ship and return to earth safely. There had been almost no attention given to the psychological state of the three-man crew.

Similarly, he had gradually shifted the attention of the journalists until they were firing question after question at him about the rewriting of the computer programmes and whether the life support systems of the Spacelab were functioning normally. Only one female journalist had ventured to question the crew's attitudes and stability and Caldor had immediately used her as a butt for a joke about women worrying more about the mess in the galley than about the status of the Dynostar device.

She had not spoken again.

An awkward moment had come when a veteran television journalist from N.B.C. had asked why the live television coverage from Spacelab had been stopped. He had made strong innuendoes about something which had happened to a crew member which was being kept secret.

Caldor had lied again, knowing that he would have to account for the denial at a later date. He gave as a reason that power supplies on board Dynostar were running low and that all power had to be conserved as far as possible.

It was his most anxious moment, but it passed.

As the room had gradually emptied and technicians had begun to dismantle the battery of television and newsreel cameras, he had sensed a new attitude among the journalists. Over the weeks prior to the conference, when speculation about the safety of Dynostar had been at its height, he had been subjected to the public need for a media scapegoat. But now the view seemed to be that he was coping successfully with a highly balanced operation which had put the lives of the Spacelab crew in jeopardy.

Irene Andler sat in Caldor's office waiting for his return from the Communications Room. She was examining seven blank sheets of paper held in magnetic clips on a steel wallbar. Each paper was labelled with a different name: Lucas, Neumann, Walters, Townsend, Patterson, Van Buren, Freeman, Hayward. Taped to the wall above each paper was the appropriate photograph. On a separate sheet of paper alongside, were the names: Fischer, Lyall, Sicura, Hart, Lasalle, Sigmund, each had a line struck through.

With a growing sense of frustration, she recalled the events of the previous four hours and realised that the pressure of time had entirely prevented her from conducting even the basis of a standard Maudsley interview.

The interview had been devised in the early fifties in a London Hospital of that name and was a highly structured and standardised method of establishing background data on a patient. It was designed to probe into every aspect of a patient's background. Family history, school activities, job achievements, reactions to stress were all included in an attempt to create the flesh and bones of a person's most likely behaviour pattern. The interview took a minimum of six hours and could stretch on into many daily sessions of several hours each.

She had had no such time available.

Irene Andler had first visited Camille Patterson and then moved on to Nicole Lucas who had Gerda Neumann, the mother of Theo Neumann, staying with her for the duration of the Spacelab Dynostar flight.

Finally, she had been unable to contact Joan Townsend, who had gone into the nearby town.

She stared at the blank sheets of paper. First had been Camille Patterson, the exotic name belying the tall, tousle-headed and large-boned woman. In New South Wales she had been known as an outstanding Pentathlon athlete. To the other wives, Andler had discovered, she was something of a joke, with chaotically untidy household and early morning jogs around the lakeshore in a bulky, shapeless track-suit.

Despite her complete lack of the more studied chic she had discovered in Sarah Van Buren and Eunice Walters, she had found that the other wives were fond of her in a slightly maternal fashion. She offered no real threat to their husbands or social affairs.

Her cooking always ended in disaster and it was a standing joke that when her turn came to entertain the other families, an ambulance, complete with stomach pumps, was standing by, hidden in a nearby wood.

Her closest companion was Joan Townsend and the two spent much of their time together. The friendship had originated during Patterson's secondment to the Culham Fusion Research Centre in England, where Bob Townsend had been working on the later stages of the Torsatron machine, a precursor of the much larger and more complex Dynostar.

Camille had proved to be completely open as a personality and had launched into a hard but enthusiastic description of her husband. Her two children had been present throughout the interview and it had been obvious from their easy affectionate bluntness towards their mother that theirs was a close relationship.

Will Patterson was revealed by his wife as an obviously

brilliant nuclear engineer who had been responsible for much of the design of the intricately interwoven magnetic coil assemblies of the Dynostar.

Devoted to the outdoor life, he was a man who hunted duck regularly during the season in the hundreds of small lakes surrounding Minneapolis. But he was also given to occasional bouts of hard rye drinking, sometimes ending in brawls in local bars. Irene Andler had caught just a hint of fear at the back of Camille's grey eyes when she had described one particular episode.

In complete contrast to the Patterson household with it's clutter of toys and general friendly untidiness, the Lucas household had been more like a monastic cell.

There were no carpets, but bare swept floor boards, not over-varnished as in the case of the Van Buren, house, but cleaned and bleached. There was a minimum of furniture and one central marbled-topped table with square brass legs. On one wall was a large black and white abstract painting.

On a low sideboard stood a sparse series of small figurative sculptures in white stone, and on another wall a large square of dyed Fijian bark-cloth was pinned onto a pine frame. The general effect was austere and intellectual, a scene to fit a Bach violin sonata. There were no concessions to the more congested American décor.

Gerda Neumann, Theo Neumann's mother, had been a total surprise. Before meeting her, Irene Andler had visualised a cliché German frau, but instead Gerda was a tall, elegant white haired woman in her early sixties. Her face was fine-boned, delicately formed and still beautiful. Amused patrician eyes caught Irene Andler completely off guard. She reminded her of the wives she had so often met at academic gatherings in Vienna during her post-graduate studies.

She had an easy unshakable confidence and had deflected Irene's attempts to probe her son's background with a charming ease.

It was as if she knew all the conversational gambits and almost before Irene had finished the enquiry, she had responded by asking after the health of the other crew members. She had given no credence whatever to Caldor's original description of the conditions aboard Spacelab.

Irene Andler had finally discovered that the older woman was delicately and persistently drawing more information from her than she herself had obtained.

Nicole Lucas was a classical Lycée-Sorbonne product. She had a short, dumpy figure, close cropped black hair and large dark eyes. She wore no make-up and was dressed in a black polo-necked sweater and white cotton slacks.

Her conversation had been abstract and even her description of her husband's family and background had been given with a quick, bird-like intelligence, but without any obvious evidence of feeling. Even when Irene had probed into the possibilities of any prior history of breakdown or abnormal reactions to stress, there had only been a "how could you suggest such a thing", but said with a careful, measured control.

Throughout the interview her eyes had been watchful, and Irene felt intuitively that the calm attentive interest failed entirely to fit with the quick intelligent quest of the eyes. Although there was obviously deep concern for her husband's safety, she had passionately argued the anti-environmentalist case, "Who were these people to ruin the years of work which her husband and the others had put into the project?" Her arguments, obviously reflecting those of her husband, showed biassed and subjective opposition to the environmentalist arguments that Irene Andler had offered.

Gerda Neumann had looked on, interjecting an occasional amused comment.

Irene Andler drew a small asterisk on the paper bearing Lucas' name.

Caldor began talking immediately he had closed the door: "Freeman's dead, he electrocuted himself in a sealed part of the ship. Hayward considers this proof positive of the man's guilt and the other crew members apparently accept this."

Caldor glanced down at one of two watches strapped to his wrist: "We're only four hours from shut-down, so it's all set now." He yawned suddenly and slumped into the chair behind the desk. "There's little point in your continuing the investigation. Incidentally, thanks for your help." He leant forward and put his head down on his hands.

"You've made up your mind?" queried Irene Andler.

He looked up surprised and nodded. "After separation they'll de-orbit and land at Marshall base. Then the law can take over. The F.B.I. have been told and I've no doubt they'll be waiting."

"So you've no doubts about Freeman?" she persisted.

"No reason," he paused. "I'll be in the Communications Room till shut-down and separation. There could still be technical problems. I think we have the human one licked."

Her face showed no reaction as he turned and went out.

*　　*　　*

159

In the main Communication Room seven men were seated in front of the complex array of controls. Four adjacent television screens showed details of the Spacelab Houston computer interchanges. Every few seconds a screen would clear, only to be replaced by a three-colour display and numbers, and the cryptic words that machines use for conversation.

Caldor sat back, his legs hunched up, watching the cascade of figures. It was clear that the operation was progressing well.

Each programme in the automatically controlled computers in the monitor can of the Spacelab was successfully being rewritten and injected back by the jury rig in the control sector. The control of the runaway Dynostar was slowly but steadily coming back under the command of the crew.

On the voice communicator he listened to the verbal exchanges between the Mission Control engineers on the one side, and Lucas, Neumann and Van Buren on the other. Caldor smiled to himself as he listened to Hayward's voice as it over-rode the others. It still sounded confident, even allowing for the distortions of transmission across space. His choice had been correct.

Whatever the repercussions which were to follow, Caldor reflected, and he knew he personally would have to fight the battle of his life, there was little doubt that Hayward would return to earth as a public hero.

He mentally re-examined the early days of the Dynostar enquiry. The leader of the Council of Twelve had, so far, only privately accused him of suppressing information. There was no doubt in his mind that when the Council decided the moment was most opportune politically, they would make the accusation publicly.

He tried to assess the situation objectively. The worst he could think of his own actions was that he had allowed a misrepresentation by omission rather than commission.

The figures on the effect of the Dynostar magnetic field on the ozone layer had always lain open to more than one interpretation.

It was the rule of physics: thesis, antithesis and experiment. No one man could dogmatically assert that his view was the only one, that he alone was right. He concluded that his own actions had been honourable and that a successful defence was not only possible but right.

He was the last in the room to notice the fading of the picture on the read-out screens from Spacelab. Then the voices of Hayward and Van Buren also dwindled to silence.

The men seated at the panels leant forward anxiously, scanning the complex arrays of meters and panel indicators.

Caldor jerked upright in the chair: "What the hell's happened?"

A technician spoke without turning: "Power failure."

"Here or there?" Caldor queried.

"On board," the technician replied. "It's big, there's no signal gain at all."

Every part of Caldor's mind rebelled as his mood of confidence exploded and swept away. He turned and swung into the glass cubicle. Quickly unlocking the controls, he activated the tear-off scrambler system and pressed the call button to the space shuttle. Time and time again, he pressed it, but there was no reply. He pressed the talkback control to speak to the men in the Communications Room outside the glass:

"Anything?"

"No, nothing!" came the reply.

Caldor pressed the call button again. There was no answer. Why couldn't they reply? Was there anyone there to answer?

CHAPTER TWENTY-ONE

The Spacelab was beginning to die around its crew. An array of television monitors flashed briefly through red to green and then snapped off, dwindling to a small bright spicule of light and then to darkness.

Bank after bank of indicator lights flicked off. The alarm bell gave one short burst of angry clamour, then stopped. The background noise of whirring servo-motors lurched downwards in pitch and the soft hiss of the air conditioners faded to silence.

The fluorescent tube lights dimmed once and then blacked out, leaving only dim swirling patterns of light in the tubes. Finally, they too extinguished.

The vast and once elegantly integrated bulk of Spacelab was silent and in the total darkness except for a slowly wheeling shaft of blue sunlight streaming in through the heavily tinted glass of a porthole.

Van Buren moved quickly over to a switch panel and pulled a switch up and down repeatedly. There was no response.

"Emergency circuit's out. That's main batteries. Get the torches!"

Lucas had already opened a small perforated panel and was unplugging four self-charging torches. He lit one, the yellow beam reflecting faces glistening with sweat, like primitive cavemen in the firelight.

Neumann was moving from console to console quickly trying different combinations of switches:

"There is no current on the main distributor line, all four voltage regulators are out."

"That confirms main batteries," Lucas said, swinging quickly over to another panel. "Twenty-eight V.D.C. is now zero, yes, it is."

The main energy store of Spacelab Dynostar was contained in two rectangular arrays of forty-eight silver oxide zinc batteries stowed in alloy frames behind a curved panel in the crew quarters.

Lucas was the first to reach the panel, followed by Neumann and Walters. The others followed. Lucas undid the eight Dzus fasteners and floated the panel away in the harsh shadowed light of the torches. He reached inside the darkness of the space behind the panel and undid three over-centre clips and pulled at the first array of batteries which swung out of the panel on a pivotted frame.

"Somebody get back to control and confirm the main isolators are out," Van Buren said. "We could have a bad voltage surge."

As he spoke, the distant tinny sound of the space-shuttle call-signal buzzer echoed eerily on its ship repeater down the darkened central access tunnel. With relief, Hayward realised that at least part of the shuttle was still operational.

Townsend had already started back up the access tunnel, but Hayward was uncertain whether his exit was solely in response to Van Buren's command. The call-signal buzzer continued insistently, but Hayward ignored it, reasoning that Caldor would continue to keep the line open until he got a response. He decided to wait until there was more to report.

Lucas had clipped his torch to a Velcro fastening on his chest and was carefully examining the six by eight array of matt silver cells, each interconnected by heavy red and blue insulated cables. He attached a small test meter to the main output lines, the needle remained on the zero mark.

"More light, give me more light," Lucas said.

Walters and Neumann floated forward and pointed their torches over Lucas' shoulders into the cavity of the battery compartment. Lucas swung the first array of cells back into position, pulled out the second and repeated his examination with the test meter. Again there was no movement of the needle.

Van Buren pushed himself up alongside Lucas: "The main output lines."

He thrust his arm into the cavity and then suddenly shot backwards with a cry of pain. There were ugly brown scorch marks across the pads of two fingers and a thumb.

Lucas quickly shone the torch and swore softly. The others crowded around the Frenchman.

In the beam of the torch, connected between the heavy aluminium bars of the two battery output lines was a roughly coiled wire, looking like a heavy gleaming spring. It was about two feet in length and three inches in diameter. It had obviously been first wound round a cylindrical former, which had been removed and the two ends connected across the main battery output terminals forming a short circuit.

Van Buren gripped his seared fingers: "Don't touch it, it's still damn near red hot!"

"Resistance wire," Lucas breathed. "That is clever! The silver oxide cells, they would discharge their energy as heat through the coil."

"Is that right?" said Walters. "We would have seen a dip in the forward voltage indicators long before failure. The voltage regulator alarm would have gone off."

"Not so," Lucas replied. "The silver oxide cell does not gradually lose voltage, it continues at a fixed potential, then falls to zero in seconds."

Walters reflected for a moment, then slowly nodded his head in agreement.

The sense of fear in the crowded compartment was overwhelming.

There are two main psychological props that astronauts need. First, the already withdrawn ability to get outside the ship in space-suits, and second, to feel that there are reserves of power available for emergencies. Both are to some extent irrational since it is not possible either to return to earth in a space-suit, nor, in some magical way, can energy for all eventualities be drawn from the batteries.

In the harsh unhealthy light of the torches, each man stared at his fellow, unblinking.

Each man seeing his own death. One man wanting it.

"Maybe Freeman did it before he chopped himself," Townsend said.

In the silence that followed the noise of the repeating call-signal buzzer echoed more and more insistently down the central tunnel.

"Not possible," Lucas replied. "This bank had a four hundred amp-hour capacity, the discharge through such a resistance would only take perhaps four minutes."

"And Freeman has been dead for nearly an hour," Neumann said.

"Minimum," Hayward said grimly. "And the seal on the airlock was still there."

The full horror of the implication settled on their shoulders, like the hand of death itself.

Hayward gripped hold of a bulkhead, looking from face to face, Lucas, Neumann, Walters, Patterson, Van Buren and Townsend. Which one was it?

He had been wrong about Freeman.

Townsend's furious accusations repeated in his head: "You've hounded an innocent man to death!" He felt the surging vertigo. Fighting it down, he spoke to Lucas:

"What other power reserves do we have?"

The repeating call-signal in the shuttle seemed louder.

Lucas shook his head slowly: "You had better answer Caldor, it is our only link now."

As Hayward pulled himself along the handholds in the darkened central access tunnel, he was unable to marshall his thoughts into any reasonable order.

It was not until he reached the fully lit sanity of the space shuttle interior that he was able to start reasoning out the possibilities. Automatically, he tore off the last patch code sequence, punched it into the scrambler until orange digital tubes flicked into agreement. He pressed the speech switch:

"Hayward. Spacelab Dynostar. Do you copy?"

There was a short pause. Caldor's voice was urgent:

"John what the hell's happened? We read a major power failure here."

Hayward gave a concise account of the main battery failure and the discovery of the resistance wire and their realisation that Freeman could not have been responsible.

"Then who?" Even across the distortion of space, the shock in Caldor's voice was obvious.

"I've no idea," Hayward replied wearily.

"How far were you from shut-down?" Caldor asked.

"Around two hours," Hayward replied. "Plus or minus eight, ten minutes."

"Can you recharge the batteries?"

"Lucas says no, but they're talking it through."

"Right, I'll get Mission Control on to it right away. We'll have to get back to you through this line if your communicators are out. Take care John."

Hayward switched off without replying and pulled himself downwards and forwards towards the docking collar.

CHAPTER TWENTY-TWO

In forward control, Lucas had fixed the four torches into wall clips. In the yellowish light their faces were shining in the ghastly ochre hue of the beams. Hayward launched himself towards a corner of the perforated floor mesh and locked his heelpads firmly into its pattern. No one turned as he entered. No one attempted to include him in the discussion. Lucas was speaking:

". . . and so if we've got no stored wattage, we could reconnect the ventral solar panels directly into the power buses in forward control. There are snags, but it's possible.

"No good," said Walters. "The programming units we've rigged must have a voltage stability of less than ten millivolts."

"So why can't we get that?" Neumann demanded impatiently.

"Because we could not guarantee the attitude of the panels to the sun exactly enough. The angle of incident flux is going to vary too much."

"We can orient the ship using the vector jets," Patterson offered.

"The vector jets are oriented on electro-mechanical servo-gymbals," Van Buren interjected. "There is plenty of stored nitrogen in the Dewars to make them work, but no power to change their direction. We'll spin like a top."

"We could maybe repair the M.H.D. generator in the monitor can," Walters said.

"No one's going to last in there more than a minute, even if it was working," Hayward intervened. "There's enough hard gamma to halve your white blood count in twenty seconds. That's not including any plutonium dust. It's sealed off at the moment, and it's going to stay that way.

"Matter of fact, we'd better have a Geiger probe up there in the tunnel, then we'll know if it leaks out." He turned to Walters: "Will you see to that?"

He spoke to Lucas: "The power failure must have pulled the plug on the computers up there."

Lucas' face looked more pained than ever. "Commander, the computers in the monitor can were driven off the main battery store."

"Good, so they're kaput?" Hayward replied.

"In the event of failure, they were automatically programmed to switch to a local power supply up there in the can. There is a small array of silver zinc oxide batteries—of six hundred amp-hour capacity. More than enough to run the start-up procedure twice over!"

"What about the power can under Dynostar?" Hayward persisted.

"We can't get out to it," Townsend said. "Forget it, Commander, the Dynostar is going to start up and there's not a thing in hell we can do about it!"

"Are you certain the batteries are finished?" Hayward asked.

"The plates and core electrodes will have been distorted beyond repair by such a massive discharge. They are so much junk effectively." Lucas swung round and turned his back on Hayward.

"Commander," Patterson said, "we're on a dead ship. We've lost the absorption pumps, all refrigerated parts of the ship will be warming up. Deodorisers, heaters, coolers, water iodine injection pumps, air fans, the whole bloody issue. It's all ballsed up. We've had it!"

"There are just two possibilities," Lucas said. "First, we could manœuvre Spacelab, using the shuttle thrusters. It has fourteen vernier jets and we could. . . ."

"Forget it!" Townsend interrupted. "If we do that it'll break the docking collar. There's too much inertia by a factor of ten."

"And then," Lucas continued imperturbably, "there are the shuttle batteries."

"If we use those, how do we get down again?" Neumann demanded.

"There is some risk," Lucas continued calmly, "but if we start the back-up turbo-generator in the shuttle, we should keep pace with the power drain here. I cannot be sure, but I think so."

"You . . . think!" Townsend exploded. "To get shutdown—you'd lose the only chance we've got of getting back alive! Who the bloody hell are you?" He shot forward to grab the Frenchman. Hayward quickly moved between them. He braced himself against a bulkhead, wrenched Townsend's hand away from the Frenchman, and swung him around, the effort sending their bodies spiralling round each other like dancers. The others pulled back in dismay.

Townsend's saturnine face was working with fury: "You bloody murderer. You'll kill us all, like Freeman!"

Hayward floated, poised, with one hand still gripping the bulkhead. Then slowly and deliberately he braced both feet and swung his other hand back and then forward, hitting Townsend a tremendous blow on the side of the head. Immediately he let the force in his arm expend itself by following through like a golfer making a swing.

Townsend's head snapped back and his weightless body somersaulted backwards, cannoning into the wall of the ship and rebounding in a confusion of flailing arms and legs into the other crew members. Collecting himself, Townsend launched himself off the wall with his feet, swinging his fist at Hayward, his teeth bared.

The blow failed to connect as Hayward pulled himself easily to one side, and once again Townsend cartwheeled out of control, smashing into the opposite side of the ship. The others had collected themselves and had formed into a group almost surrounding Hayward. They began to close in towards him.

"Get back!" Hayward shouted. "Cool it, all of you!"

The men paused in their advance. For several moments each one remaining absolutely still in the dim light. Townsend was holding his head in both hands, knees up to his chest, rotating slowly. Hayward moved across to him and pulled his hands away to examine his head. There was only slight bleeding. He turned to face the others.

The mood broken, the men began slowly to move back into their previous positions. Townsend watched Hayward warily, anger still smouldering in his deep-set eyes.

"We'll have to use the shuttle batteries. There's no other choice," Hayward said.

"There is," said Patterson turning. "We just get into the shuttle, de-orbit and get away. They can get another crew up—we've bloody had it—all of us!"

Hayward looked around the faces, his mind still rebelling against the certain knowledge that one of them was a murderous psychotic. He grabbed a bulkhead and wheeled: "You don't give a goddam what happens do you? The next crew'll just pick up the pieces, the ozone will be gone, there'll be a gaping hole in the atmosphere and half the earth'll be dying!"

He stopped. Dully he realised that their years of research on the Dynostar project had given them an intractable bias. They all still totally believed in its success, and one of them was prepared to do anything to get it to work.

"One thing you'd better keep in mind," Hayward continued. "How you propose de-orbiting the shuttle, let alone landing it."

There was a pause and he was aware of their attention. He went on: "Does any one of you know how to hit the re-entry window on the nail? Can you put it down on the ground? It lands at two hundred eighty. You haven't a chance. I'm the only shuttle pilot and you know it.

"So get this. No one leaves this ship till we've shut Dynostar off."

The long silence that followed was broken by Neumann, he spoke coldly: "I think we would have to make you."

"You can't take us all on," Townsend grated.

"Look," Hayward said. "I don't give a shit whether I get back or not. Either I drive the shuttle or you do. And you'll either fry yourselves or hit the desert floor."

It was Walters who finally broke the silence, a smile coming and going over his open salesman's face:

"Powerful logic I'd say, Commander, real good that!" He turned to the others. "You heard the man, so why don't we get the thing over with, instead of sitting around here?"

Lucas and Neumann had already begun to turn back to an examination of the jury rig, the others followed slowly. Only Townsend stood his ground: "That's only half of it, isn't it?" he said. The others turned. "You're forgetting something. One of us is a bloody murderer!"

Hayward saw the men stiffen, the unspeakable had been mentioned.

"And your judgment's the last thing we can trust," Townsend continued.

"Meaning?" Hayward asked.

"Freeman. He's dead, remember?" Townsend replied.

Hayward felt his control of the situation slipping and then suddenly remembered the diagram of the space-suit system he had found among Freeman's possessions. He reached into his tunic and pulled it out.

"You haven't seen this. It was in Freeman's locker." He unfolded the paper and held it out in a torch beam for the others to see. He pointed to the tube ringed in felt pen ink: "This oxygen connector's missing from one of the suits."

Townsend snatched the diagram from Hayward's hand. He was shaking with anger: "My God! Is that all you had? That and a drug trip? I'll tell you exactly what that diagram was doing in his locker." He paused.

"I gave it to him! He had a curved tracheotomy tube in the medical unit, it had the right radius of curvature and we talked about resistance brazing a couple of small plates on each end, to repair it. Not to wreck it! To patch it up!"

In the silence that followed, Hayward saw only a circle of faces in the dim light, eyes accusing.

Townsend jabbed a finger: "You can't answer that, can you? You had to nail somebody, so you chose Freeman.

Well one thing for certain, you can forget the Commander bit. From now on, you're nothing. You don't give any more orders."

Patterson moved forward anchoring himself in the middle of the circle, facing Townsend: "No one's asking you to take orders. Or anyone else. He's said his piece, you've made your point, so's Jean. We're stuck here till Hayward gets us off this ship. There's sweet nothing we can do about that, so let's get the hell on with shut-down!"

One by one, over the ensuing minutes, the men moved silently back to their positions, Patterson and Townsend unclipped one torch and carefully inched their way into the blackness of the central access tunnel to the workshop. Lucas and Neumann picked up a second torch and floated into the docking collar on their way to the space shuttle to examine its power supplies. Walters and Van Buren began to peer at the complex of bare printed circuits and cables on the jury-rig.

Hayward felt suddenly at a loss, he had no function. With a burst of fear, he noticed that he was breathing more rapidly than normal and that the air in the ship was warmer.

CHAPTER TWENTY-THREE

Caldor's first action on hearing of the attempt to take power from the shuttle batteries was to give the Mission Control chief in Houston the instruction that unless specifically requested by Hayward, all further communication was to be directly through the lines at Clear Lake, to conserve power on board.

With Irene Andler, he wasted no time on apologies: "I was wrong about Freeman, but whoever the man is, he's blown at least one cover. Freeman would have almost certainly been indicted and the man would have got back to earth and walked away scot free.

"So now we've got an entirely different situation. Whoever it is, is past all thoughts of saving himself or anyone else. He's obviously sufficiently clever to mask his thoughts and obsessions and stop all efforts at shut-down."

She studied her hand: "It makes for a very interesting group situation."

Suddenly, without warning, he crashed both hands down on the desk. She looked up in alarm. The studied diplomatic manner had vanished. In its place, Caldor now sat forward at his desk, his body tensed, jaw set. His grey eyes were frightening in their intensity and he spoke with a compressed, tense, fury:

"This is not just an interesting situation! It's lethal

and I want yes or no answers from you on everything I ask. The way you people go to work amazes me! When you come to a point of real responsibility you duck behind jargon and statistics. So just get off your academic ass and start giving me some ordinary straight understandable answers!"

She sat immobile, her heavy lids blinking rapidly.

He continued: "Now I've already given orders that all the wives are to be brought here under guard." He looked at his watch. "And that should be in just a few minutes from now.

"Once they're here, I'm going to talk to them myself and I need you there. You are going to look for every shade and meaning you can find. Anything at all, a nuance, a piece of family history—anything which'll give you some fragment we can build on."

He got up and began to pace the room. "I'm holding the meeting in the seminar room. It will be taped. I'm going to tell them every last detail of what's happened. It may shake one of them loose. Any comments?"

She shook her head. He continued.

"They will be driven to their homes and kept there under guard. Then you and I and your colleagues will go to each home in turn to see whether they have found anything further to say or to show us—documents, anything."

He leant forward. "On my responsibility, if any one of them offers any resistance or attempt at concealment, they'll be held in restraint and their homes searched."

"One point," she said. "I think we'll do better on our own. A six-man team doesn't make any more sense to me than two. Particularly if we're after confidential information."

Caldor nodded quickly: "Agreed. We can feed your people all the material we get—if any—and let them debate it." He looked at his watch. "It's one thirty a.m.—a good time for questioning."

"Quite classical," she remarked evenly.

* * *

All six women were already assembled in the seminar room. Two armed National Guardsmen were on duty and locked the door behind Caldor and Irene Andler as they entered. Dexter, the base administrator and Sue Annenberg were already present, fending off a barrage of anxious questions. Caldor got up on the rostrum.

Sarah Van Buren and Eunice Walters looked completely different without make-up and with their hair in disarray. Caldor reflected that they at least shared a degree of vulnerability.

Nicole Lucas was also dressed and sat by herself, nervously picking at her nails. Gerda Neumann, Camille Patterson and Joan Townsend were still in nightclothes underneath overcoats and dressing gowns. Sarah Van Buren wore an angry frown and Eunice Walters was trying to calm her down, her own expression, a slightly condescending smile.

Without preamble, Caldor plunged into a full and true account of events on board Spacelab Dynostar. Irene Andler sat beside him, her black eyes flicking from face to face, assessing reactions.

Caldor gave a deliberately full-blooded description of events and as he finished there was a shocked silence, broken only by Camille Patterson who had begun to sob. Nicole Lucas' face was deathly white and Gerda Neumann put the palms of both hands to her face and bowed her head.

Out of the corner of one eye, Caldor noted also that Sue Annenberg was equally affected and suddenly realised that it was the first time she had heard the full story. Only Eunice Walters showed a different reaction. She seemed excited by the situation.

Sarah Van Buren rose unsteadily to her feet, her eyes blazing. The normal studied tone of her voice was replaced by a rasping aggression: "What in God's name are you doing keeping them up there? Why weren't they brought down?"

"Perhaps I wasn't clear enough about the Dynostar situation," Caldor said.

"I don't give a fuck what you think the situation is!" she exploded. "What do you think you're doing? You've got all our men up there and all you're goddam thinking about is that machine!

"Why don't you get them down right now? What more do you want from them?"

"They'll stay there until the Dynostar is shut down. There is no question of any return until that has been achieved." He spoke quietly, but there was no mistaking the chill of authority. Sarah Van Buren remained poised for a few moments, then, her face crumpled into tears and she slumped back in her seat. Eunice Walters put her arm around her shoulders.

"I do not understand the reason for this." It was Gerda Neumann who spoke. "Why are you asking this terrible sacrifice? I do not understand."

For the first time Caldor's voice softened. "Mrs. Neumann, if the Dynostar starts, it will almost certainly destroy a protective layer in the upper atmosphere and let

179

in lethal ultra-violet rays from the sun. This will blind anybody exposed to the rays, it will blind animals, kill crops and destroy much of the fauna of the earth, probably for ever.

"No man should have to take this sort of decision, but I have had to balance the lives of your menfolk against the deaths of thousands, perhaps millions of people, either from the radiation itself, or from starvation." He dropped his arms to his side. "There is nothing else I can do." He paused, no one spoke.

"One of the men—one of your men—has given way, he is no longer in touch with reality, he's living in a world of his own construction.

"He's not a criminal in any ordinary sense. He is not responsible for his own actions any more and no one here wants to penalise him. He needs a lot of help, very quickly. It's his life as well remember."

He looked slowly round the circle of faces. "To get that help I need your full and absolute attention over the next four hours.

"I want you to think back over the lives of your men, every small detail of behaviour, anything odd you may have noticed, it doesn't matter how small. Reactions to stress is important. And don't restrict yourselves to your own husbands, anything you may have noticed about any of the others could turn out to be vitally important." Caldor hesitated for a moment.

"Now you are not going to like this, but I'm having you taken to your homes, where you'll remain under guard. You can imagine what would happen if the news got out. There would certainly be panic in the cities and great loss of life, so your 'phones have already been disconnected. During the next few hours you will remain in your houses. . . ." He paused again, "If you make any attempt to leave you will be restrained.

"Food and any services you require will be brought to you. As soon as possible we'll be round to question you and by that time I want you to put together everything you can think of, evidence, conjecture, rumour. Rack your brains, anything you think may help us to find this man. Your husbands' lives, your lives, your children's, are all in the balance now." He stopped pacing. "That's all. Are there any questions?"

"Just one I think," said Gerda Neumann. "Would we not be sending this man to his execution?"

"You're thinking of a different age and time Mrs. Neumann," Caldor said searching the woman's face. "There is no question of the state taking that sort of revenge. He is a very, very sick man and he will be treated as such. You have my word." He nodded his head and turned to go.

A few minutes later, back in his office, Caldor turned to Irene Andler. "Anything come out of that?"

"I'm not sure," she replied. "I'll replay the tape with my colleagues. Three of the women will be very difficult. One could be impossible."

"Where do we start?"

"Mrs. Walters."

"Why her?"

"She will enjoy talking." She smiled thinly. "She's a bitch."

"That's the first ordinary remark you've made!"

Caldor glanced at Sue Annenberg for her reaction, but her face was set and preoccupied. He imagined her shock at realising that one of the men she had looked after, almost mothered, was a dangerous murderer. Perhaps she knew something?

As if in answer to his thoughts, she looked up and, seeing his gaze, smiled warmly. He again felt her enormous friendly attraction.

Irene Andler said, ignoring his remark, "The other person who interests me is Mrs. Townsend."

CHAPTER TWENTY-FOUR

The fifty-six-day crew period of life aboard Spacelab Dynostar had been designed using all the available skills of science. Psychologists, ergonomicists and engineers had all combined their expertise to ensure that, within the inevitable strains of weightlessness, with its attendant train of sensory and metabolic disturbance, there was the maximum degree of comfort and human support.

Living at such close quarters inevitably led to intermittent episodes of flaring anger and disagreement, but these had not gone beyond the bounds of the psychological stability of each man.

Each one knew that it was in his own interest that any apparent hostility on the part of another crew member should be absorbed, as far as possible, without overt reaction. They all knew full well that their lives could depend on their ability to co-exist.

Now the haggard, exhausted crew, already strained beyond any reasonable limits of control, found their last psychological support snatched away by the battery failure. The additional knowledge that one of them was both insane and a murderer, had completely stripped away the remaining veneers of ordinary civilised behaviour.

Now, one by one, the elegantly balanced systems of the great Spacelab complex were failing around them. The inertial ship orientation systems had ceased to work, so that the ship was no longer rotated to even the heating effect of the sun's rays and they were now beating down on the dorsal surface of the ship.

The brief cooling period as the giant complex swept around the dark side of the earth was not sufficient to re-radiate the accumulated heat back into space. There were no fans to circulate the air, no refrigerators to keep their individually chosen food trays fresh, and the waste freezer, containing the bodies of the dead crew, as well as their accumulated excreta, was already approaching blood heat.

Humidity controls had also failed. And the dust extractors and carbon-dioxide absorption membranes were completely inactive.

The most sophisticated mechanism ever designed by man had become a drifting, motionless, hulk: a prison in space.

The first changes were in the air.

The skin of the ship over their heads had begun to give off heat like a central heating radiator and, since hot air weighs the same as cold air in space, the only disturbance in the atmosphere was created by the movement of the crew as they raced to finish the re-routing of power cables from the shuttle. Any movement towards the heated skin of the ship meant exposure to the equivalent of noonday desert heat.

The men had already discarded their tunics and T-shirts in a desperate and ineffectual attempt to evaporate the sweat that glistened all over their bodies.

Theo Neumann seemed to be particularly affected by the humid, unfiltered air. Each breath he exhaled was accompanied by a high-pitched asthmatic wheeze, which irritated the others. He breathed intermittently from a facemask attached to a space-suit secondary oxygen pack, while the others watched, jealous of his greedy consumption of the vital gas.

Only Patterson seemed relatively unaffected, remarking, with a sour humour appreciated by no one, that it was no worse than parts of the Australian outback.

In the foetid dimness, lit only by the torches and a single bank of blue electro-luminescent panels still working on a standard cell, fear became a palpable presence in the nightmare gloom as the men edged their way through the silent ship.

Conversation dwindled to the minimum necessary for the task and each man reacted to the physical presence of his fellow with all the hostile tensions of cat meeting dog. Muscles tensed, eyes searched to read expressions. Any sudden or unexpected movement produced a shying away and a fearful attitude of defence.

*   *   *

Only one man remained immune from the tentacles of fear spreading into every corner of the ship. All events around him were directed towards his actions. Even the pattern of shadows made by the torches were of important significance.

There were no doubts in his mind.

His pulse rate, alone of all the others, was normal and he failed entirely to react to the terrible atmosphere in the ship. It all fitted together into a pattern which he understood fully.

*   *   *

Lucas had been the first to lose control. He had suddenly screamed at Neumann to stop his wheezing.

185

Townsend, now reacting suspiciously to every word or gesture on the part of anyone else aboard, had provided himself with a long combination plench tool, stuck ostentatiously in his rear pocket for instant use should he be attacked. A joking remark by Patterson who had tried to remove the plench almost led to a fight between the two men. Only Hayward's intervention and Patterson's cool reaction saved one of them from injury.

By far the most serious effect of the deteriorating situation was felt by Hayward.

All the resentment of the others seemed to centre upon him.

If they were wary with each other, they were doubly so when Hayward appeared. Work would stop when he entered the control room, hands would reach for screwdrivers, any tool that could be used as a weapon. Muttered conversations would cease and he would be watched warily until he'd delivered his message and left.

Despite his efforts at reassurance, he found that he was a totally negative influence upon the work and was obliged to shut himself off in the space shuttle rather than risk the disruption of the shut-down operation. The crew had made it perfectly plain that they were not going to work while he was in the vicinity. The fear and hatred that had first focused upon Freeman, now, with Freeman's death and almost certain innocence, was directed at him. On top of the ennervating effects of the heat and humidity, the effect of this semi-ostracisation was almost impossible to bear.

Even the normally friendly Walters had withdrawn into a shell of his own and answered Hayward's queries with gestures or, at best, with reluctant monosyllables.

He saw as his only remaining task the need to ensure

that the man was unable to carry out any further acts of sabotage. One more "accident" and he knew that there would be no holding the crew. One more act of violence and he was in no doubt that he would be attacked and forced to fly the shuttle down, or be killed.

Finally, Hayward realised that he could not hold on physically much longer. His whole body ached with fatigue and his balance canals were releasing bursts of intolerable nausea and vertigo, often sending him reeling out of control to strike the wall of the ship. In the semi-darkness it was impossible to grab a handhold in time.

In each shadow he saw the dead white face of Freeman, the wire around the head, the eyes accusing.

He could find no real defence to Townsend's charges. He saw all too clearly the bias in his own decision and realised that Freeman alive would have been invaluable in the present emergency.

The cockpit screens of the shuttle above his head suddenly flashed into scintillating brilliance as the ship rushed silently into the sun from the dark side of the earth. Hayward shielded his dark-adapted eyes against the glare.

The light galvanised his mood. He felt a massive surge of anger against the man who had cold-bloodedly planned not only the deaths aboard, but even the wildfire of destruction which would follow the removal of the ozone layer.

His control vanished in a raging fury where he wanted only to injure the man, to kill him, to fling his body into space. Then his anger turned against Caldor. What kind of back-up had he had? Nothing! A half-baked academic making noises about behaviour patterns and categories. They'd obviously written him off, along with the rest of the crew, otherwise they would have given him more help. Bastards! They were all written off.

"Sons of bitches, we're all dead to you now!" He realised with a shock that he had shouted aloud and looked guiltily up at a panel to make sure that the communicator leading to Spacelab was not switched on. With relief, he saw that it was not.

He gazed out through the screen panel at the impossibly clear blues and browns of the daylight earth hanging overhead. He thought of people he had known, of mothers dressing their children ready for school, of all humanity spread out before him. He thought of all those people going about their daily tasks, ignorant of the lethal machine sweeping by over their heads.

He had a sudden unbearable picture of his two sons, staring up at a dark violet sky, their eyes white with the cataracts of blindness.

Tears came to his eyes in a surge of self-pity. There was only one remaining possibility: to appeal to the crew, to tell them what would happen to their own people on earth, to touch their humanity.

Simultaneously, he realised dully that the men would merely see this as further evidence of weakness. There was only one realistic course: to be vigilant, to record and to watch, to catch him in the act; to note down any unexplained movements to another part of the ship; to keep tabs on everyone. He cudgelled his brain to remember the most probable behaviour patterns that Caldor had given him, the signs of—what was it—psychosis.

He lingered in the temperature-controlled environment of the shuttle, unwilling to exchange the clean, cool air for the malodorous humidity of the Spacelab.

In his mind's eye he started once again to re-examine

the crew: their personalities, their conversations, their actions.

Eddie Van Buren. Back on earth he had seemed the most reliable of all: a veteran space scientist, with immense experience of leadership, a public figure. And yet he had broken almost completely and was now a vacillating personality, weak and only intermittently competent.

Why had he broken?

What was the cause?

Van Buren had certainly staked his remaining career on the success of Dynostar. Although that applied to the others, he stood to gain the most. Almost any political office in the United States would be open to him. He had the right face, family and background and the success of Dynostar would have capped an almost perfect pedigree. Was he that determined to make Dynostar work?

Was his ineffectiveness an ingenious cover?

A picture of Lyall's dead face swam into his mind. There was no way he could reconcile the two images. Sabotage was just possible, but murder was unthinkable.

Jean Lucas. Electronics scientist, almost universally recognised as a genius of real originality. Hayward recalled the sad lugubrious features.

In European terms, his rewards would have been as great as Van Buren's. He was a staunch patriot of almost Gaullist ideals and was again well-known as a public figure in his native France since his selection for the Spacelab Dynostar project.

Then Hayward realised that Lucas' special knowledge had been vital to the whole operation of constructing the jury-rig. Every circuit, every computing programme had been personally supervised by him. All the Frenchman had to do would be to feign illness or at the last moment build in a false circuit which would perhaps explode and ruin all their efforts.

Perhaps, as a final twist, Lucas had deliberately designed the whole system so that it would not work. There was no one else aboard of equal competence in micro-lithic electronics who could possibly judge the validity of Lucas' designs.

Finally Hayward realised that even the circuit designs which had come through from Mission Control on the read-out screens could easily have been misdirected by Lucas. There was no protection there.

He tried to piece together the picture he had formed in his mind about the movements of the crew members around the time of Lyall's murder, the wrecking of the space-suits and the discharge of the batteries, but the patterns of movement had been such as to show that almost anyone could have done anything. There had been a continuous movement of men between different sectors of the ship and without getting them all together and grilling them, which was out of the question in the circumstances, there was no help to be had there.

Theo Neumann. Hayward reflected that he knew least about the quiet German.

What did he know? Slim, efficient, almost aristocratic in his demeanour, he remained an enigma as a person. He had always been studiously polite, but he seemed always to use the minimum number of words and, although never curt or rude, he gave the impression of finding it an effort to speak, that he would rather just think.

Caldor had told him that Neumann was independently wealthy from directorships in two family firms, and he recalled that one of them had, in competition, been awarded the contract for the airlock modules of Spacelab. At the age of thirty-five he was unmarried, a skier of near Olympic standards and obviously cultured with a broadly based knowledge of music. His contribution to the music tape library aboard had ranged from Monteverdi motets to Beethoven's last quartets.

The contract and his directorships obviously involved him in the success of Dynostar, and it was possible that he had an even larger and undeclared financial stake in the Dynostar project. Hayward tried to probe further into his recollections of Neumann, but found a dearth of knowledge almost everywhere.

He needed to know much more about Theo Neumann.

He passed to the third American, Russ Walters. Partly because of their shared nationality, Hayward felt that he knew Walters as well as anyone on board. His own background had also been mid-western and he had actually visited Walters' college and knew the pattern of his career almost as well as his own.

What came across most strongly in his personality was an over-riding personal ambition. Like the other men, he had invested nearly the whole of his intellectual potential in the Dynostar design and had worked for years in the rarified and intensely difficult field of theoretical plasma physics to find ways of designing a hyper-stable magnetic field structure to retain the sun-hot plasmas of fusion successfully.

On board he had shown himself to be the main ideas man. He seemed to be able to generate concepts for solutions quicker than any of the others, and was the first to admit, with an easy laugh, that most of his ideas turned out to be lead-bricks anyway, so what the hell. He would often start on a complicated chain of reasoning and work it up, then suddenly abandon it, covering the break with a joke.

He tried as hard as he knew to get behind the cheerful charm of the other, but try as he would, he could not see a premeditated and ingenious killer. Walters seemed to have little or no interests beyond his own subject of plasma physics and his recreation aboard had been books. He had brought several books on extra-sensory perception, telepathy and precognition aboard and had often amused the others by attempting to explain the paranormal phenomena reported in the books by using the laws of physics.

Townsend and Patterson remained for consideration. Both were powerful and aggressive individuals. Both were capable of physical violence and, although he had no means of deciding whether either would stop short of killing under stress, once again his judgment reacted strongly against them as premeditated and mentally disturbed murderers. But he could not forget that Patterson alone had remained unmoved by the sight of Lyall's disfigured corpse.

Hayward had been glad of the man's pragmatic approach at the time, but now he wondered if lack of reaction equalled pre-knowledge. Also Patterson had been the first to challenge his authority when he came aboard and his role in subsequent events had been ambiguous, sometimes taking Hayward's side, sometimes opposing him.

Now, partly by virtue of his physical strength and laconic confidence, he had almost taken Hayward's place as leader. Although he gave no orders, the others looked first towards him before acting. If there were another act of sabotage sufficient to panic the crew, Patterson, he reflected, would be able to manipulate all of them into any course of action he chose.

He cast his mind back over some of the prior events. It seemed that whenever a breakdown had occurred, Patterson had been near. It was Patterson who had found the damaged space-suits; Patterson who had been at the E.V.A. hatch when Sicura had died and Patterson who helped to find Freeman and then, again without reaction, drag his body down to the waste freezer.

His apparent support of some of Hayward's decisions could easily be a cover. He was certainly a likely candidate.

Although Townsend's northern English origin had perplexed Hayward on first acquaintance, he had very soon come to understand the blunt taciturn aggression of the nuclear scientist. Although he clearly had a large chip on his shoulder and was an automatic enemy of authority, his type was often essential in a hazardous situation. To the manner born, he would always question blindly-given orders, would always look at small print on rules and regulations.

Always suspicious and mistrustful: the great virtue of his type, thought Hayward, was that they could never be bought.

Townsend was certainly resentful to the point of a real paranoid tendency, but he was unable to decide whether it was due to a real personality defect or whether it stemmed more simply from the working-class background he so often referred to.

He had already made two attempts at physical attack and to some extent, Hayward reasoned, this was against the idea of a disturbed man who kept his affliction hidden. Or was it that the once secretive man was now finding his own internal conflicts too powerful to conceal? With his black temper and moods of fierce resentment, he too was more than likely as a suspect.

Hayward pulled himself up to the instrument panel and started the scrambler communicator to Caldor at Clear Lake.

He got through only to Colonel Robertson, Caldor's aide, and was told curtly that there was nothing to report.

As he snapped off the communication switch and made his way down towards the docking collar, all the feelings of resentment and anger returned. There was no help.

CHAPTER TWENTY-FIVE

As the car drew up alongside the Walters' cabin, to Caldor's surprise, Irene Andler made no attempt to leave. Instead she passed him one of two portable tape recorders:

"I think you should talk to her by yourself."

"Why? What reason?"

"Because she will react against me and tell us nothing. I'll talk to Camille Patterson, it'll be a better use of time, she's much more likely to talk to another woman."

Caldor paused for a moment and then got out of the car. He glanced at his watch:

"I'll pick you up at the Lucas' cabin in thirty minutes." He nodded to the driver and walked quickly up the gravel path and knocked on the wooden frame door. The car accelerated away, throwing up sprays of pebbles from the rear wheels.

"It's open."

Caldor walked into a long, low-ceilinged living room with yellowed pine timbered ceiling and ornate wrought-iron bracket lights set around the wall. The main centre pieces were an upholstered red-velvet sofa and a glass coffee table with reproduction Victorian brass frame, which supported a lamp with a pink tasselled shade.

Scattered around the edge of the room were several spindle-legged side tables and on each one was a highly glazed group of porcelain figurines. The open doors of the drink cabinet were panelled in damasked green leather.

Eunice Walters was standing beside the cabinet, a half-empty tumbler-sized glass in her hand. She swayed very slightly and her voice was loud and confident. She raised her glass as he entered:

"Well hi! Can I pour you something? I'd guess you're a scotch man?"

Caldor shook his head and sat down. "Nothing, thank you."

Eunice Walters turned back to the cabinet and re-charged her glass from a bottle of Jack Bean. Caldor noted that she had poured at least two double shots and then quickly disguised the volume, by topping up the glass with soda. She took a heavy gulp while her back was still partly turned to him.

As she turned to sit down, some of the drink spilt unheeded on the arm of the chair. He noted that she had changed out of her night clothes and was wearing a heavily frilled negligée. Her shoulders were bare. She leant back in the chair, smiling directly at him, shaking her long blonde hair back over her shoulders. She crossed her legs slowly, the garment falling away revealing the top of her thighs. She raised the glass:

"It's not often I get night callers. Certainly not Sec . . . Secretaries of State," she faltered slightly over the words.

Caldor sat, poised. "You've had a chance to think now."

"About Russell?" She put her head back and laughed and then took another deep swallow of the drink. "What can I say about Russ? Let's think now." Her manner seemed almost unbearably grotesque to Caldor. She continued:

"Russell doesn't know the meaning of neur — neurosis or whatever. Why, if you all want to find some nice juicy skeleton, you should look around my side of things. Why my little faggy brother now. . . ."

"What about his relatives?" Caldor broke in sharply. "Is there anything there. Any history of mental problems?"

She shook her head. He noticed that she had carefully made up although it was two-thirty in the morning.

"What about the other men? Do you remember hearing anything?"

"You're trying to get me to gossip," she drawled. "That's not polite."

Seeing the growing tautness of anger in Caldor's face, she continued quickly, the drawl giving way to a more definite but slightly slurred delivery:

"Well now, where am I going to start? Take little English Mrs. Townsend now. She's a good case for you, little lady sweetface."

"I said I haven't much time. Keep to the point."

"I am, Mr. Secretary, I am. Mrs. Townsend's got two lovely little children and . . ." she paused, ". . . she puts out for every goddam man on the base." She leant back waiting for a reaction, but getting none, continued: "I mean all's fair in love and space, but. . . ."

"What about your husband?"

Again she laughed. "What, Russ and little old Joany Townsend! Mr. Secretary sir, my husband's not . . . shall we say a sexually driven man."

"Then who?"

"Why, I don't exactly keep a score card." She smiled again and swallowed the remains of the drink. "But you ought to ask Jean Lucas. I mean you've just got to take a look at Nicole, all she's got going for her is big boobs, Jean Paul Sartre and a moustache."

"Who else?"

"Why Eddie Van Buren of course. He's an eye for all us ladies." She paused. "And there's Bob Townsend's buddy, Will Patterson."

"Does Townsend know about all this?"

Eunice shook her head in mock alarm. "With that temper of his, he'd kill them all!"

For a moment Caldor did not reply. The overheated room, the perfume, her drunkenness. How much could he believe. How much was just malicious invention. As if in answer to his thoughts, she continued: "Is that the kind of stress you're looking for?"

Some minutes later, after more questions, with relief he heard the car draw up on the gravel outside. There was a tap at the door. He got up to go. She waved the empty glass without rising:

"It's been a great honour, Mr. Secretary sir, come back any time."

Caldor slumped back on the car seat. "Oh boy!"

"Wasn't she helpful?" Irene Andler's voice held only the slightest trace of irony.

"According to her, Joan Townsend is an easy lay, Lucas, Van Buren and Patterson share her round and Neumann is queer!" He handed her the recorder. "It's all there, you listen with your people. How'd you make out?"

"Camille Patterson's terrified of her husband. She loves him, but his violence keeps her in a constant state of anxiety. She's a two-year history of tranquillisers—I wondered about the way she walked when I first saw her. She's still in analysis, she thinks his violence is all due to her shortcomings. She has a tremendous guilt feeling about it."

"Did she talk about Townsend?" Caldor asked.

The car wound through the trees, there were patches of night mist, drifting across the headlight beams.

"Only that he's a drinking partner of Patterson's."

The car drew up outside the Lucas' cabin, and Caldor turned to the psychologist: "From now on we do this together." He remembered the austere and patrician intelligence of Gerda Neumann. "This time, you do the questioning."

He opened the car door and sprang out.

The atmosphere in the Lucas household was palpably hostile and both Nicole Lucas and the aristocratic Gerda Neumann went onto the offensive the moment Caldor and Irene Andler entered.

Both assumed that the order to shut down Dynostar had originated in the United States for totally opportunistic reasons. The men's lives were in the balance solely because the Americans had persuaded the remainder of the European Dynostar management team of the dangers after they had succeeded with their own ground-based fusion device.

Caldor reflected that there was a grain of truth in the argument, since the Americans had, in fact, made considerable strides with the development of their own earth-bound machine, the stellerator nine. Although the giant toroidal complex in the Brookhaven laboratories was far from completion, he could understand how the two distraught women had been all too ready to exaggerate the accounts they must have heard from their two men.

As he had listened to the tirade, he had felt wave after wave of fatigue that had been almost impossible to resist. He had recognised the futility of trying to combat the stream of accusations and counter-claims and wondered whether the story was also believed by Townsend. Could it amount to enough circumstantial evidence of his guilt?

Finally he lost patience, jumped to his feet and strode to the front door, flinging it open. Outside, two uniformed policemen were waiting, he beckoned them in.

"I want this house searched from top to bottom for any papers belonging to Jean Lucas or Theodore Neumann. Deliver anything you find to my office straight away." He gestured at the two women. "If they show any resistance, restrain them."

Disregarding the furious outcry from Nicole Lucas and taunts of "Nazis" from the older woman, he brushed past the two marshals. Irene Andler followed. Once inside the car, he ordered the driver to the Townsend home.

Again fatigue started to wash down through his senses. "That was pretty damned unproductive. Did I handle it as badly as I think?"

She paused, then replied evenly: "In your shoes, I'd have done exactly the same."

Through the tension and fatigue, he felt a moment of gratitude towards her. It had been the first glimpse of anything like approval for his actions.

Inside the Townsend's living room, Caldor was surprised to see that the two children were still up, sitting with their mother deep in a board game which was unfamiliar to him. Then, at a second glance, he recognised the popular ecological game "DOOMWATCH" which had become a world favourite since its invention some fifteen years previously.

After the children had been sent to bed, Caldor sat back and let Irene Andler lead with the questions. He studied the English woman.

Her manner was easy and straightforward. None of her

features would have found their way into orthodox descriptions of beauty, but together the general impression was one of open attraction. Caldor felt that she was preparing to be entirely honest.

The picture of her husband that emerged was that of a taciturn, self-centred man with an apparently obsessional interest in his work as a nuclear scientist. His wife gave a frank but obviously resentful account of evenings where she had spent long hours preparing special meals only to have them eaten without recognition or comment by a group of men who talked only of toroidal fields and plasma stabilities.

Townsend had so completely adopted the chauvinist male image that when he finally stopped talking shop, he would turn the conversation round to his other over-riding interest in American football.

Finally, although he appeared to his wife as a morose and quick-tempered man, he also clearly possessed a real concern for the under-dog and a respect for human life. He had, she said, been approached on a number of occasions by the English Atomic Weapons Research Establishment, to work on laser-triggered fusion bombs. Each time he had firmly rejected the offer.

She also explained that any of his friends when ill or down on their luck would automatically receive practical help, although it was usually given with a gruff refusal to accept thanks or gratitude.

She responded easily and openly to Irene Andler's questions and gave a full account of Townsend's early poverty in a Tyneside slum in the North-East of England. She gave no hint or suggestion of mental instability and no amount of questioning revealed any relevant family background.

Caldor gradually led the conversation round to Patterson and immediately met a determined reticence. She kept to a too obviously neutral description of their friendship with the Patterson family, which she said had started when the two men had been working on the Torsatron Two at the Culham fusion station in England.

Finally, he broke through her reticence with a sharp and brutal reminder of what would happen to the two men if the situation in space was unresolved.

In response to the horrific images which Caldor had raised, with an almost visible relief, she began to talk about Patterson in an entirely different way. Beyond the aggressively male image, so similar to that of her husband, a man with a natural understanding of women emerged.

It seems he was a man who had established an easy relationship with her children. Uncle Will, as they called him, had often spent long hours with her when her husband had been seconded to the Max Planck Institute in Germany. Patterson obviously had only an amused tolerance for his wife and spent as little time as possible at home.

With only a slight change of emphasis, Caldor asked the obvious question and the answer had come just as easily.

"Will? Yes, we have an understanding. It just grew up, that's all."

"Does your husband know?"

"He never gets away from his work long enough to see."

"Do you worry about that?"

"Yes, I do, but Will's really good to me and the kids." She paused. "It means rather a lot to me."

"Who else is there?"

"Pardon?"

"I said who else?"

"You're making me sound like the camp whore!"

"There's no time Mrs. Townsend."

She hesitated. "Well, last year Will was in Europe, Bob and I were having a bad time. There was really nothing left. He went off to the West Coast—Caltech. It was winter here. I'm not used to that sort of cold, it just got me down."

"Who was it?" he asked gently.

"Jean—Jean Lucas. He's so gentle, he's the gentlest man I ever met. He made me feel wanted." She suddenly put her head down in her hands.

Caldor persisted: "Did your husband know about Lucas?"

For a moment she was silent, then she looked up and shook her head. Her cheeks were wet:

"If he did find out, what do you think he'd do? Would he damage them? Kill them even?"

She shook her head firmly: "No, never! He's a bad temper, but he couldn't—Bob couldn't kill a man!"

"And Will Patterson?" It was Irene Andler who had caught a sudden hesitation in the other's tone. "Can you tell us about him?"

Joan Townsend's gaze clouded, she looked away without answering.

"Answer the question," Caldor said. "What about Patterson? Did he know about Lucas?"

"No, no," she gave a frightened shake of the head. "He couldn't have."

"Mrs. Townsend," Caldor said, "we need to know everything. What is it about Patterson?"

She hesitated.

"You have to tell us," Irene Andler said. "Otherwise there's no hope for any of them."

Her voice faltered. "Can I be absolutely sure . . ." she began.

"Of course," Caldor said. "What is it?"

She dropped her hands into her lap in a gesture of defeat. "It was . . . about five years ago now, there was a demo . . . outside the Culham station. The students arrived in a great hoard, they'd blocked the road outside. There were police everywhere.

"You see Culham is an open station, there's no really secret work there, it's quite easy to get through the fence. Anyway, the students broke in, they were against fusion, against Dynostar, against everything! It was a green-earth, back-to-nature thing. The placards . . . they had all the names of the team under headlines saying things like: 'Destroyers of the Earth'." The words were tumbling out. "Will's name was on the list. He'd been drinking, there was a fight, a sort of riot, Will was in it. . . ."

"How do you know all this?"

She hesitated: "I . . . I was there, with Will in his office . . . Bob was away."

"Go on."

"This man—a student. Will caught him in the corridor, he chased him out, there was a terrible fight." She looked at the two, her eyes pleading. "He provoked Will—he really wanted to fight."

"What happened?" Irene Andler asked softly.

"He—that is—the student, died.

"The police found him, there was an enquiry, a press hunt. The police were accused of it, but it was just a fight. Will didn't mean to kill him. We didn't know he was dead. There was so much confusion. Everybody run-

ning everywhere. We didn't know what to do. In the end
—well—we didn't do anything."

She stopped suddenly and looked at them, realising the
implication. "That doesn't make Will a murderer!"

In the car, Caldor and Irene Andler remained silent for
several minutes. Finally, he turned: "Something to go on,
we've got a man who can kill."

She paused: "And that's all we've got!"

The car turned into the drive of the Van Buren home.

CHAPTER TWENTY-SIX

As soon as Hayward felt the increase in his breathing rate, he pulled his way urgently back to the space shuttle. After a few moments he felt the compulsion to drag more air into his lungs diminish.

The atmosphere control systems of the Spacelab complex had been at a complete standstill since the main power failure. The oxygen supplies were contained in twelve steel-lined fibreglass tanks each four feet in diameter and nearly six in length. The nitrogen to balance the seventy-five percent oxygen-rich atmosphere was stored in twelve four-foot-diameter Titanium steel spheres.

In normal operation, the humidity, heat, and carbon-dioxide levels were controlled by a series of power-driven fans which pushed the air through beds of activated charcoal to remove unwanted odours, and through molecular sieves to remove water vapour and carbon dioxide. Each sieve and bed was duplicated for safety but now, in the absence of powered circulation, the carbon-dioxide levels were rising rapidly.

Hayward realised, unless something was done quickly, they would not survive for long if they didn't leave the Spacelab and get into the shuttle. He reasoned from his early training in space physiology that they had probably less than thirty minutes to go.

As his head cleared in the cooled and dehumidified atmosphere of the shuttle, he also realised that the carbon dioxide contamination would also soon begin to diffuse through the open docking collar into the shuttle itself.

As quickly as he could, he called the Clear Lake base and reported the situation. He talked only to Colonel Robertson, who had no useful advice. Mission Control also had been without practical help.

Then, unclipping a portable oxygen pack from its mount under the pilot's seat, he opened the demand valve and strapped the mask into position over his mouth and nose.

The scene inside the Control room reminded Hayward of a casualty clearing station he had once worked in during the great killer smog in Los Angeles in 1979.

A single fluorescent tube threw a harsh cold glare into the fogged atmosphere.

All appeared to be unconscious. Neumann was floating upside down to Hayward, his chest heaving and his legs twitching and jerking like an epileptic.

At the jury rig control, Van Buren, his face a terrible blotchy violet in the glare, had his arms entwined in the alloy frame. Next to him Townsend was muttering to himself, wheezing with bubbles of froth breaking away from his gasping goldfish mouth. He was still attempting to work, but his mind was obviously disconnected, his movements were jerking, robotic and purposeless.

Lucas had gripped his legs around a jockey seat and was scrabbling his hands towards the row of portable oxygen packs on a magnetic bar over his head. His eyes were staring and he was grunting with the effort. As Hayward entered, Lucas' movements began to diminish in strength, his eyes closing. Towards the central tunnel opening, he could just make out something curled up like a giant drowned spider.

As he moved forward, he saw Walters, his face contorted and his chest heaving in a desperate attempt to suck enough of the foul air into his lungs. Next to him, Patterson was floating nearly unconscious, a dribble of viscous vomit still attached, like an amoeba, to his wide open mouth.

Hayward braced his feet against a bulkhead and launched himself at the row of oxygen packs, ripped them off their mountings and strapped them onto each man as quickly as he could.

Lucas, because of his small body bulk, was the first to recover.

Slowly, one by one, the others came to and began to look bemusedly around as if they were recovering from an anaesthetic.

Hayward whipped round to Lucas: "We have to vent the carbon-dioxide—now—quickly. We've got to get fresh oxygen!"

Lucas gazed back at him, his normally bright eyes dulled and only partly comprehending: "We must get out of here into the shuttle."

Fighting a sudden wave of nausea, Hayward braced himself and shook the other man, his voice muffled through the facemask:

"No, we have to flush out the ship. Do you read me?"

The others was gradually collecting their senses and crowding towards Hayward. He tried desperately to remember the accident sequences he had learned in training. He remembered that flushing, in the event of atmosphere control failure, was a last resort. It could only be done once.

The sequence was to open solenoid-operated vents in the waste freezer and start to exhaust the ship interior to the vacuum in space, but to prevent the internal pressure dropping dangerously low; and at the same time to turn up the oxygen and nitrogen flow to replace the carbon dioxide-contaminated atmosphere howling into space.

With no power supply, he realised dully that the solenoid-operated vent would not function and would have to be operated by hand, by one man, at the same time as someone else turned up the oxygen and nitrogen supplies.

"But how do we synchronise it?" Lucas demanded.

Hayward looked around at the row of eyes staring at him over the oxygen masks: "I'll go aft to the freezer." His mind rebelled at the images in store for him. "I'll open the vent myself."

"But how will I know when you start?" Lucas queried. But Hayward had already picked up a reel of fine wire. "Tie this end round your wrist, I'll pay it out behind me and as I open the vent, I'll pull it. Directly you feel the tug, open up tanks one, three and five to full, leave the nitrogen until the paramag shows the oxygen level over twenty percent, then cut in the nitrogen silos, right?"

The Frenchman nodded quickly and Hayward turned and propelled himself into the blackness of the access tunnel, the dimming beam of his chest torch just picking out enough detail for him to see ahead. He unreeled the wire behind him.

The air in the tunnel seemed even more stagnant and close. It clung to his face like a wet cloth. He was soon saturated with a mixture of water and sweat, which broke away from his wet T-shirt and skin. His eyes filled with fluid and his vision was partly obscured by the rivulets of water coursing weightlessly to and fro over his face.

As he reached the waste freezer aperture, his senses

revolted at the stench of rotting food from the crew's quarters, compounded with the unbearable carrion reek of the bodies beyond the hatch, which lay partly open due to the failure of the electrically operated solenoid retaining bolts.

Bracing himself, he swung the hatch upwards. Immediately he was engulfed in the nauseating smell of corruption as he forced himself into the darkness.

He unclipped the torch from his chest and shone it into the steaming blackness. Dimly, in the waning light beam, he could just make out the irregular bulky outlines of the polythene sacks with their dreadful contents.

He floated across to the far side of the compartment searching for the exhaust vent, and carefully trailing the wire behind him looked anxiously to make sure that it was still running freely and not trapped on any obstacle. Finally he reached the vent valve and, shining the torch only inches away from it, he could just make out the manual over-ride lever painted in a bright fluorescent orange. It was covered in a protective metal grille held by two flynuts.

Quickly, he spun the nuts off their bolts and tore the grille away, exposing the lever. He made ready to pull it, bracing himself against the release of pressure he knew would follow. Suddenly he realised he had released the end of the reel of wire, it had floated away into the darkness. Frantically, he probed the shadows with the now obviously failing torch beam.

Immediately he cannoned into one of the tethered bags. As he shone the torch, he saw the dead face of Lyall staring through the opalescent plastic, the bloodied mouth still open in a silent scream. He backed away, shuddering in the humid darkness, his senses appalled by the growing patches of dissolution which had spread over the dead glistening face.

The clinging claustrophobic presence of death slowly and steadily sapped his remaining strength. Eventually, he reached up for the orange lever with one hand, still looking for the wire. He found it and drew it tight, seeing it straighten. Then, with all his remaining strength, he jammed the lever down, at the same time as he jerked the wire.

The silence was split by the roar of escaping air, magnified and resonating like a rocket motor against the confined walls of the compartment. Again and again he jerked the wire attached to Lucas' wrist at the forward end of the ship.

The roaring thunder of the venting air rose to a shriek and a whirlwind tugged and battered his body. His chest tightened, held by an agonising band of constriction. Desperately, he fought for breath as the air pressure fell around him.

His ears roared and crackled as the air trapped in his middle ear tried to burst his eardrums outwards. The whirlwind around his head had picked up packets and papers which flew around the compartment like trapped birds. The pressure in his ears grew to an intolerable pain. He drew quick shallow breaths, screaming in pain as he exhaled. His vision began to fail. The corpses in the bags had broken loose in the gale of escaping air. Loose clipboards and sachets of food tore insanely round in the turbulence.

With his last remaining strength, he lunged forward and jammed the orange lever upwards. Abruptly the tornado of air ceased. There was complete silence.

He breathed in once, then again and again. The air was clean. Lucas must have got his signal.

Gratefully, he inhaled time and time again. He could feel the oxygen, like a wine, tingling through his limbs, clearing his senses. The pains receded, he found he could move more easily. The movement of the loose objects in the compartment were slowing down; gradually, they came to rest, some against the walls, others hanging, spinning slowly on their own axis in the air.

He turned to leave.

Monstrous, distended shapes were blocking his view! Like giant Christmas balloons, the air inside the bags containing the corpses had expanded in the reduced pressure and now each dead man lay like an embryo in a womb of plastic.

The distention of each bag was slowly diminishing as the compartment air returned to normal pressure. The awful vision snapped his control completely. Launching himself with his feet towards the ballooned bags blocking his exit and moving obscenely from side to side in a silent dance of death, he pushed too hard and struck his head on a bulkhead, rebounding back and striking one of the bags. With a soft plop it ripped open releasing a flood of foul, putrescent liquid which sprayed out into the weightless air. Retching and scrabbling, he fought his way between the bags, eventually regaining the entry hatch.

Slamming the hatch behind, he clung onto a hand hold, fighting for control. It was minutes before he felt any sort of command return to his senses. He looked around the crew's quarters. The air had cleared of fog. The unbearable smell was weaker. He felt the tension in his ears returning as the pressure of oxygen built up in the cabin. He swallowed and sucked the air in and out of his lungs, a pulse throbbing in his neck. Finally, he floated to the water feeder, put the tube in his mouth and pressed the pump release.

Suddenly he retched violently and spat the water out. The power failure had caused the elecromagnetic iodine metering valves to jam open.

The water was undrinkably contaminated with iodine!

A few minutes later, Hayward had finished a search of the galley and collected a number of soft drink sachets which he took with him to forward control. The drinks revived the exhausted men and they turned back to work with renewed vigour. He heard Walters' voice in the semi-darkness:

"We're going to connect the main cable to the shuttle battery pack now. O.K. Commander?"

Hayward nodded quickly and Walters, followed by Patterson and Neumann, disappeared through the airlock of the docking collar.

It was fully three minutes before Hayward realised that he had let three men into the unguarded shuttle. Three men were next to the last remaining source of power. Mentally cursing himself, he dragged himself quickly into the airlock.

CHAPTER TWENTY-SEVEN

Sarah Van Buren's first reaction had been suspicious and unco-operative, but Irene Andler began to play upon her self-appointed leadership of the Clear Lake community, and gradually drew her co-operation.

Her account corroborated most of the information they already had and, when questioned about Eunice Walters' innuendo about her husband and Joan Townsend, she countered with the statement that Russ Walters had had a similar episode with Sue Annenberg.

Caldor registered the accusation, realising, at the same time, that he would no longer be able to rely on Sue Annenberg's impartial summaries of the other women.

Sarah Van Buren ended the interview by angrily defending her husband against any possible accusations. Then, as if hunting around in her mind for anything to draw their attention away from him towards someone else, finally told them that there was a part of Russ Walters' life which he normally concealed. She was unable to supply full details, but she had heard Eunice speak of a mysterious relative he sometimes visited and had pleaded with her never to mention.

* * *

As Caldor entered the over-decorated living room, Eunice Walters was standing by the fireplace. She was swaying.

"Hello again." She raised her glass.

"Sit down," Caldor said.

Her eyes narrowed as Irene Andler followed Caldor into the room. "Do we need Dracula's mother here?"

Caldor noticed the colour rise in the psychiatrist's cheek. He intervened: "There's some information I want from you, quickly."

Eunice launched herself from the fireplace and made her way unsteadily over to the sofa, flopping down, her negligée dropping away from her full breasts. "Anything at all Mr. Secretary. Like a drink?"

"Quite a lot of what you told me last time was accurate," Caldor said. "But there's one thing we didn't talk about. Your husband has a relative he sometimes visits. Tell me about that."

The remark sobered her. She put the drink down and pulled the open negligée together; her shoulders hunched.

"Well?"

She looked down at her hands, her brow furrowed. "I don't know what you're talking about."

"You're lying," Irene Andler said evenly.

"He doesn't like me talking about it."

"About what?" Caldor asked.

"It's none of your concern, either of you."

Caldor suddenly grabbed both her shoulders and shook her. "We've no time left, sober up. I need to know who that relative is, now! And why he won't talk about it."

She broke free of his grip and aimed an ineffectual blow at his face. "Keep your goddam hands off me!" she shouted.

Deliberately, Caldor leaned forward and slapped her face, once, twice and then three times. Her head jerked from one side to the other, with the force of the blows.

"You son of a bitch! You dirty mother. . . ." She leapt at him and he hit her face once more with the back of his hand.

She collapsed back weeping on the sofa. Caldor got to his feet looking coldly down at her. "Get this, if I don't get what I want from you—now—voluntarily." He reached down and grabbed her by the jaw, pulling her face forward, his grip tight. "There are men waiting outside, who have my authority to get it, by any means they care to use!"

Irene Andler moved forward to restrain him, he wheeled on her, his eyes blazing. "And you keep out of this!" He turned back to Eunice, releasing his grip on her jaw. She fell back on the sofa, her hand to her face, eyes widened in fear.

"Now answer my questions, one by one," Caldor continued. "Who is the relative? And why does he keep quiet about it?"

"She—she's his—Oh Christ! He'll . . ." She broke off.

"Go on," Caldor said.

"She's an aunt. She—she's in Nevada. It's a sort of a home. Old people who aren't. . . ."

"Aren't what?" Caldor leaned forward, she put up her hand.

"Aren't well," she faltered, "all right in the head."

Caldor caught Irene Andler's gaze.

"What's wrong with her?" He continued.

Eunice shook her head clumsily. "Russ wouldn't say exactly. She's just crazy. She talks all the time about angels and things."

"Why didn't Russ get her treated?"

"He didn't . . ." She hesitated looking up at him. "I shouldn't be telling you all this."

Caldor's voice was quieter: "You are and it's very, very helpful. Now go on. Why did Russ keep her shut away in the home?"

"He thought if it got out it would stop him being chosen for Dynostar. I told him it didn't matter. So what if you've got a crazy relative! Who hasn't? It doesn't make *him* any more likely to go crazy, He knew that. He just had this fixed idea—that it would stop him getting up there."

Her face suddenly clouded with anger. "It sure costs a hell of a lot of bread to keep that crazy old bitch in luxury. We could use the money." She looked up suddenly. "Now that doesn't make him crazy. So don't you go using that. Russ is peaceable, he's not. . . ."

"Is he always peaceable?" Irene Andler asked.

Eunice nodded eagerly: "Yes, everyone likes him. He's got no hate in his heart for anyone. . . ." She halted confused as if remembering something.

"Anyone?" Caldor probed.

"Except for Dr. Risbach."

"Who?" Irene Andler asked quickly.

"Dr. Risbach. He was Russ' departmental head at Caltech. After Russ had done all the work he claimed the credit."

"Credit for what?"

Russ did most of the theoretical work on the field shapes for Dynostar—topology was his subject." She went on. "Risbach took most of it and published it under his own name in *Physics Letters*. There was a hell of a row.

"Russ wrote to the editor threatening to sue, but Risbach was Dean of Science there—he didn't stand a chance. To rub it right in, Dr. Risbach thanked Russ for his assistance in an acknowledgement at the end of the paper."

"You mean Russ believes Dynostar is his idea?" Irene Andler enquired quickly.

Eunice looked up and nodded vigorously: "It is his. Honest to God it is. It broke him up. You know how it is. In that field it's all split-second cut-throat competition. They were all racing at it. In England and Russia, they'd got basically onto the right track. But it was Russ who used topology to break it."

She rose to her feet and started to pace unsteadily. "You've seen the television, the papers, they made Risbach the great inventor. Can you believe it! They gave that mother all the credit. Jesus, it's no wonder Russ . . ." She broke off.

"Russ what?" asked Caldor.

"He—he can't stand hearing Risbach's name. It tears him apart. He goes almost crazy." She stopped. "I don't mean . . . Oh God! I didn't mean that—he's not the only one who hates that son of a bitch. You ask Will Patterson, Bob Townsend as well.

"Risbach's got a hell of a reputation for stealing. He gets people like Bob Townsend to do post-doctorates with him. It's never obvious, he just soaks up what they do, goes away, takes it a little further and then publishes. He's a hundred percent opportunist shit. Ask Will and Bob."

*   *   *

In the car on the way back to the Clear Lake headquarters, they reviewed what they had. Patterson, a man who had killed in rage, Walters hiding an insane relative. And now Risbach, who had left an indelible mark on three of the crew.

218

Caldor held the radio-phone, he was speaking to Robertson:

"Joe, I want you to get Risbach. I don't care how you do it. Just get him over here now. If he won't come voluntarily, bring him all the same. It'll be less than an hour by jump-jet from his home. Clear it with Lorimer base now." He put the receiver down.

"Do you know this man?" queried Irene Andler.

Caldor turned: "Walters could be right. When I took over responsibility for Dynostar, Risbach expected to get the science directorship. He wheeled and dealed his way right up to it. But I did a lot of sampling, everyone said the same thing, he's very good, but he's a shit. Nobody'll work with the guy. So I dropped him. I don't suppose he's forgiven me for that."

The car drew up alongside the entrance to the Administration Building. It was almost 5 a.m. and the sky to the east was beginning to lighten with streaks of duck-egg blue breaking through the clouds.

From somewhere across the black water, the cry of a loon echoed eerily like some lost soul. There was nothing else to be seen. They could have been in a wilderness, hundreds of years before.

Irene Andler staggered suddenly on the steps leading up to the verandah. "I'm sorry, I haven't your endurance. If Risbach is going to take an hour—perhaps I could lie down somewhere?"

He looked at her in the harsh dawn light, the wind was bitter. Her face was lined and pouched with fatigue, she looked years older than the person who had first walked into his office so confidently a few hours before.

"Yes, of course." His voice was gentle. "I'll send someone to wake you as soon as he arrives."

After she had gone, Caldor suddenly left the weight of his own fatigue.

In the darkened office, he slumped in the chair, tilting it back and swinging his feet up onto the mass of papers on the desk top. He closed his eyes and immediately felt an irresistible curtain of sleep filming down through his senses.

There was a slight rustling noise. He quickly swung his legs down and snapped on the desk light.

Sue Annenberg, her long hair lying partly across her face, was asleep on the couch, a coat lying loosely across her shoulders. Her long legs were stretched out and slightly apart, a brown leather skirt rucked up over her thighs.

Almost in a daze, he got up and walked over to her and stood looking down. Her face, relaxed in sleep, seemed unbearably innocent and attractive. She stirred slightly, her head moving to find a more comfortable position. He could just sense the musky perfume of her body.

He knelt beside her and then, without thinking, tenderly brushed the long auburn hair away from her face. Her eyes flicked open, startled. And then, recognising him, softened. He drew back and stood up suddenly in embarrassment: "I . . . I didn't mean. I just wanted. . . ." He realised his hands were shaking uncontrollably. The four days of strain had taken their toll. He looked away.

Then he felt both his hands being held, pulling him down again towards her. She looked up at him, her lips parted. She was smiling, her eyes still half closed.

He felt an overwhelming sense of care and concern coming from her. He bent down and she put her arms up around his neck. "Don't talk," she said. Her kiss was warm, reassuring.

There was no awkwardness, no declaration, nothing that

could have broken through the moment. As he entered her, all he was aware of was a soft, gentle rhythm, the fragrance of her skin, her enveloping hair, her body drawing up to his in climax, draining all the fears and tensions out of him.

Long afterwards, he lay completely still, exulting in the closeness of her body. Neither of them spoke.

Somewhere, in the distance, a telephone was ringing. She stirred. "I'd better answer it." She got up and walked over to the desk. He watched her beautiful silhouette against the dawn light of the window.

CHAPTER TWENTY-EIGHT

The power supplies and battery stores of the Orbiter Four Shuttle Vehicle were situated at the rear of the craft and only reached by a narrow cylindrical tunnel connecting the forward control cabin and the rocket motor turbine room. The tunnel stretched beneath the floor of the one-hundred-an-ten-foot cargo bay, and was just under a metre in diameter. It was divided by three airlocks so that either the rear or forward sections could be maintained at differential pressures as required.

Hayward waited anxiously by the forward access lock to the tunnel. After some minutes Patterson emerged, followed immediately by Neumann and then, after a few moments delay, by Walters who was holding a reel of thick electrical cable, and paying it out behind him into the tunnel. Neumann was still ashen white and breathing stertorously. Only Walters seemed entirely in command of himself. Patterson's face was set in a grim mask as he started to swing the airlock hatch back into position, but Hayward moved to restrain him.

"Hold it. I've got to do a systems check in there," he said.

Patterson's normally mobile face was hard set. "Is that right? Well reckon you'd better check what we've done too, while you're about it!"

"I will," Hayward replied, and started into the tunnel. The closeness of the narrow ribbed wall immediately started a new attack of giddiness and nausea. His mind raced back to an incident in his childhood.

Once he had started to crawl through a culvert under a highway. Half-way through, his route had been blocked by a fall of sand and pebbles. Trapped, menaced by the booming vibrations of massive trucks overhead, the experience had formed part of his nightmares for years.

He paused halfway along the tunnel, his breathing echoing harshly back from the metal walls, sweat breaking away from his face in weightless sprays.

For some moments he floated immobile in the aft compartment collecting his senses, waiting for his thudding pulse to subside.

The compartment was congested with the convoluted mass of multi-coloured tubes and control panels. At the far end were the three turbine pumps feeding the five giant Perseus rocket motors with methalox and hydrazine fuels. The pipes were separately coded in stripes of bright fluorescent colour.

On one bulkhead near a panel of instruments and indicators was a numbered list of check routines, behind a transparent panel. Hayward started to work methodically through each one, knowing that failure to be one hundred percent thorough would maroon them for ever until their slow and protracted death by asphyxiation or dehydration.

First he checked out the servo-motors driving the rocket motor steering gymbals, then the battery store capacity meter readings. With colossal relief, he saw that they showed a maximum reading, so that the small amount of power which it would be necessary to drain for the shutdown operation should, if Lucas' estimates were correct, not seriously jeopardise the operation of the shuttle systems.

Finally he came to the ammonia boilers of the ship's air conditioning system. They took the form of four two-foot titanium spheres, connected by a complex of lagged tubes connected to a finned alloy heat exchanger on the external surface of the shuttle.

One by one, he turned on the pressure cocks and then switched on the circulation pumps which started with a low-pitched purring, rising gradually to a shrill whine. Needles on pressure gauges started to swing up to precisely predetermined levels. As the ritual progressed, Hayward felt his confidence sweeping back. He was in familiar territory; the machines were working.

There was an unfamiliar sound—a harsh hissing. He whipped around, searching for its location.

Suddenly he caught his breath, the choking acridity of ammonia vapour seared his nostrils. He reeled back, the fumes were filling every corner of the confined space. His eyes burnt and watered. He searched desperately for the leak. A hexagonal locking collar was rotating slowly on a half inch diameter pipe. It was completely off its thread and spinning in the stream of pressurised vapour now shrieking out of the leak. Holding his breath, he reached up for the power switch, and pulled it down. Immediately the noise of the refrigeration pumps swooped down to silence.

He swung round and dragged himself into the crawl tunnel, coughing and trying unsuccessfully to hold his breath. The choking vapour had already spread into the tunnel, but as he dragged himself forward, he moved ahead of the vapour and the air gradually cleared.

Taking in a final deep breath, he reached the forward hatch and pulled at the central locking handle to open it.

It did not move.

He tugged again. It was stuck, the airlock door was jammed shut. He felt the first sting of the pursuing vapour, then a burning started in his mouth and nose. Again and again he wrenched at the immobile locking handle. The gas was now as strong as it had been in the aft compartment.

His senses began to ebb, there were flashes of light racing across his dimming vision. Desperately he banged on the door with his fists. He heard a thin, high-pitched scream and realised as his consciousness dwindled that it was his own voice.

The image of the culvert flashed briefly.

Then darkness.

There was a flashing yellow light. He opened his eyes. Walters was looking down at him, holding a portable oxygen mask to Hayward's face. His memory started to work and he craned his head round, but the crawl tunnel door was shut. He looked around. He was strapped by Velcro tapes to the underside of the crew seats. Walters' face was screwed up in concern, he spoke urgently:

"What in hell happened?"

The clear air in the forward compartment revived him quickly. "There's a leak back there. A junction collar's loose. I don't know how it could have happened. It's right off its thread."

Walters nodded and picked a short length of alloy bar off a clip rack. "I found this through the crawl tunnel lock handle." He moved across to the closed door, pushing it through the ring shape of the handle and wedging the two ends against projecting lugs on the rim of the tunnel. "It was like that!"

Hayward nodded slowly in understanding. He unstrapped the facemask and put the oxygen set aside. "Who else was in here while I was in the aft section?"

"Nobody I guess," Walters replied. "We were just fixing the cable through into the docking collar. . . ."

"We?" Hayward said. "Who else?"

"Just the three of us. Will, Theo, myself, that's all."

Hayward leant forward. "No one else? You're sure?"

"No, that's all," Walters replied. "I was up at the entrance to forward control, the others had gone back aft. Then I came back in here to check the voltage on the wall connectors. I heard you banging, then I saw that bar stuck through the handle."

"And you're sure no one else got back in here?"

Walters shook his head. "Right. Nobody."

"You see what that means?" Hayward said.

Walters stared back at him. "I guess."

"How long does Lucas estimate to shut-down?" Hayward asked.

"Around thirty minutes, he reckoned."

"Now listen," Hayward continued, "those two, we have to keep them away from the jury rig. When we get back inside the control sector, I want you to stay by the docking collar airlock. Make sure no one gets back in the shuttle." He jerked his thumb back over his shoulder. "The batteries are all the energy we've got."

Walters turned to a small bank of controls by the crawl tunnel airlock.

"What the hell are you doing?" Hayward queried angrily.

"I'll set the automatic baro pumps to flush the ammonia out of the tunnel. Before we de-orbit someone'll have to get back in there and repair that pipe."

Walters fished in a pocket, pulled out a small packet and launched it at Hayward. "Get a couple of these glucose tablets inside you."

Hayward caught the packet.

CHAPTER TWENTY-NINE

Sue Annenberg held out the receiver for Caldor and then turned to let down the slat blind against the morning light.

"Your Dr. Risbach sounds pretty mad!" She smiled.

Caldor's euphoric mood was abruptly dispelled by the stridently angry voice at the other end of the line:

"Where the hell do you think you are Caldor, Russia? I'll remind you we still have a democracy in this country! I've just been dragged out of bed and told some crazy story about going to Clear Lake by jump-jet. . . ."

Caldor tried to break in but the tirade continued; "One more thing . . . I'm not going anywhere today. I am giving the Franklin lecture at the National Academy meeting this morning and, as far as I'm concerned, that takes priority over. . . ."

"Dr. Risbach, please," Caldor's tone was calm, soothing. "I'm sorry, we had to do this. . . ."

"Sorry! God almighty! You will be, Mr. Secretary. When I've finished talking to Senator Vannic. . . ."

Vannic had been one of Caldor's chief adversaries during the enquiry into Dynostar.

"Dr. Risbach!" Caldor raised his voice. "Something of the gravest significance has happened to Dynostar. We must have your help, now, urgently."

In the silence that followed, Caldor balancing the phone between cheek and shoulder, stared at Sue Annenberg's large cowhide handbag on the desk. On impulse he reached out and brought it closer.

The voice continued: "What the hell help can I give? As I remember, you haven't found any need for my services until now!" Despite the angry content, the tone was slightly more conciliatory.

"You're the only man who can help."

Caldor twisted the clasps on Sue's bag. A jumble of papers, notebooks and make-up containers fell out. Amongst them were several photographs.

"You may be able to avert the most serious crisis ever to occur to man, Dr. Risbach."

"I've only read the press. There's been great speculation as to what's happening up there. What exactly is the situation?"

Caldor spread out some of the photographs on the desk, his tone was firmer. "You must know I can't disclose that sort of information over the phone. This is not a secure line."

He caught sight of some prints of Sue on horseback on a mountain track and picked one up. There was a man alongside her. His face seemed familiar.

Risbach's voice cut in: "Are you still there? I said I'll cancel the lecture. I can't tell you how inconvenient this will be."

"Thank you Dr. Risbach. You should be here within the hour. I'll have quarters arranged for you. Goodbye." He put the receiver down and glanced across at the large prints pinned on the wall. There was no mistake. The man in the picture was Russ Walters.

"There's a reading glass in the desk, if you want a real close look!" Her voice was cool, she had dressed and held two mugs of coffee.

With an icy sense of premonition, Caldor felt the warmth of the attraction he had felt for her slip away and vanish. "How well do you know Walters?" He was aware that his voice was hard, demanding.

"I know him very well."

"That's not what I meant. Have you had an affair with him?"

"None of your damn business, I'd say!"

"Anything to do with these men," Caldor gestured at the board, "is my business."

For a moment she glared angrily at him, then she turned away and sat down on the couch. "O.K. I'm not particularly proud of it. I didn't intend to get really involved with any of the guys." She looked over at the board. There were tears in her eyes.

"He's a sort of lame duck, doesn't fit in so easily. I was sorry for him I guess, so we started dating. He made me laugh, he's great to be with. He's got a sort of black, funny throw-away side. It wasn't any great shakes, it only lasted a short time. I mean you've met his wife, right? She'd castrate a bull elephant!"

Caldor got up and walked over to the row of photographs of the crew on the wall-board. Walters' alert, peaked features, the slightly too eager smile. A hint of insolence in the eyes.

He turned: "Do you know who Dr. Risbach is?"

To his surprise, she nodded: "Yes, I do."

"How do you know about him? Through Walters?"

Her manner changed. The outgoing warmth was replaced by the inward searching expression he had seen once before, while he was talking to the wives in the seminar room. She spoke flatly:

"Sometimes he'd talk about nothing else. He was like a

guy deliberately biting on a sore tooth. Really obsessed. I had to try and keep him off it, or the day would be shot to hell.

"We used to rent a little cabin up there in the mountains," she smiled. "He'd write me cute little notes." She started to rummage in her handbag. "I kept them. But when Risbach's name came up. . . ." She brought out a small bundle of papers held together by a rubber band, she pulled one of the notes from the bundle and handed it to Caldor. He read it.

It was written in short, clipped sentences, apologising for leaving early. It ended: ". . . Risbach is due here tomorrow; it makes a bad pression for me. I'll have to go over my last calculations. He's bound to attack them. It's all part of his scheme. He's already got all the staff here working for him." The note was unsigned.

"He left it on my pillow at two in the morning." Sue looked at him, trying to read his mind. "It's not Russ is it?"

Caldor did not reply.

"I mean, my God! Risbach's a bad joke around here. Will Patterson, Bob Townsend both feel as strong as Russ about him."

There was a light tap at the door. Irene Andler entered. Her eyes flicked around the room. "I hope I'm not interrupting . . ."

Caldor shook his head. He turned to the girl, his voice cold: "That's all, Sue."

She looked at him as if to say something and then began to collect the contents of her handbag from the desk. As she reached for the letter, Caldor put his hand over it. "I'll keep that."

She searched his face for some sort of response. There

231

was nothing to see in the close, thinly chiselled features. She turned and hurried out.

Caldor, without preamble, slid the note across the desk at Irene Andler. "What do you make of that?"

He paced the room as she sat down to read it. Finally, she looked up: "What do you want me to say?"

"Is it normal?"

"There is a word 'pression' some people might say that was a neologism, the writing has exaggerated curls—yes, it could be the writing of a disturbed man. That's what you mean, isn't it?"

"Can you be sure?"

"No, it's just an indication."

"Don't for God's sake start this 'yes, maybe no' routine again! Are you sure?"

"I'm sorry, but only some people agree that there is such a thing as schizophreniform writing. Not everyone thinks new words like that are important. One paper showed that apparently quite normal people use them sometimes."

He wheeled suddenly, put both hands on the desk, bending down towards her, his voice was cold and menacing: "What I want from you, now, is something you've never had to do before. I want you to write a speech for Dr. Risbach."

"What?"

"That's right. I want you to write a script for him to read over the radio-phone to the crew with just one function in mind. One of those people is a dangerous paranoiac. So far he's managed to keep his disturbances to himself. And now what I want from you is a speech for Risbach, specifically to throw the man we're looking for. I want you to deliberately send him right over the top. You can do that?"

"I can, but I won't. No doctor would debase their training in that way."

"I don't give a goddam about your professional scruples. Right now your duty is to every living soul on this planet —not to your hippocratic oath." He pushed a pad over to her. "Now get it down there—fast!"

He turned abruptly and strode out.

For some moments, Irene Andler sat absolutely still in her chair, two warning spots of colour on her cheeks, the only sign of reaction.

Finally, she picked up a pencil and began to write on the notepad.

CHAPTER THIRTY

The air in the forward control room had almost cleared of mist since the flushing manœuvre. The jury rig control was once again active and the row of indicator lights were flashing in regular sequence as Lucas masterminded the final sequence of shut-down.

Hayward remained by the control desk. He surveyed the scene. Behind him, just inside the entrance to the shuttle airlock, he saw Walters, busily pretending to check the cables running through from the space shuttle. His presence was a relief, leaving Hayward free to keep an eye on the other men inside the Control sector.

He had temporarily postponed his original intention of tackling Patterson and Neumann and attempting to confine them in the geophysical module until shut-down was achieved, because they were so involved in the intricate electronics of shut-down that any intervention could delay procedure disastrously. So he bided his time, waiting, trying not to get in the way or to appear watchful, reasoning that his presence alone would ensure that whichever man it was, the Australian or the German, would be unable to carry out any further sabotage.

The situation in the Control Room was now almost electric in tension.

Lucas looked carefully from man to man, then pointed to an illuminated digital chronometer dial on the main control panel. The liquid crystal face changed its digit pattern each second, inexorably counting away the remaining minutes to shut-down.

"We now must have complete integration," he said. "When I begin to run the new field sensor programme, that will automatically start the disconnection of the first power feed programme in the monitor can." He pointed to the row of indicator lights. "That is, if we have re-written it correctly. Then we shall see the right hand bank of lights go out in sequence from right to left."

He turned to Van Buren: "Eddie, immediately you see the lights go out, you must start the second field stabiliser withdrawal programme running."

Van Buren nodded, put the log book into a rack and took up a position to one side of the jury rig. He picked up a pair of switches taped to a small board. Wires from the switches ran into the jury rig.

Lucas turned to Townsend and Patterson; Hayward braced himself. "Then you both will see the alarm signal lights go on up there." He pointed to a row of unlit indicators overhead. "Ignore them and operate the override. You must do that within the two-second marker pulse or we shall have to begin the sequence again."

Hayward watched the men move from the control desk with relief. The control desk had to be protected.

Lucas turned to Neumann: "Theo, the input voltage level from the shuttle is your responsibility. You must use regulator set four to stabilise to plus or minus half a volt at maximum. It must not fluctuate over that, otherwise the clock pulse in the new programmes will drop out of phase."

For a moment Lucas' order did not register on Hayward. Then he saw the German move over to the control desk.

Hayward remained poised for an agonised moment of indecision, then launched himself forward, striking Neumann in mid flight. Quickly recovering as Neumann backed away from the main control, he put out an accusing arm:

"Stay away from that! Get right back away from the desk." He placed his hand on the other's chest and shoved him away. The German somersaulted backwards against the far bulkhead. The men stared at Hayward astonished and completely uncomprehending. There was an angry protest from the others. He looked back at Neumann who was clutching the far bulkhead, still bent double with the force of the impact.

Hayward turned. Patterson's hand was now resting on the control board, and he pointed to it. "Take your hand off," he said, "and get over there with him." He spoke slowly, deliberately confronting the other man.

There was a silence in the control room broken only by the whirr and click of the digital indicator.

Hayward glanced around the room. To his relief, Walters was still at the airlock entrance, clutching the metal bar in one hand. He felt a hand clasp his arm, he turned. Eddie Van Buren seemed to have recovered something of his former dignity and leadership for a moment. "Explain yourself," he said. "And quick." He pointed to the meter. "We've only got minutes."

Hayward leant over and wrenched Patterson's hand off the control, pushing the man backwards. For a moment the large Australian made no resistance, staring at the astronaut in surprise.

He jabbed a finger at Patterson and Neumann. "While I was back in the shuttle on the pre-flight check routine, I was nearly gassed by ammonia from the boilers. It wasn't just a leak, a union had been undone completely. I got up the crawl tunnel and tried to get out, but somebody had jammed the airlock with a bar of metal."

He looked round. Walters had remained at his position. "Russ will corroborate that, because he found it and let me out. If he hadn't, I'd be dead. The only others in there were these two." He pointed at Patterson and Neumann. "So they are not to get anywhere near the equipment here, do you understand? Keep them right away!"

He glanced around at the men again, but this new turn in the long agony of Spacelab Dynostar was too much for them to comprehend. Lucas' mind was still obviously filled by the problems of shut-down. Van Buren was shaking his head from side to side, uncomprehendingly. Townsend was scowling, his anger seemingly directed more at Hayward himself than at the other two. Only Walters' eyes met his with any degree of comprehension and approval.

"You're mad!" Patterson exploded. "The three of us were in there together the whole time. No one had a chance to do anything like that. If anyone's doing anything, its got to be you." Patterson went on furiously.

"If anybody's crazy among this crew, I reckon it's you, Commander. Barring the initial accident, everything that's happened has happened since you arrived on board. And you're about the only man aboard who's had the freedom to do it. The rest of us have been occupied the whole time."

Hayward felt a surge of nausea, his eyes still watering from the ammonia vapour and his vision was blurred. He was unable to focus. He fought back the rising tide of sickness and gripped the side of a control panel to steady himself.

"I reckon if anybody needs locking up, it's you, Hayward," said Patterson. "Until you take us back to earth you're going in the geophysical lab."

The Australian suddenly made a dive forward, imprisoning Hayward's arms in a bearlike grip. Hayward flexed his arms and forced him back, then flicked his foot behind and at the same time jack-knifed his body. Patterson, surprised, found himself propelled backwards and upwards. He struck the floor mesh and rebounded diving at Hayward's neck and locking his arms behind the Commander's head.

Hayward struggled for a moment and then, fighting for breath, ceased to resist. He felt someone else grab his arms from behind. "I've got the bastard," he heard Townsend's rough voice by his ear.

Lucas moved forward, glancing anxiously at the indicator: "Get him out of here and let's get under way."

"All right," Townsend growled. "Move, Commander." He gave a tug at his arm and a streak of agony shot through Hayward's shoulder as the men started to manhandle him into the central access tunnel.

There was a sudden crackle from the main speakers linked to Mission Control. A loud buzzer sounded. Someone was trying to activate the transceiver from Ground Control.

Lucas quickly switched on the main set. The speaker was repeating a loud urgent tone signal.

Patterson and Townsend released their grip and spun round at the unfamiliar sound. Hayward cannoned backwards, just managing to grab a hand hold in time to prevent himself falling through into the access tunnel.

Suddenly, the familiar voice of Caldor filled the dimness of the control sector. It sounded harsh and grating on distort.

"This is Caldor. Do you read me? I repeat, this is Caldor. Are you receiving?"

Lucas flicked down the responder switch: "Yes, we are hearing you clearly."

"I want you to listen very carefully," Caldor's voice continued, the metallic tones echoing in the confined space of the cabin. "We have now completed a complete dummy rehearsal of what you are doing now. There are some additional features which require some changes and so, therefore, I have decided to put Dr. Sven Risbach in temporary scientific direction of the final shut-down stages. . . ."

There was a slight pause. Townsend and Patterson were staring incredulously at the speaker.

"Dr. Risbach will check out each one of your final procedures, Lucas, and you will accept direction from him. Is that clear?"

Townsend swore briefly: "That's about it! That's all we need!"

The voice continued: "I'm putting Dr. Risbach on now."

Risbach's voice was clipped and authoritative: "Of course some of you are known to me, and I guess I'm familiar with much of your work. So I have been re-examining the situation and have decided that there are two possible flaws in your sequence as planned. These are final power withdrawal. . . ."

The voice continued, giving detailed instructions for changing the shut-down sequence. Townsend turned to Patterson:

"They can't be that stupid! How can that bastard possibly know anythink about what we've done up here. We've had no communication with him at all!"

"Unless he was listening to us all the time," Patterson said.

Risbach's voice continued: "Now you will remember

my own set of equations I developed for the first proto-
type. . . ."

From behind Hayward, there was a dreadful ululating
shout rising and falling, the sound of a man bursting out
of control; a figure crashed past Hayward sending him
flailing against the wall. The others scattered as Walters
shot towards the main speaker panel, a plench tool raised
in his hand. Grasping the side of the control desk, again
and again he smashed the tool against the speaker grille.
The voice continued:

"I know you're going to disagree with some of my
findings . . ."

"You've arranged it all!" Walters shouted. "O.K. I
know all about it now." He had dented the grille, his arm
moving up and down in a frenzy of attack. "You're not
really Risbach, you're a goddam lousy tape—just a re-
cording. You're not going to stop it now."

He gave one last blow at the speaker, the grille collapsed inwards and Risbach's voice snapped off. Walters
swung round still clenching the tool in his fist. His lips
were drawn back off his teeth.

Hayward started forwards but Van Buren interposed
himself between Walters and the jury rig. "For Christ's
sake Russ . . ." he began.

Walters swung the tool in a sudden backhand swipe.
Van Buren reeled back, blood spraying away from a two
inch gash down the side of his forehead. His body struck
the rim of the access tunnel, rebounded and hung, spinning
slowly in the air.

Walters turned, holding the tool out in front of him,
his words tumbled out, delivered in staccato spurts: "You
bastards think I didn't notice—all those times—you've all
been pretty damn smart—but I knew—I had good data

all the time—you didn't know that—very good data . . ."
He swung the plench smashing it down on the jury rig.
There was a flash and a harsh crackling sound. He swung
the tool at the bank of indicators, several splintered and
then went out.

"You could have helped." Walters' eyes filled with tears.
"You sold out instead—all of you. You did what Risbach
wanted—all the time."

He smashed the tool down on the jury rig again. There
was a muffled explosion and white fumes jutted from the
maze of circuitry.

"O.K. Dr. Risbach . . . make this work. . . ."

Walters reached down for the main power cable leading
from the shuttle batteries. He gave it a sudden jerk tearing
it away from the main terminals, there was a blinding
flash and the control room plunged into darkness at the
same time as Patterson and Hayward shot forward to grab
Walters. They both struck the control panel.

Walters had gone.

For several moments no one moved or spoke, their eyes
straining to pick out something—anything in the humid
darkness. The only sound was a harsh bubbling rattle from
the unconscious Van Buren.

It was Lucas who first got to a torch and switched it on.
Its power was nearly exhausted and it gave only a dim
yellow beam. He quickly moved over to the jury rig, examining the wreckage. Townsend had found a second
torch. They all quickly crowded around the Frenchman.

"What chance?" Hayward queried.

Lucas paused, unclipped a shattered programme plate
flinging it to one side. "None, none at all. It is over."

Townsend shone his torch at the airlock door leading
to the docking collar of the shuttle. It was firmly closed.

Walters had gone. Patterson grabbed at the opening lock handle of the airlock door. It would not move.

"He's jammed it the far side!"

"We can force it," Townsend said.

"No, no we can't," said Hayward. "He's in command. He has the shuttle. If we force our way in, he could do anything."

"What then? Just sit here waiting for that bloody lunatic to kill us?" Townsend's voice was very near to hysteria.

Patterson had picked up the power cable from the shuttle batteries and attached two clips from a test meter. "It's still live, nine volts RMS."

"So what?" Townsend queried.

"We can power the squawk box—talk to him." Patterson moved to unclip a small panel next to a speaker grille alongside the closed airlock door.

Hayward joined Neumann hovering over Van Buren. The chief scientist was still alive, but his pulse was weak and a stream of clotting blood floated away from the gash on his head. He helped Neumann and Lucas carry the man aft, along to the medical unit, then returned.

Patterson had meanwhile connected two thin leads to the main shuttle battery cables and roughly wound them around two terminals protruding from the space behind the panel. He moved to switch on the communicator. Hayward stopped him:

"Hold it, we don't know what he wants yet."

"How can you expect anything rational from him? You've seen him just now," Townsend demanded.

"He could have killed anyone, especially me. Instead of which he set up a trap to gain my confidence," Hayward replied. "He wants us for some purpose of his own."

"Hayward's right," Patterson agreed. "He's probably got some Dynostar pulse hero thing, take us all down with him to earth, or maybe he wants us to watch. We'd better try and talk."

Hayward switched on the communicator. "Russ, can you hear me?"

Each man froze, listening.

"Russ—you there?"

"I hear you," the voice sounded tinny, distorted.

"Open this bloody airlock," Townsend began, but Hayward pushed him aside and turned back to speak, deliberately keeping his voice calm: "Russ, what do you want with us? What do you intend doing with the space shuttle?" He looked at his watch, gleaming luminously through the dark. "We've only sixty minutes to go until the pulse. We need your instructions."

The voice came through again, a little louder this time. "Don't give me any of that crap Hayward. I'm not crazy. In fact I'm the only sane man you've got. I was the only one that saw through Risbach. If you start trying to bullshit me, all communications are going to cease. Understand?"

"I understand," Hayward replied.

"O.K. But drop that tone of voice. You're not dealing with a crazy! There's nothing I have to do now Commander. It all fits together. It's just me and Dynostar. It's the greatest goddam machine there ever was—lot of barrage there.

"You shouldn't have thought up all that stuff about shut-down. Jeeze! That was a real crooked thing to do! I know you cooked it up—I heard about it all right."

The voice changed, became almost pleading: "Can't

you see—our folks back there, they're going to need Dynostar, they need the energy—all that vital energy."

"O.K. Russ," Hayward replied. "I agree with you. What do you want?"

There was a pause. "You wouldn't let Dynostar work, so I made sure it would."

Lucas had entered the control sector from the access tunnel. "By murdering us all!" He exclaimed. There was a pause.

"I couldn't help it. The others were obstructing," Walters went on. "They were in the way. Bringing that tape of Risbach up with you—that was really something. Say that for you, Commander—that was real keen. But, you weren't careful enough.

"I mean, after a meal once, you left all your trays on top of mine—that was a crazy thing to do. It was obvious at once. It gave you all away, my data bank confirmed it."

"Russ," Hayward talked quietly. "We need to know what you want with us."

The voice pleaded: "I didn't want to harm anyone. I don't want to harm you. I want you to witness the Dynostar."

"What after that?" Hayward queried.

"We get back!" The voice was eager. "We go back down—do you think anyone's going to ask questions after it works? Do you think anyone's going to worry about five bodies when it works? It's nothing. The bodies aren't going to talk, especially Lyall!"

"Shut that maniac off! Townsend groped forward at the switch. Hayward and Patterson restrained him.

"I heard that, Bob," the voice continued. "Don't worry about it though. I've got the shuttle now." Walters' tone hardened. "So you stay where you are. If you try and get in here, I'll kill the batteries—so you'll be up here for good!"

Patterson glanced around quickly at the others, then spoke into the communicator: "Russ, this is Will. Listen to me, Russ. You can't condemn us all for God's sake! Bob here, we've both suffered from Risbach. O.K. he's a bastard, we agree, so why don't we talk about it? We could maybe think something out. Fix him for keeps?"

There was a longer pause, the voice sounded less sure: "Yeah, I'd like that! But you should've thought about it before, you'd be sure to talk to Risbach, I couldn't ever be certain. I didn't know you were with him Will!"

Again the voice hardened: "Lyall was obvious—the way he talked—he worked for Risbach. Did you find the power drill? Went right through his ribs. Boy was he surprised —me finding him out!

"You can ask some more questions after Dynostar's pulsed. Then, if my data bank checks you out, maybe we can get together."

The communicator clicked off.

CHAPTER THIRTY-ONE

In the Clear Lake control room, Caldor was so concentrated upon the attempt to contact Spacelab, that he failed to notice Dr. Risbach as he entered the room and walked over to his side.

The scientist had a short, stocky frame with a rounded sun-burnt face and small intelligently shrewd black eyes. A natural and gifted opportunist, he now gazed confidently around the room, his eyes flicking from one technician to another, mentally assuming control of the operation.

He put a hand down on Caldor's shoulder, thick square fingers gripping. His voice was firm and authoritative:

"There are several routines we should be starting. I have recalculated some of their programmes and there are certainly. . . ."

Caldor swung round and jumped to his feet, a half smile hovering on his face. Without replying he took Risbach firmly by the arm and led him out of the room, on past two waiting guards and down a corridor towards the front exit of the building. He spoke as they walked:

"Dr. Risbach, the best thing I can say about you is that your ignorance is a tribute to your vanity."

The other man turned, his over-weight face puckering into anger.

Caldor continued: "Did you really think I'd call you

246

out of the blue to take charge, just like that? You were brought here for one reason and one reason only. You have filled your role magnificently."

They had reached the door, a guard opened it and saluted, and Caldor walked through, pulling the furious scientist with him.

"As far as I'm concerned, I wouldn't give you charge of a roadsweeping gang!" He pointed. "There's a pool car waiting for you over there, your baggage is loaded. Be off limits inside the hour.

"One final thing. You might take a good look at the whole situation on the way home. Decide whether you are not ultimately responsible for a large part of this tragedy!"

He nodded curtly and turned back through the door, leaving the astonished scientist standing speechless on the step.

Caldor was unaware that two hours previously Nicole Lucas had successfully evaded her guard by climbing through a back window of her home and walking through a wood to her car in the general park. She had then driven to the gate and shown the guard her photopass. While he had been examining it, she had suddenly gunned the throttle and sped off down the road to the nearby township of Oakley. Patrol cars had taken off in pursuit, but by the time she had been caught in a local drugstore, she had already succeeded in telephoning the Washington correspondent of *Paris Soir*.

Like an uncontrollable brushfire, the entire story of the Dynostar disaster and the deaths on board the Spacelab had spread around the media channels of the world in minutes.

Crowds were already gathering in city streets looking up fearfully for signs in the sky.

The mosques were filling with the faithful, seeking help,

and Embassy guards in all major cities of the world prepared for seige conditions.

Media gurus in countless television studios intoned their own views of the crisis and hospitals began to assemble emergency burns units and eye treatment centres.

Governments met in urgent secret session.

The population of a very small planet cowered, waiting.

CHAPTER THIRTY-TWO

Hayward floated in full E.V.A. space-suit next to the inner door of the airlock in the workshop module.

In the dim light of a torch held by Neumann, Patterson was in the process of spraying a self-foaming plastic around a tracheotomy tube which he had wedged into the life-support unit of the E.V.A. suit to replace the missing connector tube removed by Walters.

"Mel Freeman was right," he said. "It'll fit—just!"

The clear viscous fluid Patterson had sprayed from an aerosol first turned opaque, then began to expand and grow around the tube in a brown spongy mass. Finally it stopped, giving off a light smoke. After about a minute Patterson tapped it with a fingernail:

"It's polymerised quite well, but don't make any sudden movements, it can't be a hundred percent airtight, although it's a closed bubble system. You'll have to take it very carefully. Don't give yourself any more than ten or twelve minutes E.V.A."

Hayward nodded and began to lower the head piece of the suit down over his head. He twisted it on the metal neck collar until it locked and looked down at his wrist chronometer.

Fifteen minutes!

Fifteen minutes before the automatic computers in the

monitor can completed their task and released the giant bolt of electric current into the coils of the shining magnetic doughnut of Dynostar.

Fifteen minutes before the injected gas plasma was gripped in a spinning vice of colossal magnetic fields.

Fifteen minutes before the contained plasma flared to a temperature of millions of degrees to turn for one brief second into a minature sun.

In the short time since Walters had made his escape to the shuttle, they had quickly reviewed the situation and concluded that there was no point in trying to reason further with him.

One possibility remained, to get outside the ship and cut some of the cables connecting the Monitor Can to the Dynostar machine as first projected before the sabotage to the space-suits. Then, finally, for Hayward to get into the shuttle through its airlock, just below the cabin window on the starboard side.

Several hazards and uncertainties remained. Since the destruction of the jury rig they no longer had any means of knowing the exact state of the Dynostar and to cut the wrong cable at the wrong time could still cause the power can to discharge into its own connections and explode.

The crude repair to the space-suit meant that they could only guess whether the foam would remain in position for long enough in space. Also, Walters might be able to prevent Hayward from opening the shuttle airlock from the outside. They had kept careful watch on the blue metalised cabin windows of the shuttle, but had, so far, seen no movement inside.

Finally, they did not know whether one of the sabotaged space-suits which Hayward had already removed to the shuttle for repair, would be refitted by Walters with the missing part. The operation needed only the plench tool which he had taken with him.

Patterson finished connecting Hayward's umbilical to the ship-mounted E.V.A. unit, realising that he would have to work without the water-cooled body garment because of the lack of power. Hayward knew that by the end of fifteen minutes, his body temperature control would be overcome without the aid of the garment and he would begin to die of heat exhaustion.

The power failure also ensured that they had no other E.V.A. equipment to use, such as the astronaut manœuvring chair.

Patterson sealed the lock door, and the air in the confined space around Hayward roared and shrieked into space.

He carefully opened the outer airlock door, but in spite of the heavily tinted face visor, his eyes, adapted to the internal gloom, were temporarily blinded by the brilliant coruscating reflection of the sun's rays from the outer skin and fittings of the ship.

Shielding his eyes with one gloved hand, he pushed himself off into space with the other, looking round to see that his umbilical was uncoiling behind him without catching on any projection.

He looked anxiously down at the demand pressure gauge on the life-support unit strapped to the front of his body. With relief, he saw that the needle fluctuated regularly with his breathing, exactly between the permitted limits.

He began to haul himself cautiously along the fluorescent orange handholds on the huge curved exterior of the main Spacelab, making his way towards a short ladder leading up to the walkway stretching between the monitor can and the power assembly underneath the gleaming coils of the Dynostar. Over his head, the brilliant blues and greens of the earth slid silently by as the massive Space-lab complex hurtled along its orbital trajectory.

Nausea and vertigo began to grip once again and it was some moments before he had regained sufficient control of his lurching senses to continue. The movement of the earth, like moving clouds behind a church tower, made it seem as if the whole ship was falling to one side, down into the atmosphere.

His breathing rate increased and, cautiously, he increased the oxygen supply, repeatedly blinking his eyes to keep out the weightless sweat which had gathered under his lids.

From the outside, the monitor can looked exactly like a thirty-five-feet-long bottle with its neck stuck into the side of the main Spacelab. Between it and the power can assembly under the Dynostar, was an alloy ladderway. The leash of heavy cables connecting the computers and the power can were held in a series of support rings rivetted to the ladder.

Like blades of a windmill, the four matt-black solar panels, each thirty feet long, protruded from the sides of the power can.

Hayward began to pull himself up the ladder leading to the walkway. He had a clear view of the shuttle cabin windows and was relieved to see no sign of Walters either in the cabin or out in space.

He reached the walkway, pulled his bulk awkwardly into the retaining hoops and started to examine the leash of multi-coloured cables. His eyes had adjusted to the blinding reflection of the sunlight from the alloy mesh-work. He brought up an arm to look at the sequence of instructions Lucas had given him, held in place on his arm by Velcro retainers. He glanced at his wrist chronometer.

Eleven minutes! He fought down panic. Was there enough time?

He pulled a heavy pair of end-cutters from his belt and studying the instructions on his arm pad once more, began to pull out the first coloured cable.

In his concentration, he failed to see a hard black shadow ripple across the surface of the power can assembly.

A sense of presence made him turn. Walters, in full E.V.A. space-suit, was standing, feet hooked into the end of the ladderway. Hayward saw that he had no umbilical and reasoned quickly that he would have had no one to operate the umbilical E.V.A. system on the shuttle. He was, therefore, relying on his secondary oxygen pack attached to one thigh.

Walters, without the security of the tethering line of the umbilical, had grabbed a retaining hoop with one hand. With his free hand, he held two cylinders mounted in parallel on a frame. Each was about a foot in length and four inches in diameter. There was a tubular crosspiece connecting the two cylinders to a long finned nozzle.

Brandishing the cylinders in front of him, Walters began to advance cautiously along the ladderway towards Hayward. Hayward glanced quickly down at the wire he had selected and cut it firmly through.

Walters was fifteen feet away.

Hayward glanced at the written sequence on his arm and cut a second cable.

Suddenly, there was a bright blue flash. He wheeled.

Walters was repeatedly pressing a button on the cylinders. Each time he did so, a spark flashed across the mouth of the nozzle. Suddenly a shaft of brilliant orange flame, fully two feet long, shot from the nozzle. With a beat of fear, Hayward recognised the portable oxy-propane brazing torch from the shuttle repair kit. It was lit by a piezo-spark.

Hayward quickly bent to cut the next cable but Walters lunged forward at him with the torch flame. He put up an arm to protect himself, but was too late. The flame slashed across the transparent vizor of his helmet. Immediately, the polished surface frosted over as the clear plastic crazed and bubbled in the heat. Temporarily blinded, he jerked his head up to see around the edge of the opaque patch.

Walters thrust the torch forward again, this time aiming at the life support unit and its piping. Hayward aimed a back-handed blow at Walter's helmet with the cutters, but missed and almost lost his grip on the walkway in the follow through.

Again Walters lunged and, for the first time, Hayward caught a glimpse of his face. It was expressionless, the eyes set in a look of total concentration.

The flame burnt across the front of Hayward's suit. Immediately, the epoxide fibre of the suit flared briefly and then charred, leaving a crumbling black scar across the suit. Part of the instrument bezel of the life-support pack softened and deformed.

He lost his grip and spun away from the walkway, striking the side of the monitor can. His umbilical suddenly tautened and sprung him back on rebound until he came to a halt, spinning in the space between the monitor can and Dynostar.

Walters kept hold of the walkway, gazing fixedly up at Hayward, then quickly turned and made his way towards the ladder leading down to the main Spacelab hull. He had turned the blow-torch down until the flame was hardly visible. Hayward watched, trying to reason out the other's action.

254

Walters had now reached the surface of the workshop module. With a terrible surge of fear, Hayward realised the other man's purpose. The flame from the blow-torch shot out its full extent and Walters grabbed hold of Hayward's life-support umbilical.

Desperately, Hayward hauled himself hand over hand down his umbilical. Walters had started to point the flame at the grey cloth cover of the line. It began to char.

Hayward's body gathered momentum as he shot down towards Walters, boots outstretched. He struck Walters' helmet a glancing blow and then bounced off, crashing heavily into the surface of the workshop module.

Walters lost his hold, dropped the flaring blowtorch and was spinning way back towards the base of the power can assembly. His feet finally entangled in the complex of alloy girders and struts and he just managed to reach out and grab hold of the blowtorch as it spun past him under the reaction drive of its own flame.

Hayward began to haul his way back up the ladder to the walkway. He peered down at his wrist chronometer through the misted visor of his helmet, holding his arm up to see clearly.

Two minutes.

He rapidly estimated whether he could cut the remaining cables before Walters got to his umbilical line with the blow-torch for a second time. The other man had started back along the walkway, torch in hand. Hayward reached the cables and pulled out the end-cutters.

Walters was just six feet away, the torch held out in front of him, flaming like a swordpoint.

Hayward braced himself and sprang at the other. But he had anticipated the move and ducked. Hayward missed completely and cartwheeled out to the full extent of his umbilical, jerking to a sudden jarring halt and then rebounding.

Walters grabbed the umbilical, Hayward spun helpless like a kite at its limit. Walters looked up and then, as if relishing his complete command of the situation, brought the flame slowly down onto the umbilical. Hayward began desperately to drag himself down the line, knowing that he would not reach the other man in time.

Without warning, the whole of space exploded into light. The Dynostar coil suddenly flashed with a violet light of such intensity that the sun itself seemed to dim. As the terrible glare brightened, a waving serpentine green ring of fire appeared briefly inside the giant coil, then grew in intensity, spinning madly, and suddenly snapped off.

The violet light flared out from the coils for another brief moment and then it too faded. Then, like ripples on a pond from a stone, wave after wave of sparkling blue radiation bands flew out from the centre of the coil, flashing away into space and down towards the earth. Complex patterns of interference laced the racing bands of colour as they swooped on down towards the atmosphere.

At no time was there any sound.

Finally, all activity in the great machine ceased and Hayward peered, half-blinded, through the pattern of after-images in his eyes and the distorted visor of his helmet. He could just see the figure of Walters.

He was completely motionless, staring fixedly at the silent coils. It was his apotheosis, he was at one with the Dynostar.

Hayward gave one sudden powerful jerk at his umbilical line and launched himself directly down at the unsuspecting man, who turned but, as if hypnotised by the Dynostar, made no effort to avoid him.

Hayward's feet struck the other squarely in the chest, breaking his grip on the ladderway and sending him spinning away. Then, without pause, he wheeled as quickly as the bulk of his suit would allow and started to haul himself back along the walkway towards the meshwork of struts underneath the power can.

As he reached the girders, he began to pull himself down to the nose of the shuttle towards the safety of the airlock.

Overhead he felt a violent shock wave strike his helmet, the girder he was holding began to tremble and buckle in his hand. He looked up in alarm, one by one, the solar panels were vibrating, pieces of the cells fragmenting and flying away into space like snow. The side of the power can had split and jagged pieces of its metal casing were tumbling out in all directions.

The walkway had started to undulate like a snake, black fumes and débris were jutting out of the disintegrating power assembly.

The surface of the earth appeared to move upwards obscuring the black of space and then continuing on in a nauseous lurch around and behind Hayward's head.

The doomed space complex had begun to spin.

At the mercy of an intolerable vertigo and half blind from the fires of Dynostar, Hayward struggled down through the crumbling framework, each step needing an intense effort of will.

A second shock-wave struck his suit and then a large piece of the power can broke away, spinning in slow motion until it struck the corrugated outer surface of the Spacelab. It rebounded and scythed through the ladder walkway which finally tore from its twin mounting and began to curl and twist away into space. The jagged piece of metal flew silently past Hayward, a pointed section just scraping one of his boots.

He grabbed quickly for support and looked upwards. Walters was following him down the twisted and disintegrating girders. He still held the blow-torch. With a wave of horror, he realised that the deranged scientist was also making for the shuttle airlock.

Anxiously, he looked back down at his umbilical. But it was in a long curved arc in space leading back to the workshop hatch, well out of the reach of the other.

The airlock was in front of him, a brightly painted orange arrow on its surface pointing to the opening handle.

Walters was gaining behind him.

Six handholds on the skin of the shuttle lay between him and safety. His breathing became suddenly more difficult. Glancing down, he saw the demand pressure indicator almost ceasing to move in tune with his breathing.

Walters had damaged the oxygen lines with the torch. They were beginning to leak.

He looked back and saw the man recklessly launch himself across space to a girder only feet away from the airlock.

Hayward had reached the last handhold. He pushed himself off towards the airlock. To his horror, he felt the umbilical suddenly tug at his life-support unit, spinning him round. He looked back aghast, the line was taut. Like a man tethered by invisible forces in a nightmare, unable to move, he could just not reach the airlock. He was gasping for breath just feet away, held by the long white line.

His mind raced, Walters was bracing himself to leap across space to the airlock. Without hesitation, Hayward pulled the end-cutters from his belt and bent the umbilical line until he held a kinked loop of it in one hand. Then,

258

with the cutters, he tore open the cloth cover and savagely ripped and tore his way through the oxygen lines and nylon tether.

Immediately, in spite of his attempt to seal the end leading to his suit with the kinked loop, he felt the agony of falling pressure in his ears as the air rushed away.

His consciousness began to ebb.

With his last remaining strength, he flung himself at the airlock, scrabbling for a grip. He flung back the two locking catches, swung the door open, pulled himself in, sealed the door catches behind him and just managed to bang open the oxygen tap and get his helmet off before a roaring tide of blackness engulfed him.

CHAPTER THIRTY-THREE

Hayward felt no sensation of elapsed time as he regained consciousness, but for several minutes he waited until his brain and senses cleared sufficiently to piece together the events of the previous hour.

Then, as he struggled towards clarity, he became aware of a low-pitched thundering noise somewhere nearby. Alarmed, he swung round to try and locate its source. In the outer airlock door, there was a small glass inspection window four inches in diameter and through it he could see the flare of the blow torch reflecting off Walters' helmet outside.

Suddenly, the flame splashed directly onto the glass port itself. Hayward looked on helplessly as the glass gave off a brilliant yellow sodium flare. He tensed, waiting for the explosion which would shatter his lungs by decompression.

Then, the flame suddenly began to diminish, finally snapping out altogether. Walters was out of gas.

The confined airlock boomed hollowly as the scientist frantically beat on the outer surface of the airlock door with the empty cylinders. Finally, there was silence and Hayward had a brief glimpse through the port of Walters' boots disappearing upwards towards the outer surface of the cabin window.

As rapidly as possible, Hayward cut away a length of the nylon tethering line from the ripped stump of his umbilical and lashed it firmly between the two inner operating handles of the airlock, then swung open the inner door to the shuttle.

He hauled himself down to the docking collar, but as he pulled his shoulders into the narrow tunnel, to his horror he could see the skin of the three foot diameter tunnel beginning to distort and buckle as the irregular inertia of the spinning ship tried to twist the shuttle off its linking collar.

Finally, he reached the airlock door leading to the Spacelab. There was a loud metallic banging from the far side. Walters had jammed the operating rings with a bar of metal. Hayward tugged the bar free and pulled at the airlock door. It stuck. He glanced at a pressure gauge alongside the lock. The atmosphere of the Spacelab was three pounds per square inch down on the shuttle atmosphere.

The exploding power can must have breached the skin of the Spacelab. Hayward yelled through the airlock door to the trapped crew: "Push it. Push it from your side. All of you!"

Bracing his feet against the airlock rim, he tugged with all his strength at the two handles. There was a sudden loud crack and then a hiss and the door swung violently open. Hayward catapulted back along the docking collar.

The five surviving crew members quickly pulled themselves along the collar and into the shuttle. Townsend dragged the semi-conscious Van Buren along, like a swimmer rescuing a drowning man.

In the lower cabin of the shuttle, Lucas quickly disconnected the cables from the shuttle batteries to the bulkhead connectors leading to the Spacelab.

Patterson was the last to enter and he resealed both airlock doors behind him.

261

As the men strapped themselves into the double row of heavily padded seats underneath the flight deck, Hayward clambered up the vertical ladder and settled himself into the pilot's seat above them. He carefully adjusted the complex restraining harness until he had optimum movement.

One by one, he activated the maze of systems controlling the giant shuttle craft: propellant pressures, avionics systems, conditioner units, vector jet servos, all were examined, tested and passed as correct by the on-board monitoring computers.

Gradually, like a giant waking animal, sounds began to echo softly through the air of the shuttle. Servo-motors whirred, vacuum pumps began their pulsing blatter, warm air began to pour through surrounding grilles. Rows of multi-coloured lights flicked on and off in complex arrays on banks of instruments surrounding Hayward. He pressed the ground communicator switch.

Immediately, the voice of Ground Control came through in the cabin as though the owner of the voice was only feet away.

"Shuttle orbiter, this is Mission Control, Houston. Shuttle orbiter, do you read?"

The completely impersonal tones reassured Hayward, he paused and then depressed his own switch. He tried to keep emotion out of his voice: "Yes Houston. I read. Good to hear you."

"Copy, shuttle orbiter. We now have ground check of on-board systems, you are free to commence undocking and de-orbit. We have atmosphere re-entry window as solid angle, four, four, zero radians. Repeat four, four, zero."

Hayward punched up the figures on the golf-ball navigator.

"Check, four, four, zero, Houston."

"You will encounter first aerodynamic response at approximately six, five point six eight minutes from deorbit burn. Repeat, six five point six eight. . . ."

Hayward became totally immersed in the ritual task of successfully undocking the shuttle craft. First, the systems were compared with measurements taken by telemetry at Ground Control. Then the manœuvre was re-computed to make allowance for the spinning of the ship. Finally, the technicians at Houston and Clear Lake sat back waiting for Hayward's signal that he had withdrawn the docking collar, closed the nose cone and disengaged from the ruined Spacelab.

*   *   *

Caldor sat watching the technicians and realised for the first time that he had no further function. He almost envied Hayward's task, now so nearly completed, and realised wryly that his own problems were just about to begin.

He got up to leave and stopped for a moment by the water cooler and took a drink, knowing that the conference room was already packed with journalists and cameras, all waiting for him to walk on stage. He began to prepare forms of words in his mind as he set off down the corridor. His pace quickened. No further evasions were possible.

The door to Sue Annenberg's office was open. She was standing by the window and turned as he began to say something. Remembering her wrath, he put his hand out

263

involuntarily and for several moments their eyes met, then she turned silently back to the window.

Irene Andler's room was already emptied of her few belongings. She had just completed the packing of a small briefcase. As he passed, she looked up at him with the same enigmatic half-smile. He searched her expression but it showed no hint of encouragement or criticism.

The double doors of the conference room lay ahead and, as he approached, he could hear a furious hubbub of voices with Robertson's voice raised above them. The two guards stood aside, opening both doors. He braced himself.

The voices abruptly dwindled away to silence as he entered. His vision was blinded by a rapid succession of flash guns as he walked towards the dais. The two guards closed the doors. One looked at the other and shrugged.

CHAPTER THIRTY-FOUR

Patterson had strapped himself in the jump seat beside Hayward on the flight deck. Neither spoke.

Hayward pushed down four bright red switches deeply inset on one panel.

There was a loud whine from a servo motor. Both men looked anxiously downwards as the gold-plated proboscis of the docking collar disengaged and slowly withdrew back into the hull of the shuttle. As it disappeared, the hinged re-entry nose cone swung slowly back into position. They both clearly heard the hiss and clack of the locking rams, followed by the brief clatter of the collar pressure pumps.

Almost imperceptibly at first, the shuttle drifted away from the abandoned space complex.

Patterson tapped Hayward on the shoulder and pointed up through the blue tinted window.

Hayward could just see the white suited figure of Walters set against the multi-coloured patchwork of the earth. He was holding onto one of the coils of the Dynostar, pulling himself from side to side.

"How long's he got?" Patterson asked quietly.

"It's got to be less than ten minutes on his secondary oxygen pack," Hayward replied. Their gaze met. Patterson spoke their joint thought:

"We'd need forty minutes minimum to suit up, and another ten to get him in."

Hayward nodded silently and turned back to the controls.

On the outside of the ship, attitude control thruster rockets began to hiss and snap. The Spacelab hulk diminished in size more rapidly.

The voice of Ground Control filled the instrument crowded cockpit:

"Shuttle orbiter. We now have monitor reports from global stations, Hawai, Odessa, Cap Richelle and Thule. Readings are consistent to a factor of point oh, four two. The Dynostar pulse was of point six seconds duration and not of one second, due to premature failure of the power can.

"Repeat, oh point six and not one point oh."

Lucas' head had appeared through the access aperture of the flight deck floor, and as he listened, for the first time, his face crinkled into the beginnings of a smile:

"So we do not have a stripped ozone layer. A point six-second flash would not be sufficient for that! You must have cut the right cables Commander."

Patterson stared through the window: "Even point six of a second could have done something!"

The ritual voice of Ground Control intoned its flat instructions. The shape of Spacelab Dynostar was now an almost indistinguishable pinpoint of light just above the cerulean blue haze of the atmosphere capping the horizon of the earth. Hayward and Patterson were both closely watching a set of changing digital indicators. As the row of tubes all reached zero, Hayward pulled two bright yellow levers towards him.

In the rear of the shuttle, the propellant turbine pumps howled into action, the whole craft juddered and shook as the bank of Perseus rocket motors fired with a deep rumbling crackle. Both men felt the seats thrust forward into their backs. Their heads went back involuntarily.

The earth's horizon crept upwards like a brilliant mottled blue curtain as the nose of the shuttle swung downwards. For exactly twenty one point two seconds the motors roared their distant metallic thunder. Then, just as abruptly as they had started, they snapped off into silence.

The shuttle was now bulleting downwards towards the outer limits of the atmosphere. The survivors waited alone with their thoughts, listening for the first external sounds of the atmosphere which would soon begin to pluck and tear at the fragile skin of the shuttle, heating the ceramic nose-cone until it burned away.

Patterson gazed out through the metallised side window as the convoluted spirals of the cloud patterns began to resolve into clearer detail. He turned to Hayward: "Eddie's all right. There's no more bleeding."

Hayward nodded, studying the swinging golf ball navigator. He moved one of the two joystick controls he held in each hand. The ball swung slowly into a new position. "When we're down, I guess I could do without the debriefing. Nobody's going to have any flowers waiting." A buzzer sounded, Hayward looked up. "Ion probe's showing, we should hear the air any second. They'll be polishing their steel toe-caps!"

Patterson grinned: "For us, not you. They're going to need a hero figure to balance things up a bit. You'll be able to write your own ticket."

Hayward kept his eyes on the swinging navigator, then shook his head: "Not this time. I've had all that. Too many years in tin cans like this. I've been away too long." He gestured at the crowded instruments. "It's the end of all this anyway!"

"Maybe," Patterson replied. "But you'll still be able to take your pick, politics, business!"

Hayward shook his head: "I've walked the carpet on the flight deck too many times, Will. Dynostar is the end of an era. What would I do? 'Confession of an ex-astronaut'—it might just sell a thousand copies!"

"What then?" Patterson asked.

Hayward looked down at his hands and the joystick. He released his grip on one of the levers and flexed his fingers, studying the wrinkled skin on the back of his hand. "There's plenty to do, I'll find something."

Outside the shuttle, the first sparse atoms of the atmosphere were creating a soft, almost inaudible hiss as they rushed past the outer hull. The earth was now filling the sky and Hayward caught a brief glimpse of land in a gap between two cloud structures. There was a river glistening between a puckered range of mountains. The scene could easily have been just inches across: a trickle of water between sand patterns on a beach.

He was suddenly able to see the altered scale of the river with an overwhelming lucid insight. All the images of his previous life as an astronaut rushed into his mind and then, just as suddenly, wavered and fragmented.

The hero-worship, the parties, the press conferences and public appearances, all seemed to lose any significance. He wondered how he had ever allowed his ego to be so trivially inflated.

For the first time in his life, he began to look forward to living on a scale more related to that of his two sons.

The rushing sound grew in intensity to a beating, juddering thunder. Flames began to lash back over the cabin windows from the incandescent nose cone as it burnt away in the tearing friction of the thickening atmosphere.

Hayward's body strained painfully forward in the decelerating course of the shuttle. Despite the discomfort, he felt at ease.

*   *   *

The fragmenting bulk of Spacelab Dynostar swept into the glaring sunlight from the dark side of its orbit. It was spinning slowly on its axis.

The skin of the main hull had begun to buckle and distort and every few moments a fragment of once-precisely fashioned metal would break off and tumble slowly away into space.

In the wreckage of the control sector, the only light came from a single heavily tinted port. Just once, a single indicator light lit dimly, flashed twice and then winked out for ever.

The atmosphere had leaked away through the many jagged rents in the hull and in the harsh vacuum of space which had replaced it, there was no sound.

In the waste freezer, the dreadful cargo swung and turned silently in the darkness.

The twisted and deformed girders connecting the Dynostar ring to the main hull began to snap, one by one.

Enmeshed in the tangled metal lay the white-suited figure of Walters.

It did not move.

The protective ozone layer enclosing the earth is maintained by a delicately balanced cycle of chemical reactions.

In December 1974, the first accurate measurements showing a definite thinning of the layer were reported. The cause was unknown.

Without the ozone layer, most surface life on earth would cease.

In the same year, a rapidly growing number of scientists in many countries began to produce well-documented evidence showing quite unacceptable dangers in the operation of nuclear fission power stations.

* * *

By the year 1978, it was reluctantly concluded by an international panel of scientists and engineers that further construction of fission power stations should stop and that existing stations should be run down to a minimum level of operation and then abandoned.

From that time onwards, all available research was directed towards the development of a stable fusion reactor and on July 8th, 1986, the Dynostar machine pulsed into action for point six of a second.

Shortly after dawn on July 9th, 1986, twenty-five miles

above a localised region of Eastern Africa, the ozone layer wavered and vanished.

The region of high Savannah land known as the Serengeti National Park was bathed in an invisible flood of short wave ultra-violet radiation. On the evening of the same day, the diaphanous filigree of ozone molecules had re-assembled itself; once again shutting out the lethal rays.

By July 10th, 1986, the ecology of the Park was in ruins.

A herd of blind Impala searched vainly for foliage. A lioness, her eyes whitened by cataracts, scented prey which she was unable to hunt. A flamingo crashed blindly into the spikes of a thorn bush. In just a few hours, the grass shrivelled and turned to a patchy ochre hue.

On July 13th, 1986, a black African game-warden and his white assistant were found dead in the wreckage of their hover vehicle. The exposed parts of the white assistant's body showed second-degree skin burns.

On September 12th, 1986, Lee Caldor resigned as Secretary of State for Energy, following a multi-national enquiry demanded by the Council of Twelve.

In the year 1989 fusion research was finally abandoned and all further work directed towards the exploitation of natural power sources.

Solar energy machines, geothermal probes, and wind generators all began to take practical form.

By the early nineties, the necessary technology for a post-industrial millennium was assembled and waiting.